Daughter of Anne-Hoeck

Also by Carol Pratt Bradley
Fire of the Word
Light of the Candle
Waiting for the Light

Daughter of Anne-Hoeck

Carol Pratt Bradley

WiDo Publishing
Salt Lake City

WiDō Publishing
Salt Lake City, Utah
widopublishing.com

Cover design by Steven Novak
Book design by Marny K. Parkin

ISBN: 978-1-947966-28-4

In honor of my eighth-great grandmother,
Susanna Hutchinson

"I will give unto you one place more which the Lord brought to me by immediate revelations, and that doth concern you all. It is in Daniel Six. When the president and princes could find nothing against Daniel, because he was faithful, they fought against him concerning the law of his God, to cast him into the lion's den. So it was revealed to me that they should plot against me. But the Lord bid me not to fear. . . ."

Anne Hutchinson
Boston, Massachusetts, 1638

Chapter One

THE TALL MAN'S VOICE CLANGED LIKE AN ECHO, THE deep timbre of another voice I had heard long ago. *Ku.* I must do as the strangers at the fort had told me and think of the English word and not the Siwanoy. *Nuxa.* Father. He had a voice like my father's.

"Welcome home, my little sister." The tall man pushed open the red-painted door.

A rush of warm air came round me as I stepped inside the house. A woman stood in the hallway, her pale face and hair lit by the candle she held. "Do shut the door, Edward. The cold is coming in." The woman's eyes pinched as she stared at me, her expression the same as the people at the fort in New Amsterdam. Anxious. Afraid.

This woman did not want me here.

"I am Katherine," she said. "Your brother's wife."

Edward, my eldest brother. The woman belonged to him. I had not seen him in many moons. *Kahtene.* The English word came to my mind. I whispered it. "Years." The sound tasted foreign upon my tongue and yet familiar, like an echo off the distant hills.

"Did you speak, Susanna?" Edward asked.

I shook my head. "*Ku.*" The woman gave me a sharp look, and I closed my lips tight.

Since I had been sent away from the village, the words people spoke around me jarred like chattering bluejays. Since the Siwanoy spoke only when needed, our days were filled with more silence than speaking. I was tuned more to hearing the voices of the trees, the bird and animal calls.

No one spoke now. A tree branch scratched against the window. The big fire in the next room crackled. This was a different silence, full of strain.

This language had once belonged to me. When I first came to the village the Indians frowned when I spoke the English, like this woman named Katherine did at my Indian words. The more I heard them speak, the more I understood, a familiar echo sounding in the back of my mind, quiet at first, then shouting.

During my two weeks at the fort, before my brother came for me, I could understand many of the English words. The people treated me as though I was slow-minded. My mind replaced the English with the Siwanoy and then back again, making it hard to speak. To understand the language was easier than speaking it.

I understood what the Dutchmen had said about me: "Will the girl be welcomed back into Boston? 'Tis a harsh place. They will not accept her, and where will the lass be then? She fits nowhere—not with the Indians and not with the English. Those Puritans are a harsh lot."

One of the Dutchmen saw my face and knew I understood what they said: "Hush yourselves, for she knows what you say. I have observed this before. The young taken by the Indians and then returned recall their original tongue with lightning speed. 'Tis a needed thing. Take pity upon this most unfortunate one."

Chief Wampage traded me to the Dutchmen. Sent me away from the village. I clutched my stomach at the familiar pains that bent me over.

"Are you well, Susanna?" It was the man, Edward, who called me his sister. His voice faded, and I could hear him no more.

੨ఆ

On the day Wampage brought me to the village, all the women surrounded me, screaming and weeping. I thought they would kill me, too, as my mother and siblings had been slaughtered. Later I learned I had been brought to the village to take the place of a girl killed by the Dutchmen, who had slaughtered many of their people. Gela was the name of the girl killed by the Dutchmen. Opala was her mother.

I was taken to the *wigwam* of the wise woman Muh-teh-qway and her daughter Opala. Opala was the wife of Wampage, the man who killed my family. A girl about my age sat in the corner. Minsi. She glared at me. She did not want me there.

The women took my calico dress and handed me Indian clothes: a skirt of deerskin, a possum shawl. Opala held out a doll made of cattail leaves. It had long black hair and Indian clothing. Minsi rushed from the corner and grabbed it away. I did not know the doll had belonged to her sister, Gela. Opala took the doll away as she scolded Minsi, then handed it back to me. I threw it on the floor.

Outside the wigwam the warriors whooped and screamed: "Anne-Hoeck! Anne-Hoeck!"

What was that name?

I did not sleep well for a long time. The terrible sorrow I felt at the loss of my family burned within my heart like a firebrand. "Mother!" I cried over and over. "Mother! Why did you have to die? Where is my family?" The woman Muh-teh-qway rocked me against her as though I were a babe. She let me weep and moan in my terrible grief.

When my tears were spent, she talked to me. "It was not the way of the Great Spirit that you go to the world of spirits with the rest of your family. You are to live."

Opala set the doll next to me. She gestured that it was mine. It had black bead eyes and a deerskin skirt. The doll my mother gave me had a dress of calico. I missed my doll. I took Gela's doll and hugged it to me.

Ntan'tet, my little daughter, they both called me. Muh-teh-qway was kind to me. She loved me. Her daughter Opala loved me, too. Minsi never did. She would sneak up behind me and whisper in my ear: "Anne-Hoeck. Anne-Hoeck." And laugh.

Wampage saw Minsi taunt me with that name. "*Luweyan!*" he shouted at his daughter. *Do not say it.* He forbade the warriors to call him Anne-Hoeck in my presence. Minsi did not stop. She only waited until Wampage could not hear.

My nights of weeping lessened. I learned to be content. I learned to belong to the village.

And then the Dutchmen came.

ʾ🌢

The voice of the woman who stood beside my brother brought me back to the present. "You must be very tired. Come and I will show you where you will sleep." She held the candle high as she climbed the staircase, stopping before a door opposite the top of the stairs.

"Do you remember this house, Susanna?" Edward spoke just behind me. "You lived here with our family." Who was this girl Susanna? Not I. I was Sisika, girl of the Siwanoy.

House? A *pitaikaon.* Two stories stacked upon another. Did I remember this place? I shook my head. "*Tak-ta-nee.*"

Katherine's lips tightened again.

"Can you answer in your own language, Susanna?" Edward's tone was soft and kind.

What was my own language? Siwanoy? English? What did *tak-ta-nee* mean in English? Another echo came unbidden. *I do not know.* I understood what they said in the English, but I could not find the words to answer back.

Edward's mouth parted in a slow smile. It felt as though lightning shot through me and made me dizzy. I had seen that smile before. Was it on the face of my father? The one I had before my village home? I could not recall what he looked like.

"This is your childhood home," Edward said. "When you were very small, you slept in this bedchamber with your older sisters, Faith and Bridget." He looked at me expectantly. He wanted me to respond.

To remember.

"*Tak-ta-nee.*" I do not know. I shrugged.

Katherine entered the room and set the candle on the table by the bed. She held up a garment, gesturing for me to put it on, and pointed to a basin filled with water. How could I clean myself in this little water? I took a daily swim and steamed often in the sweat lodge. Edward's wife would not know this. Her nose crinkled as though she smelled something sour.

It had been the same in the fort called New Amsterdam.

They took me to a house where a Dutchman's short, squat wife had also crinkled her nose as she stared at my deerskin skirt and leggings, and my shawl of turkey feathers. She spoke rapidly in Dutch. I could not understand her words. Her hand motions made it clear I was to get into the tub of steaming water in front of the fireplace.

"*Ku.*" I shook my head.

"*Je zal,*" she yelled in Dutch. She snatched at the bag I had brought from the village.

"*Ku!*" I cried and grabbed the bag tight against my chest. It held the things that meant the most to me: my two *wampum* belts that Muh-teh-qway had made, my beads and my flute. "*Ku!*" They would not take it from me. We struggled together.

Another woman came in. She spoke English. "You are frightening the girl, Mrs. Kieft. Be gentle." She reached out and fingered the porcupine quills on my skirt. "Remarkable. Such beauty. This design looks as fine as lace." She pointed down to the skirt, moving her arms as though she sewed.

"Did you make this?" I nodded my head. I had worked many days on it, soaking the quills until they were pliable and then dyeing them white.

"Have pity, Mrs. Kieft. Let the girl keep what she wants." She pointed to herself and to my bag. "I will hold these for you, and when you finish your bath, I will give them back. Safe. I will keep them safe."

Her eyes were kind like Muh-teh-qway's. I let her take the bag. She helped me remove my clothing, and the woman Mrs. Kieft dumped me into a tub of hot water, scrubbing at the white paint on my forehead and cheeks, clucking her tongue again and again.

I was stuffed into a stiff gray dress with pointed white collar and cuffs that scratched my skin. The skirt did not reach my ankles. "It will have to do," Mrs. Kieft said. There were too many layers, stiff rows of stitching that tightened around my chest, making me aware of every breath. Instead of soft moccasins, she insisted I put on thick stockings and horrible black shoes that pinched my toes.

The nice woman carefully folded my deerskin skirt and put it into my bag and handed it to me. I grabbed it close. "*Wanishi,*" I thanked her.

She lifted one of my braids. "Your hair is a beautiful red. You look like your mother, the Mistress Anne Hutchinson."

I slapped my hands over my ears. She had dared to speak aloud the name of the dead. Muh-teh-qway taught me the names of the dead died with them, never to be uttered again or bad would come of it. I swayed back and forth and began to wail. The woman fled the room and did not speak to me again.

❧

"Sleep well, Susanna." The woman called Katherine shut the door, closing me inside. I could not see the man who said he was my brother. The silence shouted at me. I could not move, as though rooted like a tree to the rough floorboards.

In the wavy candlelight, the nightdress seemed to float on the bed. Sleep time in the village had not meant a change of clothing. I only had to lay down on the bearskins in the corner of the *wigwam* where the others slept, pulling another skin over me for warmth. The *wigwam* smelled of smoke from the fires set in the center of the long, narrow room, and the pungent odor of animal furs and of fresh rushes strewn on the dirt floor.

This room smelled only of pine from the hard floor and the walls.

The woman expected me to put on the nightdress, just as the woman had at the fort. It would be more comfortable than this itchy clothing. The dress was so big I pulled the top easily over my hair and stepped out of the skirt, untied the loop around the waist and tugged downward until the stay loosened and I could pull it down my hips. I missed my deerskin shawl and skirt. I pulled off the tight shoes and stripped away the stockings and slipped the nightdress over my head.

The bed looked hard and lumpy. How could I sleep on it? I walked to the window, staring out at the shadows of the trees made by the half-moon. The chilly air on my skin made me shiver.

What was happening back in the village? They would be getting ready for the fall harvest feast. I was not there to gather the corn and squash from the fields, smoke the fish and oysters, prepare the stews. This night I would have been sitting around the fire with the others, listening to the stories of the elders.

"*Achim,*" all would chant in unison: tell us a story.

Firelight would flicker across the storyteller's face as he told again the tales the people knew well, the stories that strove to find the meaning behind living.

"When first the Great Creator formed the earth, all was water." He would remove a piece of coal from the fire and draw a circle in the dirt, adding four legs, a head, and a tail. The children would shout together, "The tortoise!" The storyteller would wait until their shouts died and then continue.

"The tortoise raised its back high out of the water, and the water ran off it and earth became dry." He placed a stick on the circle. "A tree began to grow and from it sprouted a man. Another sprout became a woman. And from them came many more."

When I first heard the story it reminded me of another from long ago. I do not remember much except a man with the name of Adam. Eve was the name of the woman.

On those nights in the village, after the last story ended, came the dancing. Everyone danced, young and old, swooping and dipping to the drumbeats, dust swirling around their ankles, making me cough as I sat beside the fire.

"The time will come when you learn to dance, salt girl," the medicine woman, Muh-teh-qway, said to me. It took many moons until Muh-teh-qway saw the salt person—the white girl—dance at last.

In the early years of my life with the Siwanoy, each dawn would bring me the hope I would be returned to my family. With the passing of many seasons came the certainty that I would remain in the village for the rest of my life. Most of my family were dead. My life in that other place called New Amsterdam was gone forever.

Then one day the Dutchmen appeared in the village to make a peace treaty, and found the white girl living with the Indians.

Wampage traded me for a pile of goods: glass beads, heavy iron axes, three black kettles, and a hoe for the women of the village to work the fields. In exchange for my return, the Indians pledged not to attack again.

The candle on the table by the bed sputtered. Soon it would go out, leaving me in darkness. I lifted my hands and knees high and began to sway side to side. *Ku.* No. This was not the time to dance. I no longer belonged to the Siwanoy. Did I belong here in this strange place called Boston?

My temples beat like the dancing drum. Where was the joy I should feel at my return? Hidden. Behind the terrible face of fear. *Ntalemi.* I am afraid.

I left the window and climbed up onto the bed, clutching my bag of treasures. The bag was made of the rushes that grew by the rivers. Opala had taught me how to dye the reeds and weave them in and out of each other, pulling them tight, and how to make the designs. Onto this bag I had woven white water lilies. The dusky odor of dirt and water still clung to the reeds.

I also made mats for the floor of the *wigwam*. The work relaxed my taut muscles and emptied my mind for a short time of the things troubling me.

The silence in the house shouted louder than the snores from the dozen *wigwams* surrounding ours. Beside me, Muh-teh-qway's would be the loudest of all. "*Guwin*," Muh-teh-qway would say every night. Sleep. She was not here to say it to me.

The mattress folded around my body, smelling of duck feathers. The blanket scratched, so unlike soft bear fur. These wood walls would choke me. I was used to spending my days in the outdoors beneath the open sky, going indoors only to sleep. I threw back the blanket, still clutching my bag. No more light came through the gap by the floorboards. No voices. I eased the door open and slipped silently down the stairs and out the door of the house into the night.

The sky rose black, studded with tiny star lights. I tracked the sky until I found what I was looking for: *a-nay-e*, the starry cluster. Muh-teh-qway said it was the path the dead followed on their journey to dwell with the Great Creator in the highest heaven.

Each night before I entered the *wigwam*, I would find the *a-nay-e* and fix my gaze in the center of the cluster where the stars were thickest. I did not speak aloud, not even to whisper or move my lips, saying each of my siblings' names only inside my head: Francis, William, Anne, Mary, Katherine, little Zuriel. Each of their faces appeared before me, just as I remembered them that last day before the Indians had come. Smiling, laughing, teasing. I tried to see Father's peaceful eyes, to feel Mother's arms around me, saying my name like soft rain. I determined never to forget them.

To my grief, their faces faded. I could no longer hear their voices. Only echoes.

Six autumns and winters passed in this way, taking me from nine to fifteen years. Time took away the memories of the life I knew with my family before that terrible day.

I could hear again the sounds of my family taken from me: the screams of my mother and my siblings as the Indians attacked, the crackling of the fire as the house burned, the smoke rising above the trees, and then the sickening silence.

That day I had gone to pick berries in the woods. Mother forbade us to wander far from the house alone. I did anyway. My disobedience spared my life, an awful irony. I should have been with them at the house. I should have died with my family. The words beat like a drum inside my head.

They could have killed me when they dragged me from my hiding place inside the split rock, their hatchets dripping red, blood smeared on their hands and bare chests. The blood of my family.

One of them shouted: "*Akim!*" They stopped, dropping their raised hatchets. The huge warrior came toward me. He had a wide gap between his brown teeth, his face striped with red paint.

"*Shiki,*" he said, touching my hair. Beautiful. His bloody hands went round my waist, clutching me beneath one of his arms. I still remember his stench: bear grease, sweat, and the sweet scent of sticky, fresh blood.

Wampage shouted over and over as he ran, carrying me: "Anne-Hoeck! Anne-Hoeck!" The others picked up the chant.

I did not understand then that Wampage was yelling the new name he had taken, that of his greatest victim. Anne Hutchinson. Anne-Hoeck.

Mother.

I heard it again, as though it were now. I dropped to my knees and covered my ears. Someone wailed as though their heart was breaking.

Hands were on my shoulders. Strong hands. The Indians had come again to take me. I screamed. The man tightened his grip, lifting me, holding me tight against his chest.

"Susanna. Susanna. It is I, your brother." That familiar voice again, the same deep timbre as my father's.

He wore no bearskin. He did not smell of blood. It was the man named Edward. My brother.

Chapter Two

M<small>Y MIND FELT AS THOUGH A FOG FILLED IT.</small> I SHOOK my head to clear it. I was not at the split rock and not in the village. I was in a place called Boston at the house of my brother.

"I thought you had run away, Susanna," he cried. "Shush now. Do not be afraid. You are here at last where you belong, with your family."

He held me firmly against his coat. I stopped struggling, but my limbs still shook. I took a deep breath and let it out slowly.

"I hope you can understand my words, Susanna. Our father and mother are gone, and many of our siblings. They cannot return. When we learned you were still alive, we searched everywhere. I hardly dared to hope. My little sister is found at last."

This man who called me sister seemed filled with sorrow. He was afraid. Like me. The roaring faded inside my head. I turned my head to look up. The starry cluster was still there.

"Come into the house," he said.

"*Ku!*" No! I pointed up to the sky. I must be able to see the starry cluster. Then I would be all right.

"What do you want, Susanna? You want to see the sky?"

What did I want? "*Tewenama!* My . . . family." I tasted salty tears.

He took my hand and placed my palm against his chest. "*Tewenama.* I am your family, Susanna."

"Edward?" It was his woman's voice, the light of a candle in her hand. "What is wrong? You must come inside at once."

"It's all right, Katherine. We will stay here awhile. Could you bring a blanket? Susanna is cold."

He wrapped the blanket she brought around my back and shoulders, rocking me like a little child. Like Muh-teh-qway had. "*Tewenama*," he said over and over. "*Tewenama.* I am your family."

"It's all right," he said to his woman. "Go inside to bed."

My shaking ceased. Edward shifted and settled his back against a tree. I was so weary. My head sunk into his coat, his chest moved in and out, his breaths slowing.

❧

When I woke, the rose color of dawn shone above the tree leaves. I lay on a blanket on the ground with another over me.

Edward was still propped against the tree, sleeping. He stirred, stretching. "Come inside, sister," he said. "You must be hungry."

"*Ku.*" I could not. The walls would smother me.

"Very well then. We will stay out here." Edward kept his arm around me. "It is all right, Susanna." That strange name again. "This is your home."

This was a strange place. He spoke to me as if I should know it. I searched for the English word but could not find it. *Nemeshatamu.* I do not remember.

The woman brought food. I could eat only a little, and she took it away again. Children peered around the corner of the house, whispering, pointing.

"Leave her be, Elisha, Elizabeth, Anne," Edward told them. "What is in your bag?" he asked me. "It must mean much to you."

If I showed him my flute and my belts and necklace, he might take them away. I held it tight and shook my head. I slept again, and when I woke, Edward was still there, my head on his arm. I squirmed away.

He stayed with me. The sun set, leaving me in the time of dusk, when it was no longer light and not yet dark. As life was for me since I left the village. I slept during the night on the back stoop, Edward beside me.

❧

"Enough of this, Edward," Katherine said the next morning. "You missed your workday, and now Sabbath meeting. Reverend Wilson will be most displeased. Do not coddle her anymore, and she will adjust more quickly. Come inside, Susanna, if you want the morning meal."

Edward took my hand. "Come, Susanna."

My stomach was so empty that it crawled up my back. I let him raise me from the ground and lead me inside. He sat me down on the bench just inside the back door. I ate a bit of the brown bread and drank what he called cider, cool on my parched throat, and slumped on the bench. When I woke again, the sun had gone below the sea and the room lay in shadow.

The woman offered me another plate of food. "Two days without much to eat." Her eyes were kinder. I tried to eat, and my stomach lurched. She touched my shoulder. "Let me help you, Susanna," she said. I shied away from her.

Edward came and took my hand and led me up the stairs to the room where I had been. He brought in blankets and piled them on the floor beside the bed.

"You can sleep here," he said. "I will be near if you need me. Can you do it, sister? Will you?"

I would do as he asked. Perhaps the blankets would be snug like the bearskins in the *wigwam*. I walked toward the bed.

"Good, Susanna. Good."

I moved to go back down the stairs. "*Alonkok*," I said.

"What do you mean, Susanna? Can you say the English?"

I pointed upward. "*Nkawi*. Then. Sleep." I pointed back into the room at the pile of blankets.

"The stars? Very well. Get into your nightdress, and we will go see the stars."

*

When I woke, the sun shone through the window. Whispers sounded above me.

"Why does that girl sleep on the floor? And why does she hold that bag?"

"Hush, Elisha."

"Do not shush me, Elizabeth, for telling the truth. It is odd to sleep like that. And her skin is brown. Did she turn into an Indian?"

"You would be brown if you spent all day in the outdoors."

"I'm afraid of her," came the young boy's high voice. "I do not want her in our house."

"Hush, brother. That is cruel. She is our aunt. She is family."

This Elizabeth sounded like an older sister. She had a strong voice. It had a calming effect on me, like the sound of water flowing over the rocks in a stream. One could tell much about a person from the way they talked.

The blankets did not keep away the cold of the floor like the bearskins did, and I shivered.

"She's awake," Elizabeth gasped. They skittered away, shutting the door again.

My stomach rumbled as I sat up. A gray dress lay across the bed, with stockings and leather shoes, and other pieces of clothing I still did not know what to do with.

"Susanna?" Katherine called through the door. "The children said you are awake." The door creaked and she entered. "The day is wasting. There is water in the basin for you to wash your face and hands. Come now."

I did as she said. The wetness felt cool on my skin, the same as my morning washings in the river.

"Get dressed now. I laid out your clothes for you. Do you need my help?"

I nodded.

She lifted a piece of white from the bed. "This is your smock. It goes on first." She put it over my head and pulled it down. It flowed in a circle halfway to my ankles. "And now for the stays." She held up the wicked item the woman at the fort had tried to put on me. I flinched away.

"Susanna," Katherine scolded. "It is proper for a girl to wear stays."

I searched for the English words to say, rubbing my ribs. "It . . . hurts . . . me." The words sounded flat to me, as though I said them into a hollow log.

"I am glad to hear you use our language. You will soon get used to the stays."

I let my body go limp. It would not do to defy her. It would make Edward feel sad. She put the stiff thing around my waist and laced up the back. I spread my ribs wide so it would not hold me so tight.

"This is your waistcoat. It is of soft brown wool and will keep you warm." After she helped me into two petticoats to go beneath the skirt, she brushed my hair, bound it up with pins, and tied the ribbons of the white coif beneath my chin.

"You are a very lovely young woman, Susanna. I must get back to the morning meal. You can manage the stockings and shoes yourself, can you not?"

I lifted the stockings off the bed and bent to put them on. The leggings I'd worn in the winters were not so different than the stockings. The shoes were stiff and unyielding, not like my moccasins.

"Come down to breakfast when you are done." Katherine turned, her shoes making a steady click down the staircase.

❧

Elisha watched me while I ate, giggling, and Elizabeth jabbed his ribs with her elbow. Anne, who looked about five years, kept her eyes on her bowl.

"Eat slowly, Susanna," Katherine said as she turned back to the fire. "It is good manners to close your lips while you chew."

She did not want me here. I was a bother. I put my spoon down, then took it again and finished the last of the gruel. I should not do more to vex her if I could help it.

When the last child pushed their bowl away, Katherine spoke to her daughter. "Elizabeth, take Susanna out back with you to scour the pots."

I set the heavy pot on the ground. The back of the house looked strange, as though something was missing. I did not know what it could be. The lot spread deep and narrow, the roof of the nearest house barely in view behind the orchard. Near the side of the house, rows of rich brown soil lay in furrows, plowed and ready for the spring planting.

"Father said if I spoke to you, you would understand me. Do you understand, Susanna?"

I nodded. It amazed me how quickly my mind had returned to understanding my native tongue. The words sounded strange, smooth and connected, unlike the chopped, clicked sounds of the Indian language.

"And I do so want to talk to you and get to know you, for you are my aunt. You lived in this house when you were very small. Do you remember?"

I shook my head. "I was not many moons," I caught myself, "years here."

"My family also lived on Aquidneck Island, along with Grandmother and Grandfather. I was born there," she said. "We did not live there long before Father brought us to live in Boston when I was but two years. I do not remember any of that time, of course. I am nearly eleven now and tall for my age, so I look older."

Elizabeth was just four years younger than I. Two years older than my youngest brother Zuriel would be if he had not . . . I could not finish the thought, throwing it away from me.

Aquidneck, she had said. I knew that name. I had lived there with Mother and Father. A picture came into my mind of a house on a narrow strip of land, a bay on one side and the sea on the other. Two waters—one clear and calm, the other with white waves that crashed upon the road.

"I do not remember my grandparents," Elizabeth said. "Your parents. Nor do I remember you. My sister Anne was born here in Boston only two months after the Indians killed Grandmother and the rest of your family. They named Anne after Grandmother."

Elizabeth stopped scouring and put her hand over her mouth. "Forgive me. Father told me I shouldn't speak of that time to you."

I bent and took the rag from her and scrubbed at the leavings in the second pot.

"Father wept when we were told that his sister was alive and living among the Indians. He wept again on the day we heard you were coming back."

Lepakw. He wept for me. A lump rose up in my throat. It would choke me.

"Do you miss the Indians?" Elizabeth asked. "I do not think I could. Did they make you a savage, Susanna? You do not look it to me, except for your tanned skin, of course. I heard

Mr. Winthrop's new wife tell Mother at meeting that you do not belong here because you lived with the savages. All the women think so."

Winthrop. The name sounded another echo from long ago. I tried to remember the emotion that accompanied it. Fear? No. Dread. Wariness.

Elizabeth leaned close, and her voice dropped to a whisper. "Father told me once that everything Governor Winthrop says must not be taken as the truth. He warned me though not to say those words outside of our house."

The pot was clean, but I kept scrubbing. Did I miss the village? I ached with it. I wanted to go back where it was familiar, not like this strange place. I missed Muh-teh-qway and her quiet ways that had brought me to acceptance of my fate.

Elizabeth put her hands over mine to stop me scrubbing. "Father wants you to be happy here. As I do. You will try, won't you?"

Chapter Three

KATHERINE APPEARED AT THE BACK DOOR, CLUTCH-
ing at her apron. "There is someone here to see Susanna.
Wash your faces and hands at the well, both of you. Quickly now.
And come into the best room. Oh, I do wish Edward were here."

A broad man stood by the window, encased in black cloth.
The points of his stiff white collar were smudged with dirt. He
fixed his stern gaze on me, and I felt like the deer in a hunt. The
man's eyes pierced like freshly sharpened arrows.

"I am John Wilson, pastor of the First Church of Boston." His
arms seemed to puff out as he spoke, like a turkey preparing to
gobble. He did resemble a turkey, his nose like a long, curved
beak above his thin mouth.

"And you are Susanna Hutchinson. Governor Winthrop
informed me you were traded back by the Dutch, and you have
forgotten your family and your native language. You came away
from the Indians with much reluctance, he said."

This Governor Winthrop sounded as though he knew my
very thoughts, knew me better than I did myself. How could he?

"You much resemble your mother in appearance, though I
hope you do not prove to be her equal in haughty demeanor or
outspokenness."

He said no more, his stern, accusing eyes never leaving my face.
In a flash, I was back in the village, gathered round a fire with the
other children as the Mesingw, dressed head to foot in bearskin, a

mask painted red and black hiding his face, came again to frighten disobedient children. The Mesingw always succeeded.

Pastor Wilson's face was red as a painted Indian mask, and his black coat like the skin of a great black bear.

Unlike this man, the Mesingw did not talk, only shook his rattle of turtle shell to communicate his displeasure. One man in the village was selected to represent the real Mesingw, who roamed the forest on the back of a great stag, caring for all the animals. He did not come to the village only to reprimand the children, but also to bring strength and comfort to those who were sick. He was both stern and kind.

This man they called Pastor Wilson only looked to be stern.

After the Mesingw came, the children took offerings to whatever place they thought the real spirit dwelt. Some chose the tallest tree they could find, or a large rock or at the base of a waterfall. They took a handful of leaves or a stick they had carefully carved, or flowers.

When we first moved to the empty farmhouse in New Amsterdam, I would sometimes find those offerings, but did not know then what they were.

Did this man want some offering from me? Should I answer him? Tell him I would be obedient, not outspoken like my mother? *Noo ha.* I would not.

He did not appear to expect a response from me. His own words seemed enough for him.

"I consider myself to be a compassionate man." The man's mouth stayed in a straight line. His eyes were hard. "I hold out some hope for you. Perhaps your youth and your time among the savages has already humbled you, as nothing humbled your mother." He puffed out his chest. "It was an act of Divine Justice that brought her to her tragic end, to reveal without question the wicked fruits of her rebellious actions."

I clenched my hands together. What was this man saying? That my mother deserved to die? That the people of Boston were benefited by her death?

I would speak. My words came out in the language I first learned as a small child. "My mother . . . was . . . a good woman."

The pastor's face and neck bloated like a turkey, puffing in and out. "I see my task is clearly cut to bring you out of ignorance and blindness."

So, this was the offering he wanted from me. I could not think of the Indian word, only the English. Obey. I lifted my gaze from the floor and stared into his eyes.

"You do have her rebellious heart. I will break it."

Skirts swished behind me as Katherine came into the room. "Forgive me, Pastor Wilson. I sent my son Elisha to fetch my husband to visit with you."

"That will not be necessary, Mrs. Hutchinson. I have ascertained what I need in order to proceed. I will return with Reverend Cotton on the morrow, following the afternoon meeting, and we will begin our task."

"And what task is that, Pastor Wilson?"

"The reclamation of this savage." His boots beat a path to the door, and its wooden thud shut him out.

"What did you say to him, Susanna?" Katherine put her hands to her face. "The conflict is beginning again. I knew it would, with your return. I tried to warn Edward. Perhaps he will listen to me now."

Katherine did not want me. Perhaps Edward did not want me either.

"Not *now*," she muttered, pressing her hands together so tightly her knuckles whitened. "When the storm has finally passed, when we can hold up our heads in the streets without hearing constant whispers around us." Katherine's face was flushed and pale at the same time. "Not now, when I feel so poorly."

"Are you ill, Mother?" Elizabeth stood at the door.

Katherine put her hand across her mouth. Her fingers shook as she tried to calm herself. "Do not concern yourself unduly, child. I am well enough."

I clutched the edge of the table, wishing I had not spoken to the man. Muh-teh-qway said that silence was better than a hasty word uttered aloud.

What was this afternoon meeting the man mentioned? Would I be required to go? There would be people there. They would stare, like the woman at the fort and this preacher Wilson. And when the men came to the house again, they would try to make me obey.

I could find my way back to the village. Then I would not have to face any of these strangers or feel the heavy feeling of the air in this place. Of trouble. Like black clouds brewing a storm. I ran past Katherine and Elizabeth, through the keeping room and out the back door.

I tripped and fell on my hands and knees. The cool soil stuck to my palms. I raked my fingers slowly through it. The remains of plants revealed themselves. What other plants had grown here? Before the harvest and the turning under of the soil?

Life in the village had been timed to the turning of the soil, the planting and the harvest, season after season. In the springtime, when the tribe returned to the village from our winter spent in the forest, the men hunted for food. I worked with the women who grew the crops to feed us: maize and beans, squashes and sunflowers, pumpkins. I spent much of the day working in the soil, the warmth of the sun on my back. I loved to watch the seeds emerge, the green shoots growing up day by day, yielding their fruit for plucking.

"You have a need within you to make plants grow," Muh-teh-qway said. "It is a gift given to you by the Great Spirit, Kishel-emukong, who created the world."

I scooped a handful of dirt into my right hand and closed my fingers around it, breathing in the damp smell of earth.

"The earth is our mother, our *Manito,*" Muh-teh-qway had taught me, "charged by Kishelemukong to carry us and nurture us."

I missed Muh-teh-qway with her wise, wrinkled face, who spoke little, all of it wise.

"There is a spirit in all things," she had said. "In every storm, in every plant, in each new bud when the long winter is over."

The trees in the orchard behind the house stood gray and bare, their gold and scarlet cloak of leaves strewn across the ground. As though the trees were dying and would never again return to life. Inside them, the sap still flowed. When the warmth returned to the land, they would come again to life.

That last day in the village, before the Dutchmen took me away, Muh-teh-qway spoke to me alone in the *wigwam.* "You have felt this way before, young one. On the day you lost your first family. And, once again, as you leave us who became your new family. Remember this always: one must wait out the winter and the spring will come, just as it has before. The trees will flower and sprout leaves. It is the way of the Great Spirit. Wait."

Muh-teh-qway put something on my lap. A *wampum* belt. She'd given one to me after I came to the village. It told the story of my coming. "I have made you another *wampum* to take with you when you return to your former land." She fingered the rows of white and purple shell beads. "You are our daughter. Our family. This will help you never to forget. You will always belong here in my heart." She pressed another thing into my hand. A necklace made of the precious shells.

"I will remember," I said to Muh-teh-qway.

Near the garden plot stood a white oak, the deep ridges in the grayish bark rough to my touch. The Indians believed the morning sun imbued strength and healing into the bark of the trees. When we stripped the bark from a tree to make water buckets or bowls for storing and cooking, we only took from the east side of the tree.

I stepped out of the shade and took off my coif to feel the warmth on my hair and on my face. If the sun could strengthen a tree, it could strengthen me.

"Susanna!" The name sounded strange to me. Someone was calling me, the sound far away, an echo on a hill. I turned. Edward stood at the open door.

Chapter Four

I WOKE TO THE SOUND OF MY ENGLISH NAME.

"Susanna must go to afternoon meeting," Katherine said. "It will help her fit once again into society."

"I am not certain it is wise to push her too quickly," Edward answered. "We cannot comprehend the confusion she must feel."

They were down in the keeping room, their voices rising up the stairs.

"She has only had time to be idle. She sits in the orchard, as still as a hunted animal. I worry about her effect on the children, especially Elizabeth."

"She is my family, Katherine. My sister."

"She is, but must we have her with us?" Katherine said. "She could go to the farm with Faith and Thomas Savage in Mount Wollaston. It is only ten miles, and you can visit her there."

"No, Katherine. I want my little sister here, where I can protect her. I was away in England, far away from Boston, when Mother and Father needed me most. Perhaps I could have done something, said something, to convince the authorities to let my mother alone. To prove she was not a threat to them." I heard anguish and regret in my brother's voice.

Katherine softened. "I understand you took in Susanna out of your guilt, that you were not with your family when the trouble broke loose. You have been of much use to your parents. You helped them to settle in Aquidneck Island. Your signature lies on the charter below your father's. What more could you have done?"

"I could have done more. Much more. I should have stayed in Aquidneck with them and not come back to live in Boston."

"We have been over this many times before, Edward. Your duty is to look first to the needs of your own wife and children. It is best for them to be raised here in the city, not in some isolated wilderness. You take care of your father's business affairs. You run his merchant business, care for his properties, and protect the family home. You could do none of that in Aquidneck Island or in New Amsterdam."

"As the eldest son, I should have gone with Mother to New Amsterdam. If I had reviewed the sale of the land, perhaps I could have determined that the deal she made with the Dutch for the land from the Indians was not complete. If I had done so, my family might not have been killed."

I peered over the railing into the room below. Edward sat at the table with his head in his hands. Katherine put her arm across his back. "We cannot change the past, no matter how much we wish it. We can only go forward."

He lifted his head and took both her hands in his. "Understand this, Katherine. I cannot bring my family back, but I can care for my sister. I must care for her. You can help me do this, wife. We can give aid to Susanna."

"Well," Katherine said, "if you insist she stay in our home, she can be of use to me. She can do chores the same as our children do."

"I agree. Do not hurry her. She requires time to adjust to our ways again. I do not want her to think she is one of the servants. She is to feel part of the family," Edward said.

"She has known our English ways before. She was born into them. It need not take her long to adjust, if we do not coddle her as though she is a babe in arms."

"Think of our Elisha, wife. He is a few months younger than Susanna when she was taken to live with the Indians. I do not think it would take Elisha long to forget his life here. Children adapt very quickly to their circumstances."

Katherine clucked her tongue. "And just as swiftly back. She can understand what we say. I wish she would speak English rather than using those Indian words. She will adjust better if she understands our expectations of her."

"She needs time to adjust. I do not think she should go too soon to church. Imagine what John Winthrop will do when he sees her."

"The governor may not be at meeting. Martha said her husband has not felt well of late." Katherine stared out the window. "I'm afraid trouble will begin again. I feel him watching us from his windows."

"It has been over ten years since Mother was put on trial and banished," Edward said. "Perhaps in his ill health, John Winthrop has tired of trouble."

"Ten years seems only yesterday. We must give the authorities no reason to suspect rebellion in our household. Remember our maidservant cast out of the colony for persisting in errors of doctrine?"

"Judith Smith. It was unjust what they did to her for believing in my mother's teachings."

"That is my point. We have little reason to determine the trouble is entirely in the past, Edward."

"I pray daily to God it is."

My heart hurt at the sadness in my brother's voice.

"Susanna can stay with the younger ones during Thursday meeting today," he said, "and you and I will go."

"We do not know if she can be trusted to care properly for them. If she is to remain at home, Elizabeth must be with her."

"My mother used to say that even as a toddler Susanna already had the qualities of a mother. She will do well with Elisha and little Anne."

"We do not know what habits and attitudes the Indians have instilled in her. You remember her in your mother's house. The Indians have changed her. Surely you see her strange ways? We must tread carefully."

"I hear all you say, Katherine, but she is our sister."

"*Your* sister, Edward. I will trust her when she has earned my trust and only then."

Edward offered no answer.

Katherine's voice came again. "What of the pastor's promised visit after meeting today? He will bring Pastor Cotton with him. What will you do?"

"I will tell them Susanna needs solitude and rest to adjust to her new surroundings, and they need not see her at this time."

"Pastor Wilson will not listen. He always has his way. You will not be at home, and I am left to face them."

"Very well. I will send an assistant to meet the ship with our goods, so that I am here when they arrive."

I backed away, careful to step lightly so the wood floor would not creak with my weight. Katherine spoke the truth. My presence here caused trouble. Edward would regret bringing me and want to give me up. Questions swirled like a dust storm in my head. Why did Pastor Wilson despise Mother? Why did they make her leave Boston?

And the greatest question of all: why did my family have to die?

Chapter Five

THE KNOCK ON THE FRONT DOOR CAME IN THE moments before dusk, as the sun slid beneath the water in the bay.

Edward scoffed. "They come so late in the day. I could have gone to the dock."

"Lower your voice, Edward. They will hear you," Katherine shushed.

"Take Elisha and Anne upstairs, Elizabeth," Edward said.

Elizabeth shook her head. "I want to stay with Susanna."

"You can best help your aunt by keeping the young ones occupied," Edward said.

"Very well, Father." Elizabeth smiled at me as she herded the children from the keeping room.

Edward opened the front door. The flames in the hearth jumped to the beatings of my heart. I recognized Pastor Wilson's sharp tone.

"We have come to see your sister."

"Good evening, gentlemen. I appreciate your helpfulness. As Susanna's nearest kin, I ask she be given more time for solitude," Edward said.

"We serve as her ministers, as we do to you and all your family. We deem it best to speak with her," Wilson said.

"You need not worry, Edward," came another voice, deep and slow. "We will be kind."

Edward appeared at the keeping room door and beckoned to me. He put his hand on my shoulder as we moved into the best room. "Come, Susanna. Do not be afraid."

The man called John Cotton was also dressed in black. His pale hair hung in thick curls to his shoulders, a white collar like snow on his neck. His expression as he looked at me did seem kind, a smile on his bowed lips and in his sleepy eyes. He exuded calmness as though nothing could perturb him. Cotton took my hand in his. His fingers were cold.

"Susanna Hutchinson. I have known your family since our days in old England in Lincolnshire. We have endured much together." He looked at Edward. "Not all of it in happy circumstances. Yet we must remember the good that ever overrules the unfortunate." Cotton did not appear to notice Edward's shoulders stiffen as he continued. "You have returned to Boston and the fellowship of the church. We are glad of it. You have conformed well."

The words appeared to be praise mixed with disapproval. "We have come to rejoice with you, Edward, on the miracle of your long-lost sister's return, and to establish that she is firmly set on her path to reconciliation with her people and her church." He spoke as though Edward was a disobedient child who had chosen at last to obey.

Cotton's eyes widened as he turned back to me, still holding my hand. "Your hazel gaze, your sun gold locks. You look much as your mother did when she worshipped with us in the church in Lincolnshire. She was part of my special congregation. I called them my lilies among thorns. How much good your mother and I did together then as she helped me to care for the flock."

He sighed, putting his hand to his chest as though he had lost something once precious to him and which was no longer. I pulled my hand from his limp grasp.

"You also bear a resemblance to your older sister, whose name you bear. Susanna was sixteen when the terrible year of plague in Alford took her, along with young Katherine."

I looked at Edward. Was it true I had two more sisters who had died young in England? Edward nodded. I must have known this once and forgotten.

"She is a silent one," Pastor Wilson said. "Can the girl understand English? Governor Winthrop said she had forgotten her native language and wished to remain with her captors."

Edward's hand tightened on my shoulder. "Susanna understands everything we say."

"Do offer us a seat, Edward," Pastor Wilson said.

The two pastors seated themselves on the long bench facing the fireplace. Edward remained standing beside me. The two men looked me up and down as though I were a horse they considered purchasing. My face grew hot. I raised my gaze above them to the wooden beams of the ceiling, but still felt their stare.

John Cotton spoke first. "Susanna was very young, as I recall, when your mother came to trial."

"She was but four years of age," Edward said stiffly.

"That could be an advantage," Wilson interjected.

"It is what she has been taught in the years since that concerns us. Her years in Aquidneck Island and New Amsterdam under her mother's care," John Cotton said in his mild tone.

"Also, her years as a captive to the heathens," Pastor Wilson added. "The false teachings taught in her mother's house are of most grave concern to us." The end of Pastor Wilson's long nose dipped downward as his lips moved. "This must be corrected."

"My sister has been returned to us only a short time. If there be faults in her spiritual understanding, as her eldest brother I will teach her."

The two pastors turned to each other, exchanging a long gaze. "This is one of the reasons for our visit today," Cotton said. "Our concern is since you are her brother and your mother's eldest son, you may not be the wisest guide."

Edward's neck flushed. "I made peace with the church long ago."

Pastor Wilson snarled: "You defended your mother at her trial. That was a most grave offense."

Cotton nodded slowly, his languid eyes half open, then leaned toward Edward. "Do you recall the words I spoke to you and your brother-in-law, Thomas Savage, at your mother's excommunication trial?"

"Much time has passed since then," Edward answered. "I am not certain I can recall all of it."

"Eleven years past," Pastor Wilson said, as though proud to know the exact time, while John Cotton's full mouth turned down in a sad frown. Was he truly saddened? I could not tell.

"Allow me to bring it to your remembrance," Cotton said. He turned toward me. "I will trust your brother's word that you understand our language. Listen with the greatest attention, my dear child. You may use my admonition as a guide for your future conduct."

Edward said, "I am not certain it will aid any of us to recall the details of that time."

"It will," Wilson snapped. "To prevent any recurrence of rebellion against the church. None of us would wish that, would we?"

Edward looked weary. "No, we would not."

Reverend Cotton leaned forward, his gaze intent on Edward. "At the excommunication trial, you vigorously defended your mother. A most admirable trait for a dutiful child to strive to honor a parent, as the scriptures teach. You were not a mere child then, but a man grown and married. It was a terrible time. The very survival of the colony was at stake."

A few moments ago, Reverend Cotton had talked warmly of his long association with my family. Yet now he scolded my brother as though he were a child.

Reverend Cotton continued, his voice mellow as honey. "I take care to remind you of the dire circumstances in which we all found ourselves at that dreadful time. We sacrificed much to come to a land where we could serve our God without censure. I myself was forced to flee England or face imprisonment. We here in Boston became a beacon on a hill like our Governor John Winthrop had envisioned. Then came dissension and rebellion."

Cotton looked around him. "In these very rooms of your parents' house, your mother taught her heretical ideas. She fomented rebellion. In her heresy, she claimed the Holy Spirit spoke directly to her. The Holy Spirit speaks only to those with authority in the church. Certainly not to a mere woman. Because of her, the very survival of all we had striven to build on this new continent, this New England, was threatened."

Cotton ceased speaking. His words hung heavy in the room, like clouds swelling with unshed rain. Edward did not move, not even to blink.

"Your mother's influence came to threaten the colony. She grew arrogant and, in her pride, dared to ascribe her beliefs to *my* preaching." Annoyance flashed for a moment in his eyes and then hid behind his tranquility. "I remained her confidant and ally until I could no longer countenance her words or her actions."

I kept my eyes on Edward's white knuckles. He breathed deep and even, as though to keep himself calm.

"Edward. I rehearse to you the words I spoke to you that fateful day in which the court voted to expel your mother from the colony." Cotton turned his languid gaze on me. "I hope you understand me, child, for you will be wise to do as I advise."

The bell of the lantern clock on the table pierced the silence. Once. Twice. Thrice. Until seven times, and still Cotton did not speak. I looked down at the floor, away from his gaze.

"I admonished you at that time to consider how ill an office you performed to your mother—to harden her heart and nourish her in her unsound opinions—by your pleading for her. Instead of loving and natural children, you proved vipers to eat through the very bowels of your mother, to her ruin. I warned you to take heed of your flattery over her, your applauding of her rash thoughts and actions. It only served to hinder the work of repentance in her. You could have performed the part of faithful children if you had brought her to a sight of the evils in her . . . to reduce her. You should have divided your reason against your loyalty."

During the long speech his voice did not raise, nor did he gain in speed, each word measured and weighted the same. I thought again of the Mesingw, come to the children in the village to scold and to frighten them into submission.

Pastor Wilson shook his finger at Edward. "Consider yourself warned once again. When you appealed to return to Boston and the fellowship of the church, you were required to prove before us you had sufficiently repented your foolish ways. You were deceived by your strong-willed mother. We trust that, for your sake, you are deceived no more. As your spiritual authorities, we demand you reveal to your lost sister the foolishness and, indeed, the offensiveness of your mother's heretical opinions. Teach her they are from the Devil himself."

Edward stepped forward as though he were an old man, instead of one not yet forty years of age. "I thank you gentlemen for the esteem of your visit to my home, and your interest in the affairs of my family. As the hour is late, I will detain you no more. I give you leave to return to your own homes to rest."

"You will do as we say, Hutchinson?" Pastor Wilson looked severe. "Make certain this girl sits in meeting twice weekly to hear the word of preachers and thus of God. Teach only truth to her ears."

I took a step closer to my brother. His hands clenched into fists as though he fought to control himself. "I give you my promise," Edward said. "Susanna will be taught the truth."

"Teach only what we determine to be truth and nothing else," John Cotton said. "We are watching."

Wilson turned to me. "Girl. Do you understand what we say?"

The men stared at me. I must answer. "I hear you."

"Excellent," Cotton said. "You have not forgotten the English language. I am most pleased."

"Because she speaks a few words is not sufficient evidence to satisfy me," Reverend Wilson said. "Laws have been enacted to ensure the proper education of every child in our community. They must be taught to read and to write. We need to determine whether Susanna can do so."

"My sister learned to read and write years ago."

"We have already considered that fact," Wilson said. "You do not realize the influence of her years among the savages. Your sister may have forgotten much of what she learned at such a young age. For this reason, we have determined that Susanna must have a trial to ascertain if her knowledge is sufficient."

I looked at Edward. A trial. They said my mother was put on trial. My mouth dried up. I could not swallow.

Edward set his arm around my shoulders. "As I said before, my sister has only just returned. I beg leave of you to allow me, as her elder brother, sufficient time to determine what she requires in her education."

Cotton and Wilson looked at each other.

"Very well, Edward," Cotton said. "You may have one month, after which Susanna will submit to trial. And we the authorities, not you, shall determine her needs for the proper education."

"That is not enough time for Susanna to prepare for what shall surely be a rigorous examination," Edward said. "She needs at least until the New Year begins."

"That is several months from now. What think you, Reverend Wilson?" asked Cotton.

Wilson frowned as he stared at me. "The twenty-fifth of March is too long away. January will suffice," he answered.

"February," Edward said.

Wilson pointed his finger toward Edward, shaking it. "I warn you. Do not challenge your authorities. You well know to what end it leads."

"I do not challenge your authority," Edward answered, keeping his gaze upon the man called Cotton. "I appeal to your compassion concerning the ordeal Susanna has suffered. Grant my sister sufficient time to adjust and to relearn the ways of her youth."

"Understand this," Wilson inserted. "If your sister's skills are proven insufficient, and we as the authorities deem it necessary, she will be removed from your care and placed in a home where she can receive proper instruction."

They spoke of me as though I were a dumb animal, incapable of comprehension. A savage. My nails dug into my palms.

"In mid-November Susanna will turn sixteen," Edward said. "She is no child, almost a woman grown, and therefore not tied to statutes meant for the education of children. There may be no need then for a trial to prove her competence."

Again, the two men looked at each other. "We will acquiesce to your plea for more time," Cotton said. "February, then."

"Come, Cotton. Our business is finished here," Wilson snapped.

The two men rose. The front door closed behind them.

Edward's face drained of color. "Before God, Susanna, I will not let them win. You will never be sent from this house. They only want me to teach you what they deem to be truth. I *will* teach you. I will tell you of tyranny and the blindness of men. I will tell you a grand and tragic story of constancy and courage. I will tell you of our family. I will tell you of our mother."

Chapter Six

A STORM CAME DURING THE NIGHT. THE WIND YOWLED at the windows like a frightened animal. In the darkness, I lay on the pile of blankets on the floor. I need not fear those men who called themselves preachers. Edward would keep his word to me. He had promised to tell me the story of my family.

It would be like the evening story times in the village around a great fire, sparks spitting at the sky, Edward's face like the medicine man's shining in the firelight. He would talk of the meaning of things and help me unravel the tangled threads. The men spoke of truth. Edward's truth seemed to differ from theirs. What was truth? One thing to one man and another to someone else? Surely not.

Cold seeped into me from the hard floor. I took the blankets and smoothed them across the bed and slid beneath their warmth.

Next morning, Edward was not in the keeping room.

"Where is my brother?" I asked Katherine.

Katherine handed me a bowl of mush. "A shipment of goods has come from England. It will keep him at the dock until late. Hurry, Elisha, or school will begin with your seat empty."

She gestured to a folded paper on the table. "Edward has had a letter from your sister Faith. She cannot come as planned next week, for the children are sick with a fever. With the winter cold coming, your other sister Bridget will not be able to come from

Aquidneck Island until spring, so you must wait to be reunited with more of your family."

She handed me another paper. "Bridget has sent you your own letter."

"I . . . cannot . . . read it." I set it on the table.

Katherine reddened. "Of course, you cannot. Forgive me." She turned to Elizabeth. "Read it to Susanna while I finish mixing up the pudding."

Elizabeth sat beside me, stretching the paper flat on the table. I stared at the curved black lines. I used to know these scribbles. They'd had meaning to me.

"*My dearest little sister,*" Elizabeth began. "*It is with the greatest joy and gladness in my heart that I write to you, my sweetest sister Susanna.*" Elizabeth leaned over the paper. "It is hard to read, for there are splotches blurring the ink. I think they are tears."

My sister Bridget cried as she wrote these words to me.

It has been seven years since I last bid you goodbye. You were eight years of age when Mother began the journey to New Amsterdam—a little girl, and now you are fifteen years. A young woman! With all that has happened, I thought never to be able to see you again. And now, to know that you are living—my little sister. I remember your shining, red gold hair, your eyes so full of fun, playing games with my children, helping me in my kitchen, climbing trees with a book in your hands to read as you sat among the leaves. My greatest desire is to see you once again. As soon as we are able and the weather is fair, we will hurry to you, dearest Susanna.

All my sisterly love to you, Bridget.

Elizabeth refolded the paper and held it out to me. "This belongs to you. You keep it."

I took the note and held it in my palm. Bridget's hands had touched this paper as she wrote these words and wept. She remembered me. She loved me. I could not picture her face nor recall her voice. I stuffed the paper beneath the belt at my waist.

Katherine did not ask for my help, not even to assist Elizabeth with her chores. She must have taken Edward at his word to leave me be. My body chafed at my inactivity since I had come to Boston. I was used to being in the fields all day and itched for physical work. If I did my share, perhaps Katherine would want me here.

"I would do chores today," I said.

Katherine looked at me sharply. "It is house-cleaning day. You may help Elizabeth. She will show you what to do."

We washed the bedclothes in the great pots in the back yard and hung them to dry on a rope strung between two of the trees in the orchard. We scoured the planked wood floor in the keeping room, swept out the ashes in the hearth, wiped each windowpane until the outside light shone through.

My body felt invigorated, and my mind began to ease.

"Now we must dust the best room." Elizabeth handed me what she called a feather duster.

An oak table sat beneath the window, a large book sitting atop it. It was beautiful with its rich brown leather binding and golden brass edgings.

I had seen this book before in our house in Aquidneck Island.

I set down the duster, unhooked the two clasps and opened the cover. Its white pages were filled with curved lines like the letter from Bridget. How strange the curves looked, weaving together in a straight line. Words. Written words. English words.

There had been no books in the village. The Siwanoy had no written language, only spoken, clipped sounds upon the tongue. Sounds that meant something, that conveyed feelings, told stories, only mute unless uttered aloud. These written words did the same but in silence. They needed no voice to make them come to life in the mind.

I traced the black letters with my finger. The feel of a book seemed familiar. I must have liked to read. That was years ago. Once I had known these symbols, read them both in silence and aloud. They taunted me to remember.

Anne called out behind me. "Susanna is touching the Bible. Mother! You told me I mustn't, so she cannot either."

I drew my hand back. The pages rustled softly as they fell back upon each other. I closed the spine and the words disappeared.

"Susanna can look at the book," Elizabeth scolded. "She is not five like you."

Anne stomped her foot. "I am learning to read. I go to the Dame school. Can you read, Susanna?"

"Of course, Susanna can read," Elizabeth said. "She would have learned at your age."

Anne stomped to the table and reopened the book, pointing with her finger. "Read this word."

The black letters below Anne's finger jumped in front of my eyes.

"I told you she cannot read," Anne trumped.

"Hush, sister," Elizabeth said. "Leave Susanna alone."

Anne huffed out of the room.

"Your sister speaks truth," I said. I turned away from the book.

"Look how well you understand English and speak it again, Susanna. You can read. I know it."

It was true. The speed of the language returning to me was almost overwhelming, as though a floodgate had opened in my mind and water gushed forth.

Elizabeth removed the duster from my grasp. "You knew how to read before. Your mind has not forgotten." She turned to the front of the book and pointed to the black curves. Tall rounded letters sitting beside the small.

"This is a B, the first letter in the word Bible." She put my finger on the page and traced the straight black line, then the two curves. "Surely you remember?"

"B," I whispered.

"And this is an A. There are twenty-six letters in the alphabet, and these are the first two."

Elizabeth turned the page to the very front of the book. "This is the family Bible. These are the names of our family. Father said this book is very old. Grandmother Hutchinson brought it with her on the ship from England." She pointed. "Here is your father's name: William Hutchinson. And your mother, Anne Marbury Hutchinson."

"They are dead," I said. "You must not speak the names of the dead."

"Why ever not?" Elizabeth said. "How else will we remember them?"

Surely Elizabeth did not mean disrespect? To remember the dead by speaking their names was true to her, but not to the Indians. Which was right? Perhaps both.

I looked again at the words on the Bible page. *William. Anne.* My father. My mother.

"Written below your parents are the names of their children." Elizabeth touched each name with her finger, counting aloud to fifteen. "Here is your name. *Susanna Hutchinson.* Their fourteenth child."

Susanna. I touched my chest. It sounded like my Indian name—Sisika. Each with two of the curved letters Elizabeth called "s."

Written here for all to see were the names of my brothers and sisters, the ones I had silently rehearsed each night to the stars.

I could not make myself speak them aloud as Elizabeth did with such ease.

"I have an idea!" Elizabeth exclaimed. "Wait here. I will only be a moment." Her shoes clattered up and down the stairs. She ran back into the room, holding something in front of her. "This is my hornbook."

A flash like lightning shook me. I had seen this. I had taken one of these things to the split rock on the day my family died.

Elizabeth held it out to me. It had a handle at the bottom, a sheet of paper attached to the wide top. "Here. Take it." The wood felt rough and cool and familiar to my hands. "See? This is the alphabet, in both small and large letters. These are the vowel sounds: a, e, i, o, and u. Below them is written the Lord's Prayer."

The Lord's Prayer. I had repeated this over and over in the village.

"Tell it . . . to me." I shoved the hornbook toward her.

"*Our Father which art in heaven, hallowed be thy name.*" The words flowed over me. "*Thy kingdom come. Thy will be done even in earth as it is Heaven. Give us this day our daily bread and forgive us our debts as we forgive our debtors. And lead us not into temptation but deliver us from evil. For thine is the kingdom and the power and the glory for ever. Amen.*"

"More." I repeated some of the words with her. Bread. Debts. Debtors. Temptation. Evil. Kingdom. Forever.

"Again."

Our voices blended together until we reached the Amen.

I pressed the hornbook against my chest. This had been part of my childhood. I stared at the letters. "How . . . do I read?"

Elizabeth pointed to the symbols at the top. "First, you need to learn the letters and the vowel sounds."

I repeated the sounds after her: "a, e, i, o, u." They sounded an echo in my head.

Elizabeth squealed and jumped up and down. She pointed again to the first letter. "What is this one?"

Its name floated away from me.

"A." Elizabeth turned back to the writing on the first page of the Bible, pointing to it: two slanted lines connected by a line. "You say it."

"A." The sound tasted like warm bread on my tongue.

Katherine stood at the door in her apron, a frown on her face. "Has this room been dusted?"

"Mother, Susanna is remembering how to read! Is it not wonderful!"

"It is," Katherine said as she closed the door.

I gripped the hornbook with both hands. "Teach me. Now."

"Of course, I will teach you. It is a fine day. As soon as we finish the dusting, let's go out to the orchard. I know you prefer to be outdoors."

The girl's soft heart covered me like a blanket.

We sat in the grass below an apple tree, skirts tucked beneath our legs. The sunlight warmed my shoulders and neck below my coif.

"Let's begin by reviewing each letter," Elizabeth said. I repeated each sound aloud as she pointed to it: first in the alphabet row, then in the Lord's Prayer.

When the sun shone straight above and our long shadows disappeared beneath our skirts, a servant girl brought two plates with slices of meat and cheese and bread for our midday meal. She also handed Elizabeth sheets of paper and quill and ink. "Your mother sent this," she said.

We ate hungrily, then set the plates aside. Elizabeth handed me a slate and a piece of chalk.

"Write, Susanna."

The chalk shook in my fingers. "Spell my mother's name."

Elizabeth wrote it out on the hornbook.

I formed an A first, trying to curve the harsh lines in the same way the family names in the Bible were written. I studied the letters of Mother's name. Two small n's. An e. Letter by letter, Mother's name appeared on the page. The letters seemed to shout, sounding a single drumbeat in my head. *Anne.*

Elizabeth squealed. "That's wonderful, Susanna."

"Father's name."

Elizabeth took the chalk and spelled it out. "W-i-l-l-i-a-m." I copied out each letter below Elizabeth's. Two drumbeats sounded in my head, the first loud, the second soft: *Will-iam.*

"Now write your own name." Elizabeth wrote out the letters. *Su-san-na.* Three drumbeats. She spelled out the last name: Hutchinson, and I wrote it. Also three drumbeats.

I jumped up and ran into the house to the Bible, turning to the front page with the handwritten letters. I touched my father and mother's names then Edward's, the eldest child, down the row to my own, and Zuriel at the bottom. My family was here. Each one of them. Woven together with words.

Elizabeth put the slate, chalk, and hornbook down on the table beside the Bible, along with the paper, quill and ink. Then she left the room. She seemed to understand my need to be left alone with the wonder that swirled inside me.

Should I laugh? Cry? Dance? Sing? I could not remember how the English sang. Only the beat of drums and wailing.

I stayed in the best room until the sun's late afternoon rays slanted across it, painting the far wall with light. I filled one of the papers with the names of my family, folded it and put it in the pocket of my apron.

Later, as I chewed the supper of fish stew and bread, I kept my right hand in the pocket, wrapped around the folded paper.

Chapter Seven

I SHIVERED THROUGH THE LAYERS OF CLOTHING, WRAP-
ping the cloak tighter around my shoulders, tucking my
hands in its folds. The backless bench in the meetinghouse cut
the back of my knees. I sat on the end of the row, Elizabeth next
to me, then little Anne, and Katherine. Edward and Elisha sat
with the men on the opposite side of the room. A door stood
in the center of each of the four walls, two windows on each
side, and a tall slender one behind the raised platform holding
the carved wooden pulpit. The afternoon sun from the nearest
window slanted across Edward's solemn face.

Reverend Wilson grasped his thick hands around the pulpit,
his thumbs keeping a steady rhythm on the wood. My aunt kept
still, her hands folded in her lap. Even little Anne and Elisha
kept as quiet as the village children when the Mesingw came. In
the quiet forest, I could sit motionless for hours, like the trees
and grasses when there was no wind. Within these four walls,
surrounded by strangers, my body would not be still.

I stretched my aching legs out beneath the bench in front of
me, and Katherine shot me a reproving glance. A sharp-nosed
woman down the bench leaned forward and fixed her eyes
upon me. Another woman sitting on the end of the row in front
turned, peering at me from beneath her white coif, whispering
to the woman beside her.

I eased a hand into my pocket and rubbed the smooth chestnut I'd found beneath a tree before the service began.

Reverend Wilson's harsh voice sounded like the scraping of a saw on wood. The sands in the hourglass on the pulpit made a tiny mountain as they streamed through the narrow neck to the bottom. Elizabeth said that sometimes, if the minister had more to say, he would turn the hourglass over to begin again. The last of the sand trickled down through the narrow opening onto the mountain.

Let the long meeting be done or the scream churning in my middle would release! Katherine would be furious and Edward disappointed if I lost control.

Wilson did not touch the hourglass. Instead he picked up the psalm book. There would be no more sermon. My held breath whooshed out and Elizabeth giggled, stifling it with her hand across her mouth, bringing another sharp glance from Katherine. Elizabeth picked up her psalm book and hid her face in its pages.

"Let us now raise our hearts and voices together in praise with Psalm number 98." A man sitting on the bench below the pulpit stood and faced the congregation. "Make a joyful noise . . ." he sang. Elizabeth moved the psalm book closer to me. The high voices of the women blended with the men's low tones as they repeated each line of the Psalm.

I knew the words. Elizabeth and I had been practicing every day; but I did not sing, letting the sounds wash over me. It made me think of the flute tunes the Siwanoy boys played to attract the attention of the female they fancied. As a bird calling and another answering. If I had my flute with me, I could play to the beats.

I counted six beats. Eight. Six. Eight. The Lord's Prayer I had written on the hornbook also had beats. I'd copied it again and again: "Our Father which art in heaven." Eight beats. "Hallowed be Thy name." Five beats. "Thy kingdom come, thy will be done." Eight. "On earth as it is in heaven." Eight.

Words. Spoken aloud. Spoken in silence. It was the same. *Shiki*. It is beautiful.

I closed my eyes, feeling the movement of the music in my center, below the steady beat of my heart. It made me think of the sounds the wind made as it plucked at the trees, like an angel's harp. The whoosh of water waves on the beach. The splash of canoe paddles as a boat moved through the river.

"See how the Hutchinson girl does not sing." An old woman's voice came from behind me. "Living with the savages has rendered her dumb." The music receded behind the woman's harsh words.

Another voice. "That girl does not belong in Boston."

"Neither did her mother Anne Hutchinson."

"She looks like her."

The singing ended, psalm books thumping closed. I put my hand on the swinging door beside me. No one moved from their place.

"Now we will pray to God." Pastor Wilson said, and all stood. I turned toward the back of the room. A man stood in front of the door, blocking the way out.

"Preserve our absent leader, Governor Winthrop, and relieve him of his ailing health. Bless our land with peace, Oh Lord. Allow no more evil to return among us. And if it be so, let it be rooted out."

The scream rose up inside me, a painful lump that would choke me. I tried to swallow the lump down. It shoved downward against my heart. I wrapped my fist tighter around the chestnut in my pocket and tried to slow my breaths. If only the preacher would cease praying. If only I could get out of these stifling walls.

A dark-eyed man sitting on the back row met my gaze. He looked to be younger than my brother Edward, with thick brown hair tightly curled above his ears and across his forehead. He nodded toward me. He could not mean kindness, only jeering like the others. Yet another person to stare and scorn me. I looked away.

Silence came at last with the preacher's amen. The congregation stirred, and a few people moved toward the open door. I fled, knocking against the old woman.

"Savage," she muttered. "The men are to file out first."

Cool air at last. Warm sun. The lump in my throat eased. Elizabeth was nowhere in sight, or Katherine or Edward. The mean woman came through the doorway.

I darted across the street, dodging beneath a horse, and the rider cursed at me. I ran up the street to reach the house but could find no red-painted door. Mud splattered my shoes and apron. Katherine would scold.

The street curved into a narrow lane of shops and warehouses. Beyond them lay the wharf. The tang of the salt air thickened. A few small ships dotted the choppy gray waters of the Cove, their white sails snapping in the wind. In the far distance, the brown humps of islands dotted the sea. A seabird's sharp cries pierced the air. I watched it fly low over the water, black-tipped wings arching as it lifted free into the sky.

The bird brought a memory of the village.

We sat around the fire that was set on rocks in the center of the *wigwam*, the smoke rising upward through the hole in the roof. Minsi had returned from her vision quest. At the Gamwing, the Big House ceremony that lasted for twelve days, many of the people would share the visions they had. The Great Creator communicated to man through visions and dreams.

No one shared their visions here. Not even the preacher.

Opala said that during her vision quest an eagle had flown down to sit beside her. It kept its eye upon her until the sun set, then it spread its wide wings and flew away. She was told that she would be as wise as the eagles. The new name she was given, Opala, meant eagle.

The others around my age had all gone on their vision quests. They joined with the older ones of the village in the Big House ceremonies, recounting their visions and encounters with their chosen spirit animal. I sat in the back with the other children and listened with envy. They returned knowing who they were. I wanted that.

My two mothers agreed. "She is one of us," Opala argued with Wampage. "Why should the adopted one not go?"

Wampage grunted and left the *wigwam*. Opala and Muh-teh-qway looked at me with pity. "Talk to him with few words," Muh-teh-qway said. "I will tell him to listen."

It frightened me to approach Wampage. I chose a morning when he seemed more cheerful. I made myself look him in the face.

"You brought me to your village. You call me daughter. Like Minsi, I would go on a vision quest." I kept my head up and did not look away from him.

He did not answer.

"Let me go on a quest," I said, "to know who I am."

He turned to walk away, flinging over his shoulder: "For one day only. You will be watched."

I would go. Not three days like the others. I would not be truly alone. Though it had been years since I came to the village, they still feared I would leave or be taken away.

Once, on a river run, I saw white men on the shore. Opala and Muh-teh-qway jerked the paddle from my grip and shoved me to the floor of the canoe. They raced away. I was part of the village family. To lose me would be a great tragedy for the village.

The family had lost their daughter and sister when the Dutch-man chief named Kieft slaughtered some of their people. I was the girl's replacement, and they did not want to lose a daughter twice. Her name had been Gela, Muh-teh-qway told me. The daughter of Opala and Wampage. Her name meant happiness. And now I had become part of their happiness.

&

On the morning of my vision quest, the sky was a brilliant blue and clear of clouds. I took no food or drink in my bag, only my flute. I followed a narrow deer trail in the tall grass, the forest floor soft beneath my moccasins. Gold and red leaves still clung to the branches, unwilling to yield to the coming cold. I wandered without purpose, climbing the terrain at the edge of a waterfall, timing my steps to the steady beat of the water hitting the pool far below me.

At the top, the forest parted and yielded a view of the ocean. I stood on the ledge and pulled out my flute. It was made of river cane and I loved its strong, clear tones. The notes followed their own rhythm like no song I knew. I played soft, then loud, slow and fast. The breeze lifted them upward into the blue of the sky.

My mind became as clear and clean as the air around me. Awareness of the days behind me and days ahead receded like the waves drawing back from the beach far below. I yielded to the present moment. It brought a sense of freedom I had not known for many days.

Muh-teh-qway spoke of the Great Manito, the Great Spirit who made the land and the sky, the sun, the moon and the stars. And of the Manitowuk, the spirit of the great one that was present in all of nature.

"Mankind is one with the world," she said. "The four winds are members of a family. The change of seasons are competitions between the grandmothers and the grandfathers. The grand-mother wins in the spring when her warm winds out of the south prevail over the north wind of the grandfather. The sun and the moon are brothers who light the sky and darken it. The stars are the grandfathers. Earth is the mother with the charge of caring for all the people."

On the day of my vision quest I sensed it more than ever before. All that surrounded me was created by the Great Spirit—Kishelemukong. The Great Spirit was in the sunlight that fell upon my shoulders, in the sound of the waterfall, in the rocks and the trees.

I, the lost salt girl, was part of it. One with it all.

I stood at the edge of the cliff for a long time. Seabirds soared upon the wind higher and higher and then plunged down toward the sea, skimming just above the waves to rise once again. One flew near me. I could see its yellow eye with a black center before it turned out to sea.

Another seabird landed on the ledge near where I stood. I was careful not to move so it would not fly away. The gray and black-tipped wings folded against its white body as it rocked back and forth on its golden feet. It gave me a sharp stare, and the yellow beak opened wide as it squawked. With a whip of its wings it was gone, flying into the center of land and sky.

For a moment I felt I could lift my arms and fly alongside of the birds. I would be truly free. A voice seemed to come from inside my breast saying, *Some distant day you will know what it means to fly. Now you are meant for earth.*

I turned away from the ledge and sank down on the ground, my head in my hands. *Open your eyes. Look,* said the voice. *Look upon the earth from whence you came.*

What did those words mean? Wild marjoram. Wild leek. Violets. Indigo. Muh-teh-qway had taught me to find these plants as we searched in the forest for the herbs she used. They surrounded where I sat. *Look. Look.* I plucked some of each, stuffing them into my bag. I would take them to Muh-teh-qway.

They are for you to use, the voice said to me. *You will be a healer.* A *kikehwet.* Like Muh-teh-qway.

When the day of my vision quest ended, I had an answer for Muh-teh-qway and Opala. "The white seabirds. They are my spirit animal."

"You have chosen wisely," Muh-teh-qway answered. "A bird knows much of freedom. You are fettered now. The day will come when you will know what it is to fly."

"Sisika," she said. "That will be your new name. Bird. Let the seabirds guide you. They know how to survive. They are a symbol for healing."

"Birds mean healing?" I asked.

"*Osomi.*" She nodded.

I opened my bag and showed her the plants. "The Great Spirit spoke to me. I am to be a *kikehwet.*"

"I will teach you," she said. "It will help you know what it feels to be whole."

From that time the people in the village called me Sisika. Muh-teh-qway taught me about herbs and how to prepare them, how to use them for healing.

Before my lessons had finished, the white men came and took me away.

Chapter Eight

As I watched from the Boston dock, the seabird flew away into the sun's light and disappeared. The sun hung just above the horizon, painting a golden path across the choppy water, giving the buildings a rosy glow.

The people who were my long-ago family called me Susanna, the name given to me at birth.

Elizabeth told me my name came from the Bible in the book of Daniel. "She was most beautiful and a good and virtuous woman," she said. "Susanna means a lily flower." Elizabeth showed me the wood lilies growing on the east side of the house. Their heads did not droop like other lilies. They had six reddish petals that looked upward toward the sun.

Did I remember the girl named Susanna?

The dark-eyed man I had seen inside the church stood in front of a three-storied timber structure on the corner, gazing out at the water. He did not wear black like the preachers, his doublet and breeches a muted indigo. He was very tall. Below the ruffles of his sleeves his hands looked big.

He walked toward me. I shied back.

"You are Susanna Hutchinson, are you not?" His low voice made me think of a still pool of water. I could not make myself answer or look at his face, keeping my eyes on the silver buckle on his belt.

"My name is John Cole. My father owns this inn. Are you looking for your brother's house?"

I nodded. When I looked up into his face, his eyes looked like deep water colored with the blue of the sky.

"You must have taken the wrong turn at the meetinghouse, for your house is very near to it. This is Swing-Bridge Lane. You must follow it back to High Street. It is the widest street in town. Go past the meetinghouse and the market on High Street. Your brother's house stands on the corner of Beacon Street."

The street names spun in my head. I would never be able to follow them.

He cleared his throat. "Would you permit me to show you the way? I know it well, for my father owns the house on the lot near to your father's. You and I were neighbors when you were young."

What should I do? I was lost. I did not want to follow this strange man.

"Susanna!" Elizabeth ran toward me, panting, pale curls escaping from her coif. "Where did you go? I've been searching everywhere." She grasped my hand. "Come. We will be late for supper, and Mother will be angry."

The man called John Cole stepped back and bowed. He had a face that looked like it was used to smiling. "I see you no longer require my aid. Best wishes to you, Susanna Hutchinson."

When we returned to the house, Katherine began to scold. Edward shushed her with a look. "Gather the children, Elizabeth," Katherine said. "Supper is on the table."

Sabbath meals were kept simple: dried fish, hard yellow cheese, warm bread and the huckleberries the children had picked in the wood. I ate quickly, hungry from my walk. Edward pushed back his plate and rubbed his neck. He looked weary.

The room darkened, and Katherine lit the thick yellow candles sitting atop the pewter holders in the table's center. The slender flames joined with the firelight, flickering upon the faces of the family.

Elizabeth went to the best room and returned with the big Bible in her arms. She set it on the table in front of Edward. "Susanna knows the family names, Father. She opens the Bible every day and reads them. I see her lips moving."

Edward lifted his gaze.

"Susanna is learning to read the passages I show her." Elizabeth spoke like a proud parent. I gave her my hornbook, and she practices writing."

Was it relief I saw in Edward's eyes? The same relief that was also mine?

Edward thumbed the pages and pushed the book across the table toward me. "Can you read me this passage in the Book of Psalms, Susanna?"

The letters jumped about on the page. What if I could not do it? What was the first letter? T. The second? H. Y. I knew the first word. "Thy."

Elizabeth clapped her hands as I read the rest of the passage.

"Thy word . . . is a lamp . . . unto my feet. . . . A light . . . unto my . . . path."

"This was one of Mother's favorite passages," Edward said. He thumbed through the pages again and pointed to a passage with his finger.

I read aloud the first sentence of the Book of John: "In the beginning . . . was the . . . Word."

The Word. It bore the sound of authority. Words had always been and always would be. I was reading the English words of my childhood.

Edward lifted his hand from the page, his gaze tender. "'Tis a wonder you are here with us. When you were born in Lincoln-shire, I was here in New England. Father sent me ahead to build this house in preparation for the family to come. Then I returned to England and married the woman I had loved since my youth—Katherine. The only time I have lived near you, Susanna, was the few months I spent with the family on Aquidneck Island. How old would you have been then?"

"She was five, Edward," Katherine said. "It was the same year I gave birth to Elizabeth."

I dared to ask. "Do you remember me then, brother?"

"You were never still, except to read. You would perch up in a tree with your hornbook in your hand and read aloud. Mother called you her little jaybird. She said you could never be lost because your chattering always told her where you were."

Mother's jaybird had been lost. I could not look at my brother for my shame. "Mother told me to stay at the house. I did not heed her."

Edward reached across the table and grasped my hand. "You were lost, Susanna. Now you are found."

"It reminds me of the Bible story," Elizabeth said, "about the woman who lost her coin and swept the whole house to search for it."

"Yes, Elizabeth. The coin was found. And all the house rejoiced." Edward squeezed my hand.

"What else do you remember of Susanna, Father?" Elizabeth asked.

He sat back, silent for a moment. "To Susanna, words were a song singing inside her head."

He was beginning his story, just as he had promised. He had not forgotten. I needed him to tell me of myself and teach me how to live in the world in which I had been born, where now I felt a stranger. So much of the life I'd lived before the village was only shadows. The girl I had been lived inside the shadows.

My brother told me when I was small, I had loved to read. That I loved words. I looked again at the passage of the open Bible on the table. Words were a light. A lamp in a dark room.

Katherine turned from the fire. "I remember Susanna singing as she went to sleep. Bridget would scold you for it, saying you kept her awake."

I had sung myself to sleep. Katherine remembered me. Perhaps she did not resent my presence here as much as I feared.

Edward reached into his overcoat and retrieved a folded paper. "I received another letter from Faith. She says the children have recovered from their illnesses. She will travel to Boston with a neighbor in his wagon and expects to arrive by Tuesday afternoon."

Katherine shook her head. "It is ten miles of treacherous road, and she must bring the baby to nurse. She should not attempt the journey."

"Nevertheless, she is determined to see her sister," Edward answered. "Are you happy for that, Susanna? To see your sister Faith?"

My throat was too full for words; I nodded my head.

Katherine put a hand on the small of her back, grimacing.

Edward rose from the table and went to her side, putting his arm around her shoulder. "Are you well, wife?"

"Well enough. Only weary." Katherine's shoulders slumped and she sagged against Edward.

He kissed the crown of her hair. "Come. You must lie down and rest."

"The fire needs to be banked, and the hearth swept," she said.

"I will do it," I said.

"Many thanks, Susanna," Edward said. "Katherine tells me you have been a great help to her."

I covered the glowing coals with ashes to keep the fire low. I could hear their conversation as Edward helped Katherine walk slowly toward the stairs.

"Little Katherine would have been one year old this month," Katherine sighed. "And little William three years. And our eldest son, too."

"Three of our little ones dead," Edward said. "And three who live."

Katherine was not mean. She was sad and frightened. Muh-teh-qway said that grief and fear made sharp tongues.

After I finished sweeping the hearth, I turned the Bible to the family page, tracing the names in the dimming light of the day. *Edward Hutchinson, wife Katherine Hamby.* The children's names were written below: *Elishua,* the eldest child, born 1637, four years after my own birth in England. *Elizabeth, Elisha, Anne, William, Katherine.* I hefted the heavy book in my arms, setting it down on the table in the best room.

The door bolt made only a soft click when I lifted it and slipped outside. The stars sparkled in the black sky. I found the starry cluster, mouthing silently the names of the dead: Father and Mother and each of my siblings. I added three more. Elishua, William. A babe named Katherine.

Like Elizabeth, Katherine had not shied away from speaking aloud of her dead children. Was it terrible, as the Indians said? Did it dishonor them? Or did it keep the dead close to the living? Perhaps speaking a name aloud carried more power than in thought alone. Uttered so the trees and sky might hear.

Like the family names written in the Bible woven tight together, a testament of unity that defied even death.

I opened my lips. No sound would come, though I wanted it. I must decide what I believed. The stars appeared to stay constant, unmoving. People did not. Ideas did not.

I returned to the silent house. I must try to sleep, for soon my sister would come.

Chapter Nine

KATHERINE SAID THE WAGON CARRYING MY SISTER Faith would come southwest down High Street. I paced in front of the fence. The sun warmed the top of my coif and my shoulders, though the cool breeze hinted of the coming winter. The trees stood bare, their clothing of leaves strewn orange and gold across the ground.

The house directly across the narrow street drew my attention. It was larger than the others, similar to Edward's: steep-roofed, two-story brown clapboard, a large center chimney. The door was painted a brilliant white, as were the window frames and the front gate. It looked as though it was scrubbed clean daily, even the close-clipped bushes beneath the three windows on each side of the front door.

A man stood at one of the upstairs windows, looking out at the street, his gaze fixed upon me.

At the clattering of wheels, I turned away. A wagon made its way through the road ruts. A woman sat in the front seat, a blanket-wrapped figure in her arms.

Elisha bolted from the house, running down the road. "Aunt Faith is come!"

I shrank back against the gate. Would Faith recognize me? I was not the little girl she had known. A stranger who had lived among the Indians, white skin burned brown by the sun.

Would she love me? Or would she shy away as so many in the town did, fear and anger in their gaze? I must be careful to speak only English, eat with my mouth closed, not scratch at the layers of itchy clothing, keep my coif and waistcoat straight so Faith would not frown at me as Katherine did.

A woman climbed down from the wagon. She was tall and slender, the color of her hair concealed beneath her coif. Elizabeth ran to take the babe from her arms as the man heaved her trunk from the back of the wagon.

I could not move from the gate.

Faith ran toward me. "Susanna! It is you." Her voice had a familiar timbre, as though I had heard it always. She drew me close. "My little sister." Her skin smelled of mint. "We thought you were dead. And then word came you had been taken by the Indians. We searched everywhere. We thought you, too, were lost to us." She hugged me tight.

Faith released me, cupping my face in her palms. "Why, you're nearly as tall as I am. It is truly a miracle! My little sister is here. Not the child I remember. A lovely young woman with haunting eyes and our mother's red gold hair." She touched the curls escaping from my coif.

Faith's wide mouth reminded me of Mother. Her eyes shone with an alertness that made me think of a doe in the forest watching out for her fawn. "I must ask, Susanna. Are you well? Were the Indians good to you?"

Muh-teh-qway. Opala. They treated me as a daughter. When I left the village, many of the women wept as though I had died. I thought of the gifts in my bag that Muh-teh-qway had given to me. "Yes," I said to Faith. "They were good to me."

Faith took my hands in hers. "Terrible dreams have haunted me in my fears for you. It is hard for me not to hate the Indians for what they did. There has been so much killing. Both sides wronging the other. The irony to me is that Mother had peaceful dealings with the Indians, and yet she died at their hands because they mistook her to be Dutch."

Again, I could see the fire rising above the trees as the house was set aflame, hear it roaring as it consumed my family. The sight and sound of the day had often visited me in nightmares. Now it came in sunlight. I pulled my hands from Faith's grip, shut my eyes and put my hands over my ears to silence it.

"Susanna?"

I opened my eyes. My sister was here before me, not the fire. The roaring in my ears faded.

She searched my face. "My words upset you. Please forgive me. Elizabeth, will you take Dyonisia into the house? I want to stretch my legs from the journey. Will you come walk with me, Susanna?"

We left the yard and walked past the big house on the corner. The man still stood at the window, his eyes following us. Faith kept her gaze straight ahead. I turned back. He stared at me. He looked bent and shriveled and old.

"Take no notice, Susanna. That is what we all learned to do."

"Who is that man?" I asked.

"Someone I have no wish to see again." Faith's lips pursed, a beat showed at her temple. "Let's not speak of him now." Her hand, smooth and warm, took mine.

"It seems so long since I walked these streets. We do not come often to Boston. For me, it is both sweet and bitter. So many good memories, clumped together with the bad. It feels at times as though Mother and Father still live here. Then I remember."

She talked on. "I met my Thomas here in Boston and married him in Mother's best room. After Mother's banishment from Boston, I could not travel with Thomas when he accompanied the family to Aquidneck. I was close to Habijah's birth. Mother could not attend my childbed." Faith sighed. "She attended at many births in the town. All the women loved her for the care she gave them." Her voice cracked. "How I needed her then."

She drew a ragged breath and stopped walking, staring upward. Her hand slipped from mine. She wore the same sad, weary look as Edward.

We turned off the main road south onto a narrower street. The houses thinned as we neared the Cove. Seabirds gathered above, their chatter sounding as though they laughed and cried in one sound. We stepped off the road onto a worn path through tall grasses that gave way to smooth sand. My boots slipped, and Faith steadied me with a hand beneath my elbow. We stopped at the water's edge, staring out at the deep blue waters of the Cove and beyond to the horizon, where the dark of the ocean met the whitish sky.

"Forgive me if I talk too much, Susanna. Your return has filled me with memories. I was fifteen years when you were born, and you were a toddler when I married Thomas. We moved to the farm at Mount Wollaston to work Father's farm when they moved to Aquidneck Island. Then Father died. Mother decided to keep away from Winthrop's iron hand, she must move yet again. South to New Amsterdam."

Faith stared out at the water. "Father and Mother came to Boston with such hope as they followed their beloved Preacher Cotton from Lincolnshire across the ocean. Trouble followed Mother before we had set foot on the wharf. It grew and grew until it engulfed us all."

White waves rolled, folding over themselves and crashing against the sand in a grand bow, flowing out to our feet, with white foam like lace.

"Most people loved our mother, and a few hated her. Even Reverend Cotton, Mother's greatest friend, turned away from her in the end. After her trial, during that long winter they kept her imprisoned at a house in Cambridge. The storms were so fierce we could visit her only three times."

She turned to me. "Do you remember any of that time, Susanna?"

My memories were flashes gone in the next moment. My time with the Indians stood between. Another wave crashed onto the beach. "Why could we not stay?"

"It is a long tale. It will take much time to tell you." Faith's mouth tightened so tiny lines appeared at the corners. "Our mother was not the only person to be cast out by the authorities. Our uncle, John Wheelwright, was banished not long before Mother's sentence. He went north to Maine, but a year after Mother died the authorities rescinded his banishment. He is a minister now in Hampton, here in Massachusetts. Uncle lived near us in England. We attended his church and listened to him preach. He was a great friend to Mother and Father. They were greatly troubled at his banishment."

Faith sighed. "And then Mother was summoned by the authorities and received the same sentence of banishment. So many in Boston grieved, for they loved Mother for her wisdom, her goodness, and her compassion for the sick. The man responsible is the one you saw at the window of the house across the way. The Governor John Winthrop. The other authorities, too. Mother was a faithful follower to Reverend Cotton. She trusted his doctrine and helped him with his work. He was there at the dock to greet us when our family came to Boston. At the trial, he turned away from her and condemned her with the rest of them. That hurt Mother worst of all."

Reverend Cotton, with his quiet eyes and tranquil demeanor, yet with words that cut like a knife with their cruelty.

"Why?" I asked again.

"I have tried many times to reason it out. I can conclude only two things: pride and power. It is the nature of most men and women to prove themselves right at any cost."

I thought of the man Winthrop's face in the upstairs window in the house across the way. Mother and Father were gone from Boston, both now dead. He had won, had he not? Then why did he watch us still?

The sea rolled upward, building a wave larger than any before it, crashing against the shore. It lapped up the sand as its white crest spread out toward our feet. We stepped back. Still it came. Faith laughed as we ran to escape its wet touch.

The heaviness disappeared from her countenance. "This was a game we played as children in England. We called it chasing the waves. We drew a line in the sand, and no one was allowed to cross it. The last one touched by the water won the game. We taught you younger ones to play it here in this Cove.

"Do you remember, Susanna?"

No memories came. I wanted them. Needed them.

"Come. Let's be children again." Faith sat down, tugged off her shoes and stockings and threw them back at the path. I did the same. She grabbed a wet stick and drew a long line in the sand, standing in front of it, lifting her skirts above her ankles, facing the water. "Let us see who wins the game."

We waited for the next wave. A weak one came creeping, receding as the harbor pulled it back well before it could reach our feet. A stronger one came toward us. Faith squealed, stepping sideways like a crab to dodge the swirling white foam. Too late I moved, and the cold water sunk my feet into the wet, scratchy sand.

"I won the game!" Faith grabbed my hands and we twirled until we fell, the breeze sweeping our laughter out to sea.

How like the waves were my memories: coming close, only to ebb and pull away.

I must ask. "Katherine . . . said that I sang . . . as I went to sleep. Did I?"

"I do not remember. Perhaps Bridget will remember."

The worn look returned to Faith's face. She stood up, brushing the sand from her skirts. "I suppose we should return to the house. My babe will soon need to nurse." She offered her hand to me, and we walked the path through the grasses toward town.

❧

After supper Katherine had the servant take Faith's trunk upstairs to my room. "You take the bed, Faith, with the baby," Katherine said. "We can make a bed for Susanna on the floor."

"She prefers to sleep on the floor anyway," Anne said. "I saw her."

"Anne," Elizabeth hushed her. "She does not do that now."

"'Tis a chilly night," Katherine said. "We'll keep the fire going and put an extra comforter on the bed."

"Thank you, Katherine. It will be wonderful to share a room with my sister." Faith smiled at me. "Perhaps I shall hear you sing."

After Faith put the baby to bed, I heard her go downstairs and then the low thrum of voices coming from the keeping room: Edward's, Faith's, and Katherine's. What did they speak of? Perhaps Edward and Katherine no longer wanted me. I was a difficulty to be faced. I tried to shake off my dark mood. Had they not told me they rejoiced at my return? The moon was high in the sky when Faith returned to the room. I lay in the darkness listening to her even breathing.

When I woke next morning, Faith was already downstairs helping Katherine with the morning meal. I joined them at the table.

"Is it true, then," Faith asked, "that Alice Tilley is still imprisoned?"

"Regrettably so," Katherine answered. "The ablest midwife in Boston cannot perform her work. The women have filed yet another petition, hundreds of signatures demanding her release to serve as midwife."

"How can they keep her locked up?" Faith said.

"May last, the magistrates ruled that no undue force be used against any persons during childbirth. This was certainly directed against Alice Tilley and wholly unwarranted. The injustice of it. She was tried and convicted and kept in Boston Gaol."

"She cannot have caused harm. Only good," Faith said. "Whatever her actions, they would have had that aim. The men who make this ruling do not know of such things as childbed."

"The women in Boston and Dorchester will keep petitioning until she is released. Almost three hundred signatures are on the latest petition. And Alice's husband, William, is her fiercest advocate. He has filed a lawsuit against her accuser Susannah Phillips for slander against his wife." Katherine lowered her voice. "I pray it does not take the tragic turn of Margaret Jones in Charlestown."

"What was that?" Faith asked.

"Summer last, the midwife was accused of witchcraft and hung at Boston Neck from the great elm."

Faith went pale. Katherine put her hand on Faith's arm. "There has been no talk of that for Alice Tilley. We must trust that truth will make it right in the end."

"If Alice remains in prison who will attend when your time comes, Katherine? I worry for your health. You had such trouble at your last birthing."

Katherine sighed. "Your mother used to be the midwife all the women trusted to attend their births."

"If only she were here." Faith's voice caught on her words.

My mother had been a midwife. They seemed to notice me and stopped their talk.

Faith sat down on the bench beside me. "I have sad news. I was hoping to have a longer time with you, Susanna. My neighbor sends word that with a storm threatening, he will leave sooner than expected. Thomas will fret until I am safe home again. So, I must take my leave today."

Katherine wrapped a loaf of bread in a cloth and set it in a basket on the table. "I've packed cheese and apples and a quart of cider for your journey."

"Thank you, Katherine." Faith handed the baby to Katherine and came to me. "Come. I wish to speak with you."

We stood on the back stoop. I noticed again the square spot near the house on the edge of the orchard, the soil rich and black, dotted with plants cut close against the ground.

"A garden. There." I pointed to it.

"Yes," Faith said. "That is where Mother planted her herbs. Most of the vegetables and fruits were grown on the farm in Mount Wollaston."

"Herbs." I tasted the word on my tongue.

"She planted and harvested them for healing."

Muh-teh-qway kept a garden. I helped her to water and weed and harvest the plants. Had Mother's been like it?

Faith wrapped her arms around me and pressed her cheek on mine. "It breaks my heart to leave you when you are just returned to us. 'Tis truly a miracle." She pulled back to look at me. "Your preservation is a cause of great joy to our family. I hope you feel that. Boston is a harsh place and not always kind. I suppose in your short time back you have already faced it."

"I do not want to go to meeting."

"I feel as you do. Neighbors stare. They treat you as though you were a stranger who does not belong. Boston is suspicious of anyone unlike them." Faith sighed, the crease between her eyes deepening. "It makes the air so heavy I find it hard to breathe here."

She lifted her chin. "Your presence in the town and in the church our Mother and Father did so much to build is a triumph. It proves to the enemies of our family how after everything that happened, they did not win.

"I believe it is the reason why Edward made the decision to return from Aquidneck to live again in Boston in our parents' house. He is protecting our father's business and properties, why he forced himself to make peace with the church authorities. It is not in his nature to debase himself as he must have had to do before Winthrop. I admire his bravery, for I do not have it. I would rather be miles away at Mount Wollaston."

She took my hands in her warm ones. "It is your well-being now that most concerns us. We want you to be happy. I have an offer for you. I've discussed it with Edward, and he agrees with me. You do not have to stay in Boston. You can return with me to the farm. Thomas would welcome you, and the children will love you. Life will be easier. People remember Mother there, only they do not wag their tongues and point their fingers at anyone with the name of Hutchinson. They let us be."

I looked around the yard and back at the house. I did not know the farm in Wollaston. If I remained here, perhaps more memories would return to teach me who I was. Edward had stayed in Boston. Should I do the same? Faith called my presence here a triumph.

I turned to my sister. "I will stay."

Chapter Ten

IN THE MORNING, AFTER CHORES WERE DONE, I WORKED with Elizabeth on my reading.

The hornbook became my constant companion, the wooden handle hanging from a string tied round my waist. Edward nodded when he saw it. I saw the worry in his eyes. On the appointed day before the magistrates, I must do well. The thought tied my stomach in the same knots as the string. If I did not please them, I would be sent away from my brother to live with strangers.

The hearth, the table, all fell away from my view. The awful memory came again. I was hiding inside the split in the rock, the musty smell of the soft moss that clung to the rock in my nostrils.

The whooping of the Indians as they murdered my family. I heard my mother scream. The roaring of our house afire.

"Susanna? Why do you moan? Why do you hold your ears?"

Whose voice was that? Elizabeth. I forced my eyes to open and lowered my hands. My palm slapped against the hornbook at my waist. It hit against my thigh. The split in the rock faded from my vision.

Elizabeth stared at me. "Whatever is the matter? Should I fetch Father?"

"*Ku.*" I forced myself to answer. I did not want Edward here. Not now.

"Mother does not want you to speak like the Indians. You don't want her to hear you." Elizabeth looked frightened. "I have to fetch the winter clothes from the attic now that cold weather comes. Will you come?"

The staircase at the end of the upstairs hall had narrow, steep steps that creaked beneath our weight as we climbed.

"Careful not to smack your head," she said as we reached the top step.

The sharp tang of the unpainted pine tingled my nose as we walked across the wooden floor. Elizabeth knelt in front of the trunks lining the low walls. From one she pulled out my brother's greatcoat, a black hat lined with brown fur, and thick wool stockings. In another chest lay cloaks: russet, green, gray, brown, and yellow.

"This one will do for Anne," Elizabeth said, holding up a small green cloak. She pulled out a russet one and held it up to me. "Your reddish hair will look very well with this color." She handed me a pair of gray stockings. They were soft to the touch, so perhaps they would not itch my legs. She put the cloak around my shoulders and handed me a brass fastener. "It holds your cloak. Like this." She clipped it into place.

I fingered the wool.

"Colors have meanings, you know," she said. "Russet stands for courage." Elizabeth lifted out a pale yellow shawl. She chattered on while she removed the russet shawl and wrapped the yellow one around my shoulders. "It is made of wincey. That means it is woven with both linen and wool. The best clothing is made of it. Mother said this shawl belonged to Grandmother."

Mother's shawl. It felt as though Mother's arms enfolded me. *Susanna, dear.* Her voice in my ear sounded as though it came from far away.

"Your eyes are red, Susanna. Are you going to cry?"

I turned away so she would not see and moved to the last chest tucked into the far corner. The heavy lid creaked. Inside were books and papers. I picked up a slim black volume and held it close to my face. The musty smell of the leather cover made me cough.

"What are these?"

"I've not opened that trunk before." Elizabeth left the pile of clothing and crossed the attic, lifting one of the books.

"What does it say?" I asked.

She stumbled over the words as she read it aloud: *The Short Story of the Rise, Reign and Ruin of the Antinomians, Familists and Libertines that Infected the Churches of New England. John Winthrop, London 1644.*

I stared at the strange, long words. This book had been written by John Winthrop, the man Faith said lived across the way. The man I saw in the window.

Elizabeth took it from my hands and set it back into the chest. "These must belong to Father. They do not concern us." She started to close the chest. I grabbed the lid. The contents were part of my family's story.

I lifted out a pile of papers tied with a string wrapped around the sides and top to bottom. The edges of the papers were frayed as though they had been read many times. "What does it say?" I asked Elizabeth.

I stared at the bold black words as she read: *The Examination of Mrs. Anne Hutchinson at the Court at Newtown, November 7 and 8, 1637.* My mother's name. This was recorded twelve years past, before I had reached my fourth year.

Elizabeth turned away. "Mother said we do not speak of the past. It is gone and done and not to be remembered."

I fumbled with the string.

"No, Susanna. Mother will not like it. Come away. We must get the clothing downstairs."

Elizabeth took the bundle from my hands and set it back in the chest. I saw more books. *The Examination.* What was an examination? The ministers who had come said I must have an examination to see if I could remain in my brother's house. What had my mother done that she would need to be examined by a court? It sounded as though crows chattered inside my head. My mind knew something, but it would not yield the answers.

I gathered up Edward's greatcoat and followed Elizabeth down the steep stairs, the weight of Mother's shawl on my back.

≈

"You must go to Sunday meeting," Katherine said.

"I do not want to."

"That does not matter. Wait on the porch until I get the others ready."

I could not face the cruel stares of the people. If I were not in sight, perhaps Katherine would forget me and leave for the meetinghouse without me. I crossed the yard and stepped onto the road. The November morn yielded a pale sky, the sun warm while the cool breeze ruffled the petticoats beneath my skirt.

"Come here, young woman."

Across the road, the man from the window sat in a chair in the yard. He was swathed in black, a gray shawl wrapped close around his neck. He raised his hand in a commanding gesture. "Come. Now."

My feet moved toward him, although my mind cried out to flee. Beneath his hat his black hair was peppered with white streaks, the thin nose extending from his eyes to below his ears. It made me think of a horse. His heavy-lidded eyes looked me up and down.

"I know who you are. The daughter of the woman Anne Hutchinson. You survived the massacre and were taken to live among the savages, and you became one yourself. Reverend Cotton tells me you are mute."

"I speak."

"You are not so much a savage, then?"

"I understand what you say."

"Prove it so. What have I told you of yourself?"

"Anne Hutchinson is my mother and I am a savage. You said I am mute."

"Hmmph. You are as proud as your mother." His hands twitched. "You were a young child when your family was sent from Boston. What is your age now?" His voice was deep and commanding. Like Wampage.

"I am not yet sixteen years."

"You lived long with the savages. Tell me, then, since you claim to understand my words. Do you remember the happenings in that house during your youth, or has your time with the Indians made you forget?"

He spoke as though I were a dumb animal. He would not be privy to my thoughts nor an admission of my ignorance. I set my lips together.

"So, you are mute after all." His eyes were cold.

I took a step back from him. "It was you who cast my mother out."

He took a shuddering breath, and his gaze slipped from mine. Was it uncertainty I saw flash across his countenance? He looked old and frail. His lips tightened and his back straightened.

"Your mother cast herself out when she proved herself unfit for our society. She stepped out of her place as a woman, troubling the peace of the commonwealth and the churches." He looked past me, eyes following the horizon as though he could see all of Boston. As though it belonged to him. "She had to be reduced, or she would destroy the colony that was my God-given destiny to build."

How could my mother have done all that? Trouble the peace. Destroy Boston. Unfit for society. My mother, whose soft fingers soothed my hair when I lay sick, who sang as she woke her children in the morning, who prayed over us, laughed with Father and kissed him when they thought we children would not see.

I remembered.

The man Winthrop's pointed beard shuddered. "You should despise your mother. It is *her* doing that caused you to become as the savages. It is *she* you must thank for your cruel fate." He stared at me. "You should have remained among the savages."

No wonder Faith said she was glad she lived away from this place. Was I glad I had left the Indians? Perhaps it would have been better if I had not.

A woman emerged from the house. No lines creased her face like Winthrop's; beneath her white coif, I saw brown hair. She appeared to be half his age.

"I've come to take you inside, husband. You're ill enough as it is, and you must not take a chill." She gave me a curious look. "Who might you be?"

"Do not mind the girl, Martha," Winthrop said.

"I am Susanna Hutchinson."

"I heard of your return to our community," she said.

"Martha, fulfill your duty and return me to the house," he barked. The woman turned her back to raise him out of the chair. He leaned heavily against her. The door shut behind them.

"What did Winthrop say to you, Susanna?" Edward came up beside me.

I did not wish to repeat his bitter words and thus taste them upon my own tongue.

"I can guess well enough," Edward said. I walked back with him to the porch. "Our mother did no wrong."

I stared across the street. No one stood in the window. The house looked empty, old and weathered from salt and wind and rain, like its owner.

Edward's gaze rested on the yellow shawl I wore. "The Book of Leviticus in the Bible tells of a custom of the ancient Jews. On the Day of Atonement, the ruling priests would put upon a goat the sins of Israel and then release it into the wilderness. It was called a scapegoat. That is what men like Winthrop and Cotton and Wilson made our mother. Boston's scapegoat."

The man stood again at the upstairs window, staring at us. I turned my back to him.

"Edward, you promised to tell me the story of my family."

He gave me an anxious look. "Do you really wish to know, Susanna? Perhaps it is better just to move forward instead of looking back. What lies in the past cannot be altered." He stared at the ground. "Yet it is fluid in the minds of those people who try to corrupt it for their own purposes. Like a river whose banks change."

"I would know the past from you and not the man across the way."

Edward straightened and looked in my eyes. "Well spoken, sister."

The church bell rang out across the air.

"I do not want . . ."

"Yes, Susanna?"

"To go to meeting."

"I would not have you put through it except that the threats to remove you from my care hang over us. The ministers will take note of your attendance at church. They will say your elder brother did not bring you to be properly instructed. Obedience is what they demand."

The bell clanged again.

"Obedience," he repeated. "It is the currency I must pay to remain here in Boston."

"I want to stay in this house. With you." My voice cracked.

Edward gripped my shaking hands. "Then come with me to meeting."

୬

The afternoon sun sifted through the window of the meeting-house. A shaft of light reached toward the pulpit. It fell short of Reverend Wilson, leaving him in shadow.

Eyes bored into my back like the woodpeckers on the trees in the wood, whispering. Had my mother felt this way as she sat in this meetinghouse? Did she sense the disapproving gaze of people? From across the way, Edward caught my gaze. On the row behind him sat the man named John Cole.

The day I was first brought to the village, the Indians gawked at me much like these people in the church. I was only nine years and alone in a terrifying place. My family was dead. I did not look like them: the pale-skinned, freckled young girl with red hair. They circled around me, touching me, grabbing my curls, shouting at me in a tongue I could not understand. I thought they would kill me.

I dropped to my knees and covered my head. Still they pushed and shoved. Hands grasped my shoulders and raised me up. The gray-haired woman shouted to them: "*Ikalia! Ikali machi!*" Go away and go home.

She pulled me into the trees where they could not follow. She took me to her *wigwam*. My hands were cut and bleeding. "*Kike-hel*," she said. I learned later what she meant: I heal you. She spread a salve on my palms. The bleeding stopped. Her hands clasped to her chest: "Muh-teh-qway. Muh-teh-qway." In my terror I did not know she told me her name. I shrank into the corner, shaking and crying. All that night she did not leave me. She offered me a cup that steamed and, in my terrible thirst, I took it. It tasted both sweet and sharp. It calmed me, and I slept.

In the morning Muh-teh-qway kept the others away from the *wigwam*. I watched her prepare a meat over the fire. She held it out to me, the juice dripping from her fingers. I shook my head. She put some in her mouth and rubbed her stomach and offered it to me again. I took it. I ate and she offered more. All that day I slept. When I woke, she was there. It was her family that adopted me.

Muh-teh-qway. They called her a wise woman: *lepwexkwe*. A *kikehwet*. A healer. My friend. My mother. My teacher.

When the others taunted and teased me, the salt girl, she told me: "Trees have bark to shield them against the winds and the rain. You must grow a tough bark to protect you. You can. Trees do not move. They are still no matter what surrounds them. They do not break. You can learn to be still like the trees."

I used to sit beneath a tree in the forest and practice that stillness. I had need of it now.

My back pressed against the wood of the bench in the meetinghouse, Muh-teh-qway's voice in my mind: *Chitkuwi*. Be calm. Be quiet. The twitching in my limbs ceased. My hands quieted in my lap. What would Muh-teh-qway advise me?

"You must come to know yourself," she had said. "As the Great Spirit knows you. And then you will be still."

Know myself? I had three selves. Susanna: the daughter of my parents. Sisika: the daughter of the village. And now Susanna again. I knew none of them. How can I do this, Muh-teh-qway? How I needed the wise woman. The *lepwexkwe*.

Susanna of the past. Susanna of the present. To know both, I must learn the world of the past. I pressed my back harder into the wood. The preacher's voice and the stirs of the people around me faded until I could not hear them.

It came to me what to do. I would not need to wait for Edward to talk to me. The chest in the attic. The papers and the books about my family. I would read every word.

Chapter Eleven

A T LAST THE MEETING ENDED. I WAITED FOR THE FAM-
ily outside beneath the chestnut tree. Heavy clouds blocked
the sun. I shivered in the cold. After supper, I could go up to the
attic and open the chest. No, it would be dark by then. I would
have to wait until after the chores were done tomorrow.

"Pray pardon, Miss." The man John Cole stood in front of me.
I could not see his eyes beneath the wide brim of his hat. "Your
brother Edward has granted me permission to speak with you."

I backed up against the tree. The heel of my shoe hit against
a raised root, making me stumble. His hand came out as though
to steady me. I drew back, clutching at the scratchy bark of the
trunk.

"Miss Hutchinson, you have been much on my mind. I
remember well the day we spoke on the dock." The edges of his
deep voice had the timbre of a boy's. "I feel for your unfortunate
situation. You have known hard things: the loss of your family, being raised by the Indians, and yet again ripped away from
all you have known. Perhaps the life you have returned to now
seems strange to you."

Yet again, his words were a reminder that I was a curiosity.
How dare he presume to know my feelings? His height made it
easy to avoid looking at his face.

"My father informed me that the authorities may force you to
leave your brother's house. Is that true?"

He stood waiting. I would give no answer. Perhaps my silence would make him leave. His boots were black with thick soles, so big that both my bare feet would fit in one. The boots did not move away.

"Miss Hutchinson. May I propose a solution that may help you?"

My hands clenched into fists. "I need no help. I will stay in my brother's house."

"And if they do not allow you to stay? What then? You have suffered much loss already."

His bluntness mixed with pity angered me. How would this stranger know of my sorrows? Why should he concern himself about my business? The churchyard emptied of people. I could not see Edward or the rest of the family, only this man who would not leave.

John Cole cleared his throat and scratched at his clean-shaven chin. "Forgive my boldness. I must speak. If you are willing, I could give you a home."

What did he mean?

"At present, since I am a single man and am ordered by the authorities not to live alone, I live in my father's house near the inn. He owns a house near Sudbury End, and I am to have it when . . ." He hesitated. "It is not large. I can add more rooms. It has a lovely view of Mill Cove. There is sufficient room for a garden. You would not be far from your brother's house and your family."

My silence would not make him leave, so I would answer. "I could not take your house. I would not wish to live there alone."

His thick hands tugged at the waist of his leather doublet. "Let me speak more clearly. Your brother informed me you are of age. You would not live there alone. I am . . . offering to make you my wife."

I stared at him. His gaze left my face and lowered to his shoes. "For some time, this has been in my thoughts. I know it is not the customary way to court a woman." He hesitated. "Your circumstances are not usual."

Again, he reminded me I was different.

"We could post the banns for the next three Sabbaths and then marry soon after. If this is agreeable to you," he stammered. "If this is what you wish . . . to be my wife."

"Your wife? I do not wish it. I do not know you."

"I see I have bungled my suit. My offer was meant to be of comfort to you, not a burden."

"I have no need for the charity of a stranger." My voice shook and it shamed me.

"My charity? Forgive me," he stammered. "I have offended you and it pains me. I only wished . . . My best wishes go to you, that you will be able to remain with your family."

He touched his hand to the rim of his hat. His shoes crunched the dead leaves as he turned and walked away.

How could I do it? A husband. A marriage. At barely sixteen years of age. I was still a child, a lost child, longing for my mother.

As the family left the churchyard, Elizabeth beckoned for me to come along. I trailed behind them down the road.

I could give you a home. A garden.

A home. What did that word mean to me? A place where you belonged.

Edward's house was the closest to home I had, although Katherine's words when I first arrived still echoed in my mind. She considered me a burden, a reminder of the family's past that she wanted to pretend never happened. Was she ashamed of my mother? She did not seem so when she had talked with Faith. Was it the happenings of the past that made her feel shame? Perhaps Edward shared her view and dared not say it.

If I did not satisfy the authorities in this coming trial, what would happen to me?

è

"John Cole spoke to you after meeting," Elizabeth said as we ate the midday meal. She giggled. "What did he say?"

"Hush, Elizabeth. Do not prod," Katherine scolded. "It is Susanna's affair."

The bread on my plate was soft and soaked with brown gravy. I stirred it with my spoon.

"You did not speak with him long," Edward said. "John Cole is a good man from a good family."

"I do not know him," I answered.

"Whatever he said to you, Susanna," Edward continued, "he meant it out of kindness."

"I have no need . . . of his . . . kindness." I tasted the word on my tongue.

Edward looked as though he would say more. A look passed between him and Katherine. "I spoke with John Wilson today," he said. "Your examination is set for the fourth week of December. We have much work to do."

è

A howling storm in the night made the house creak and groan, leaving a slick sheet of ice on the ground and on every bush and tree. The villagers would say a great white bear laid down upon the world for its winter sleep. In the afternoon, the wind came off the ocean in bitter cold blasts.

No one in the household went to Thursday meeting. It was a great relief. At the next Sabbath meeting, I kept my gaze forward, careful never to look over where the men sat. Behind me on the other side of the aisle, I heard the tones of John Cole's voice as he sang. I clamped my mouth shut upon the tune.

In the evenings after the children went to bed, Edward sat with me at the table by the warmth of the hearth. I would read from the Bible and copy the verses onto the hornbook. He corrected my errors and when I chose right, he praised me.

"You have come far in both your reading and writing since your return, Susanna."

The words on the Bible page wavered with the changing light of the fire. I moved the candle closer.

"What troubles me is I do not know what other things they will require of you," he said.

I could speak now of the chest in the attic. The words were on my tongue. Perhaps he did not wish to be reminded any more of the past; perhaps the contents of the chest caused him pain. I ached to read them, yet dreaded what they might show. Without my brother's permission, reading them did not feel right.

"Come." I took my brother's hand.

"Do you wish to see the stars again?" he asked.

"I want . . . to show you . . . something."

I took the candle from the table. He followed behind me as I climbed up the staircase to the attic, until we stood in front of the chest. I set the candlestick on the floor and lifted the lid.

Edward stared down at the pile of books and papers. "You found it."

I picked up the bundle of papers containing Mother's trial.

"You want to read this?" The candlelight flickered across his face.

The familiar lump clogged my throat, and I could only nod my head.

"I have not done so," Edward said. "My memories of those dark days are enough to bring back the pain of it."

"I want to understand what happened to my family," I said. "I do not remember."

"It may be just as well that you do not," Edward said. "Your memories should be of happy times with your family, not outside troubles."

"You said our mother was a scapegoat."

"It is what I have come to believe. People loved Mother and listened to her. She had much wisdom. Many people came to her weekly Bible meetings at home, both the women and the men. The authorities considered Mother a great threat. She got in the way of their authority. It rankled them that she, a mere woman, had such influence."

John Wilson. John Winthrop. Reverend Cotton. I thought again of the Mesingw who frightened the village children into obedience.

"They summoned her to trial. Any man purported to listen to her counsel was disenfranchised, their weapons confiscated by order of the Governor. They were deprived of the right to defend themselves against any attack on the colony. By the Indians or any other threat. In this way, Winthrop took away Mother's allies."

"Why was Father not put on trial with Mother?"

"It was Mother's actions the authorities did not like, not Father's. The weekly prayer meetings she held in our house. Her wisdom and ability to articulate gave her great influence. She spoke out against the war with the Pequots, believing we should live peacefully with the Indians. One of her greatest allies was a young nobleman from England elected briefly as governor— Henry Vane. When he returned suddenly to England, John Winthrop was reelected as governor. Then the real trouble began."

Edward continued, "Mother had two trials. In the first, a civil trial in November of 1637, she was banished from the colony. In the second, held the next April, they excommunicated her from the church."

"What does that mean?" I asked.

"Mother's ideas were declared to be heretical. She was thrust out of fellowship with the church."

"What did she say that angered those men?"

"She professed to believe the Holy Spirit spoke to her, advised her on what to do. If she did not agree with the doctrine taught by some of the preachers, she dared to say so. Her crime was to think for herself." Edward sucked in his breath and slowly let it out. "Did you understand Preacher Cotton's statement to me when they came to the house to see you?"

"A little."

"Our parents thought as one. Mother did not express any opinion Father did not also share. Father was proud of his intelligent wife. He'd loved her dearly since they were children. He was Mother's greatest supporter. In Genesis, God declared husband and wife should be one. William and Anne Hutchinson fulfilled that commandment with perfection.

"When Mother was put on trial, Governor Winthrop and the other authorities would not allow Father to testify for his wife. They bound him to silence. Cruel. Cruel." Edward shook his head.

"I sat beside Father and felt his agony that the woman he loved and esteemed could not have his verbal aid. It pained him more than any of us knew. I believe it led to his early death. He was only fifty-five years when he suddenly dropped. In one moment, he was gone."

Even in the dim light I saw Edward's clenched jaw. "When I tried to speak for Mother, Cotton said I did my mother a great disservice to defend her. That I should help her by condemning her. No authority should tell a son to condemn his mother. That cannot be the will of God! Mother suffered much injustice. She was kept away from her family before and after her trials. She remained all winter at a preacher's house in Cambridge."

"Faith told me of that time. I do not remember."

Edward pressed my hand in his own—hard—I do not think he realized it. He was lost in the past, the hurt of it on his face.

"In the spring of 1638 our family, friends and supporters left Boston. We settled in Providence, Rhode Island. Father and others set up a government without an established religion. People would be free to practice their own beliefs according to their own conscience. One cannot do that in the colony of Massachusetts. It is a great irony to me that those like John Winthrop who fled England so they could follow their own conscience and worship as they wished became the ones who forbade others whose beliefs differ from them to worship in Boston."

In the candlelight, Edward looked long at me. "Someday you will understand what I say, Susanna."

"It is enough for me now to hear my brother."

"We have parents of whom we can be proud. Never be ashamed you bear the name of Hutchinson. Let me tell you the story that best shows what our father thought of our mother. After our family was forced out of Boston, Winthrop sent preachers to check on us. They said they were come in the name of the Lord from the Church of Christ. Mother told them she knew of no such church nor would she own it." Edward smiled a little at the memory. "Since they could get no satisfaction from Mother they turned to Father. 'We ask for your aid in reducing your wife,' they said to him."

"What is that word: reduce?" I asked. Winthrop had said it to me in the yard.

"To reduce means to diminish. To cut down. To put back in its proper place." He returned to his story. "On that day Father took his time to respond to the preachers. His voice when he answered was calm as a still pool of water: 'I am more nearly tied to my wife than to the church. I do think her to be a dear saint and servant of God.' He turned his back on their protests and calmly sprinkled the beet seeds into the row and worked them down into the soil with his hoe. Father was right. Mother was the best of what it is to be truly good.

"People called Father weak and said he was led by his wife. They did not know his heart or his iron strength. In all things, Father and Mother worked in perfect concert. He was the most even-tempered man one could ever meet. And yet, how opposite our parents were in temperament. He was like a boat in calm waters and Mother ran the rapids. I think it is what made them so fitting for one another."

"Father looked like you, brother."

"Aye. He did. I am proud to be his son."

"Is that why you returned to live in Father and Mother's house?"

"It is something I can do for them. I can take care of their properties. I can preserve their name. To do this, I must conform to the demands of the authorities. I had to abase myself and beg to be let back into fellowship in their church. It has made me feel old, though I am not yet forty. And very weary."

"Do you believe the things they say about Mother?" I knew his answer and yet needed to hear it aloud.

"I do not." Edward leaned over the chest and retrieved another bundle of papers and a leather-bound slim volume. "Francis Marbury is our grandfather and our Mother's father. I never knew him. He died in London before our parents married. He was young when he was struck down like our father was. When Francis was young, he was outspoken in his criticism of the church in England. He did not consider himself a Puritan. He only advocated for a better-educated clergy. He was put on trial and imprisoned more than once. When he was released from Marshalsea prison, he went to Lincolnshire and became a minister in the church and taught the local school. When he spoke out again, the authorities placed him under house arrest. For three years he could not earn an income to feed his family. He decided he must conform for the sake of his family. He never spoke out publicly again for his beliefs.

"By that time the church had so many heretical priests, they could not furnish the churches with clergy. Grandfather became the priest for two parishes in London. And then he died at fifty-five years. In our family's dilemma, I looked to Grandfather's decisions. I decided what he had done was a course I must take.

"Susanna, it is a harsh truth that people can try to compel you to a belief, and sometimes the path to take is to conform. I know this," Edward touched his chest, "what is in one's own heart is seen by God alone and He honors it. I believe that is what Francis Marbury did. He did not give up his beliefs. He just chose to keep them to himself."

Edward put his head in his hands and then straightened. His eyes burned like fire. "That is what I do now because I must. God knows what is in my heart."

A breeze came and brushed the tree branches against the windows.

"Mother felt differently. She felt compelled in her circumstances to raise her voice and tell the truth. I honor her for that, just as I honor my grandfather's choices. We must each find our own way."

Edward set the two volumes down into the chest and picked up the bundle of papers and handed them to me. "Mother's story is in here. The irony is that by putting Mother on trial, every word she spoke was written down. If they had not done so, her words and wisdom might have been lost and no one would know of her life. And now you, Susanna, her youngest daughter, can read it and see who she was and what she believed."

"I thank you for the stories," I said.

"It is very late. Katherine will be seeking me. Goodnight, Susanna. Sleep well." He kissed my forehead.

I put the papers back in the chest. There was something I must do before I slept. I crept back downstairs in the silence of the house to the Bible that still lay on the table in the keeping room. My candle sputtered out. I lit another.

I turned the pages to the Book of Leviticus until I found the word. *Scapegoat.* Two sound strikes. Cruel sounds that scraped against the back of my throat as I said it aloud. I copied the three verses in Leviticus onto the hornbook, whispering them until I could say them from memory. Then I wiped the cloth over the slate.

Chapter Twelve

ON THE MORNING OF MY TRIAL, SATURDAY, THE twenty-fifth of December, I woke to a thin blanket of white. Lacy flakes stuck to the keeping room windowpanes. I traced the intricate designs with my finger on the glass. If only the sun would shine and clear the gloom. It was easier to have courage when the sky was filled with light.

What would those stern-faced men determine for my fate? They could not take me from Edward, to live with other strangers. I would not let them. I would run away. I would . . .

"Eat, Susanna. You will need your strength today." Katherine placed a bowl and spoon in front of me.

The gruel clogged in my throat. The faces of the two men who came to the house, Wilson and Cotton, loomed before me—expressions as cold as the heavy winter air that pressed upon my temples and my chest.

"Where was my mother's trial held?"

Katherine jolted as though she had been struck. She did not answer for a moment, holding the knife to cut the bread suspended in the air. "There were two trials: one across the river in Roxbury, and the second in the meetinghouse here in Boston."

"The meetinghouse. Where I go this day?"

"Yes, Susanna." Katherine brought the knife down and divided the loaf of bread into slices. "Get your shawl and muff. Edward is at the door."

I wrapped Mother's shawl around my shoulders, its lingering odor of lavender enveloping me. I walked beside Edward past the few houses down the road, our breaths shaping little puffs on the air before us as our boot prints etched the white-glazed ground. The sky, the air, the low clouds, were wrapped in silver.

A man staggered across the street. He bent in a mock bow, sneering at me. "A marvelous Christmas to you, girl."

Edward pushed past the man. "He'd best not pass the governor's house in his drunken state. The holiday is a pagan custom and has been banned in England. There is talk of forbidding the celebration of it here. The Bible speaks only of the observation of the Sabbath."

We reached the meetinghouse. My mind felt like a blank slate, as though a breeze swept inside my ears, wiping it clean of all the study I had done. Cotton and Wilson stood in front of the pulpit. I lowered my eyes to the floor. If they could not be seen, then this day would not be real.

"Your wife has not come today?" It was Cotton's languid voice speaking to Edward.

"She is feeling poorly and wishes to stay with the children," Edward answered.

"Give her our condolences when you return home," Cotton said, "after these necessities are complete." He sounded kind and concerned. I forced myself to look up. Perhaps he would be merciful.

The two men sat down on the front bench and invited Edward to sit down beside them. Reverend Wilson folded his arms across his big chest. "Remain standing where you are, Susanna Hutchinson, for your examination."

My legs would not hold me. I would sink to the floor in front of these authorities and disgrace myself. I placed my weight evenly across the bottoms of my feet and softened my knees.

"Come closer, girl," Reverend Wilson said, "so that we may hear you properly." He handed me a primer. "Let us begin. Read aloud at the page I opened for you."

It was the alphabet in big and little letters. They presumed I knew nothing. I lowered the book and rattled off the letters by memory.

"Name the consonants," Wilson demanded. I complied and, without waiting for him to ask, named the vowels.

"Susanna was well read by the age of nine when she left us," Edward said. "The language has returned very quickly to her. May I suggest you move directly to a more advanced lesson."

Wilson snorted as though he were disappointed. "One may be able to recite the letters and even words and phrases. But what is the girl's understanding?" He snatched the book from my hands, turned to a page further into the primer, and handed it back to me.

Each letter of the alphabet was accompanied by a phrase.

"Read aloud the phrase for the letter D," Wilson said.

"The Deluge drowned The Earth around."

"Now explain its meaning to us."

"It refers to the great flood during the time of Noah," I answered.

Cotton nodded. "Well done. Read the phrase for W."

"Whales in the Sea, God's Voice obey."

"To what biblical story does this phrase refer?"

"The story of Jonah, who did not wish to prophesy to the people of Nineveh, and ran away, and was swallowed by a whale." At this moment, I also preferred the inside of the whale.

One by one I explained the phrases until I had recited them all.

In ADAM'S Fall We sinned all.
Christ crucified For sinners died.

As runs the Glass, Our Life does pass.
While youth do cheer, Death may be near.

"Most impressive, Susanna," Cotton said. His heavy-lidded eyes and slack mouth made him look sleepy.

"She could easily have memorized them," Wilson said.

"As many young ones do when learning their lessons," Cotton answered. He motioned for me to come forward to look at the book in his hands. "Read to me the phrases as I point them out to you." His finger moved down the page.

> *Do not the abominable thing which I hate saith the Lord.*
> *Foolishness is bound up in the heart of a child, but the*
> *rod of correction shall drive it far from him.*
> *Liars shall have their part in the lake which burns with*
> *fire and brimstone.*
> *Seest thou a man wise in his own conceit, there is more*
> *hope of a fool than of him.*
> *Wo to the wicked, it shall be ill with him, for the reward*
> *of his hands shall be given him.*
> *Exhort one another daily while it is called to day, lest any*
> *of you be hardened thro' the deceitfulness of sin.*

Edward shifted on the bench, his mouth twitching. Had he also noticed that Cotton chose the harshest lines for me to read? Not the ones of the love of Christ or of trust or of rest. My back ached from standing, and the ends of my fingers and toes tingled.

"Surely it is proven now that Susanna's education is sufficient?" Edward said.

Cotton nodded. "Indeed, her performance is most impressive."

Wilson ignored Edward and handed me an open Bible. "Begin at verse thirty."

I began to read: *And when Jehu was come to Jezreel, Jezebel heard of it; and she painted her face, and tired her head, and looked out at a window.*

Edward stood. "If you wish to test her knowledge of scripture, I demand you pick another verse."

"You question your minister?" Wilson said.

Edward took his gaze from Wilson and looked to Cotton. "I appeal to your compassion."

"What is your objection to the verse?" Wilson demanded, his face reddening.

"My objection I wish to keep to myself."

Why would my brother object? I did not understand. Who was this biblical Jezebel that Edward should be upset?

"Perhaps we could compromise," Cotton said. "Susanna may choose a verse."

"What good will that do?" Wilson cried. "She may be reciting only from memory."

"Choose, child," Cotton said.

My mind blanked. The verse I had read last came to mind. I turned to the book of Leviticus.

And he shall take the two goats, and present them before the Lord at the door of the tabernacle of the congregation. And Aaron shall cast lots upon the two goats; one lot for the Lord, and the other lot for the scapegoat.

Edward went pale.

And Aaron shall bring the goat upon which the Lord's lot fell, and offer him for a sin offering. But the goat, on which the lot fell to be the scapegoat, shall be presented alive before the Lord, to make an atonement with him, and to let him go for a scapegoat into the wilderness.

"For what purpose did you choose these verses?" Wilson stared me down with eyes so closed into slits, I could not see his pupils.

"I have read much in the Bible since my return to Boston."

"Calm yourself, Wilson," Cotton said. "The danger lies only if she presumes to interpret its meaning. She is young and female and thus limited in her comprehension."

Wilson stared at me. "Perhaps yes. Perhaps not. It depends upon what she has been taught and by whom." He turned and looked at Edward.

Edward's eyes bored into me, pleading. I saw a barely perceptible shake of his head.

Was I getting him into trouble? "I do not presume to understand all," I answered, "as I read the Bible."

Out of the corner of my eye, I saw Edward's face relax. He resumed his seat.

Wilson leaned forward on the bench, his eyes boring into mine. "You understand it is through your spiritual teachers that you find enlightenment, not of your own volition. It is your ministers who possess the right to interpret God's word." He turned to Edward. "Your family learned a harsh lesson concerning this matter."

I heard the warning in Reverend Wilson's words.

"I am satisfied with the abilities Susanna has exhibited thus far," said Cotton. "Indeed, she appears to have no handicap from her years spent with the Indians. I have seen young men at Harvard College exhibit much less ability to decipher difficult words and their meaning as she does now."

Wilson snorted. "You greatly exaggerate, Reverend Cotton, for no mere girl can rival a man. Correct yourself."

Cotton answered, "Your point is well taken. Though a woman may exhibit intelligence, she is but a woman and more subject to error than a man." He turned to me. "Let this be a warning to you, young woman. By nature, females are inferior to men and thus subject to them. Do nothing to exceed the bounds of womanly modesty. Remember your place."

"As your mother forgot it," Wilson added. "She dared to meddle in matters that belong only to men."

"Heed our words most carefully, Susanna," John Cotton said. "As I also said to your mother at her trial: Let the Lord put fit words into my mouth and carry them home to your soul for good."

Edward stiffened.

"Nevertheless," Cotton continued, "I commend you in striving to overcome your challenges. We digress from our purpose today. Let us turn to your command of writing. For this next exercise you may be seated at the table yonder." Cotton pointed toward the table set against the wall as he handed me a hornbook.

The chair was hard and cold. I wrote out the Bible verse his long finger pointed to in the primer. My hand shook. I steadied it with the pressure of my fingers on my right wrist and wrote more slowly.

"Bring it here, girl," Wilson said. I rose and handed him the hornbook. "Hmmph. Write another," he instructed. Five times he sent me back to write another phrase onto the slate.

"Are you satisfied?" Cotton said to Wilson. "I am."

Wilson grunted. "I suppose."

"Come here, Susanna," Cotton commanded.

Edward rose from the bench to stand beside me. "What is your decision?" my brother asked.

My head buzzed as though it was filled with bees. I tried to relax the muscles in my neck and shoulders and spread my fingers wide, keeping my gaze upon the floorboards. I must not show my fear.

Cotton spoke first. "I see no sufficient reason why the girl cannot continue to live in the house of her brother. She has shown herself to be both competent and compliant. I sense no rebellion in her."

"Will she remain so?" Wilson asked. He turned to Edward. "It is her elder brother who must answer to that."

"Consider these next words to be a solemn oath, Edward Hutchinson," Cotton said. "Your youngest sister will not be taught by you or anyone the blasphemous teachings that so strayed your mother, who then infected others and indeed the whole community with her poison." The placid tone of his slow voice belied the harshness of his words.

Edward's jaw clenched, although his face remained passive. He let out his breath slowly. "I will not infect my sister with poisonous doctrine."

"That will surely harm her soul," Cotton prompted.

"That will harm her soul," Edward repeated, his voice stronger. He flexed his fingers apart.

"Say more to satisfy us," said Wilson. "I demand it."

"I do consider this to be an oath before my God," Edward stated slowly.

"We are satisfied," the preachers said together.

Cotton took my hand in his. His palm was smooth and cold. "Susanna Hutchinson, you may continue to dwell in your brother's house. Have you anything to say, girl?"

Edward stared at me, trying to convey something. Comply, his silence pleaded. Show forth humility. They like humility. They demand it.

"Prithee, thanks," I answered.

The words burned upon my tongue, my obeisance branding like a hot iron upon my forehead. They spoke about my mother as though she were some heathen, as they called the Indians. My mother, a heathen. And I, Heathen's child.

Chapter Thirteen

"COME WITH ME TO MARKET, ELIZABETH, SUSANNA. It's such a mild day and I'm up to any excuse to go out." Katherine wrapped her shawl around her shoulders. "A walk will be refreshing. I cannot bear to be shut up in this stuffy house any longer."

The snow from the day before had already melted. Without a covering of white, the bare trees looked sad and weary and gray, as though they mourned the cold. The sky overhead rose above crisp and clear of clouds, its color the washed-out blue of winter, like a garment scrubbed clean too many times.

Governor Winthrop's wife stood in the narrow yard.

"Hallo, Martha." Katherine crossed the road, and Elizabeth and I followed.

Mrs. Winthrop held her babe in the crook of her arm, her shoulders hunched.

"How is the governor today?"

Martha's chin trembled. "The fever was worse last night. He is so weak he can hardly lift his head."

Katherine touched Martha's arm. "You've a rough time of it these last months, nursing both a babe and a husband at once. I have been a neglectful neighbor. What can I do for you?"

Martha shrugged. "John had another of his Negroes brought up from his farm to help me in the house; a young girl. She tries hard, and it does ease some of my duties. She is not good with the children though. I sent my son off to school. He is much too boisterous for John's peace."

"When school is out, he can play at our house with Elisha and eat supper with us," Katherine said.

"I thank you," said Winthrop's wife. "The women of Boston are most generous, bringing food. I am worn out trying to keep him comfortable. He has been ill for months. I fear its grip upon him will not leave."

"Of course, you are weary, Martha," Katherine said. "Let me take the babe a moment and give your arms a rest."

Martha Winthrop let Katherine take the baby, its bottom resting on the top of Katherine's big belly.

"In three months' time I will have another babe of my own," Katherine ran her finger beneath the baby's chin. "I love the feel of their soft new skin."

"May all go well with you this time, Katherine." Martha twisted her hands together. "Worries and griefs do come at once. I've had a letter from England. My eldest brother is dead. He is a colonel and was killed October last. I would never have seen him again in life, I know, but it was a comfort to know he was still living across the sea. Death is a much more final separation."

"That it is."

Tears streaked down Martha's face. "And now I fear I shall lose another husband. I am beginning to believe widowhood will be my lot in life." She looked sad and uncertain, creases in her forehead and across the top of her nose.

Katherine's arm went round Martha's waist. "Is it as bad as that?"

"It is. The doctors came yesterday and give him little hope. One said it is certain he will die within the week." She stifled a sob.

"My heart goes out to you, Martha. You have been through the death of a husband once before and know full well the hurt of it."

"My first husband, Thomas Coytmore, was a captain for my father with the East India Trading Company." Martha's eyes revealed her pride in him. "He was lost at sea in Spain."

She took a deep breath and released it in a shudder. "The governor is so much older than I, almost twice my age. I thought he seemed so hardy at age sixty, and it was good to think I would not have to be alone anymore. After four long years of widowhood, I longed to be cared for again. I much prefer the security of marriage."

"Nothing is certain, is it?" Katherine said. "The longer we live, the better we know it."

"John loved his last wife dearly. They were married almost thirty years when she died of the yellow fever. 'Tis been a burden to know I would never reach her measure, though I have tried these two years."

"You are a good and dutiful wife. It could not be easy for any woman to be married to such a man of prominence."

Martha's voice cracked. "And now, I face widowhood again."

"You can bear it, Martha," Katherine said. "You have known before what it is to lose and to mourn. Your shoulders are strong enough to bear it."

With Katherine's arm around her, Martha wept.

This bond between women, who shared wifehood and mothering, I'd witnessed among the women in the village.

An Indian woman who waited to give birth was not expected to work hard. She would rest much of the day so the babe would grow strong inside her. The other women took her place in the fields and around the fire for cooking. She was not to eat liver or chicken, for the meat would be harmful to the babe. She was not to look at possums or rabbits for it would cause the babe to have a hare-lip.

When Minsi gave birth, the women of the family gathered in the hut she had built for herself outside the village. No men were present. They were not needed. I was there at Muh-teh-qway's request. I stayed out of Minsi's sight, for I knew she did not want me there. The women sang the sacred songs as they helped Minsi walk around the hut. They rubbed her belly and her back. In her birth pains, she made no sound, squatting above the leaves and rushes as the babe slipped from her body. They rubbed the babe's skin clean from the blood and white sticky substance with sand and wet rags from the river.

The women had cared for Minsi in her time of need and comforted her, as Katherine now sought to comfort Martha Winthrop.

The creases in Martha's forehead smoothed, and her shoulders straightened. Katherine, too, appeared stronger. Elizabeth moved closer to me and took my hand. There was more to my sister-in-law than the harsh things she said out of illness and weariness. She was kind and good. Like Muh-teh-qway and Opala.

A man walked up the road from the direction of the schoolhouse and turned into the Winthrops' yard.

Martha wiped her face with her fingers and took the baby from Katherine. "Good morn, Mr. Dudley," she said.

Dudley. I had seen that name in the papers of Mother's trial. He was not young, perhaps seventy years, with a thick body and a long, bulbous nose beneath thick, arched eyebrows. He held his clean-shaven chin high, his mouth soft and bowed like a woman's.

"I have come from my house in Roxbury to see the governor. I have important papers for him to sign."

"He is feeling very poorly today," Katherine answered for Martha.

"I am on important business or I would not disturb him," Dudley said. "Matters concerning the safety of the colony do not wait upon a sickbed."

Martha sighed. "Very well. Come in, and I will tell my husband." Dudley moved into the house without glancing at us.

Martha hesitated at the door. "I am sorry we have not visited much before this time, Katherine. I thank you for your listening ear."

"We are neighbors. I am here for whatever you may need," Katherine said.

Martha and her child disappeared through the open doorway.

We continued our way down the street toward the market, wandering through the stalls. Katherine picked up a length of yellow cloth.

"Will this dimity look good for new curtains in the keeping room?"

"Oh yes," Elizabeth said. "This color will seem as though the sun has come into the house."

As Katherine handed the seller the coins, she leaned onto the side of the cart.

"Momma, you look so pale," Elizabeth said.

"I do feel rather weary," Katherine answered, "and we've only begun to shop. I suppose we can finish another day." She handed me the piece of cloth the seller had secured with string, and she took Elizabeth's arm.

We walked around the corner. Katherine breathed heavily.

"It will be a relief when the babe is here at last. Will you take my other arm, Susanna?"

We walked up the road toward the house, gently pulling Katherine's weight forward, stopping every few steps to let her rest.

Mr. Dudley came out of the Winthrop house, a parcel tucked beneath his arm, coming toward us with long strides. "Weakness," he sputtered. "Weakness." He passed by us, his shoulder knocking against my arm.

"The deputy governor is most displeased," Katherine said.

"My guess is he did not obtain what he came for. Mr. Dudley is of such a determined nature that he forces his will to happen. Not to get his way this time must surely vex him."

❧

Martha Winthrop's fears came to pass. Her husband did not last the week, dying the twenty-sixth of March, the day following the New Year. I watched the servants drape the doors and windows of the house in black cloth.

Katherine took one of the two meat pies meant for our supper and crossed the street to the Winthrop house. She was gone the good part of an hour.

The funeral would not be for a week, in order for people to gather from the towns in the colony, in particular his eldest son John in Connecticut.

"This will be a grander affair than any Boston has seen. Do you expect we will receive an invitation?" Katherine asked Edward. "We are close neighbors."

"That will be reserved for the prominent and the wealthy. I would not expect it. We are Hutchinsons, remember, and my mother was the governor's enemy."

A few days later, just before supper, a knock came at the door. The maid entered the keeping room, carrying a box. "'Tis from the Winthrop house," she said.

Katherine lifted a pair of men's gloves. "Edward was wrong," she said. "He is asked to attend. And there is a pair that must be meant for me. And also another." She held up two pairs of women's gloves, black, of soft kid leather. "Perhaps there was a mistake. I must return the other pair. Surely she did not mean they are meant for you, Elizabeth? You're still a child."

She lifted out a folded piece of paper from the box and read it. "The third pair is for you, Susanna."

Why would I be expected to attend? The exchange between John Winthrop and I had not been friendly. He had looked at me as though I still wore the clothes of an Indian woman.

Phrases from the papers in the attic played in my head, in the voice of Winthrop: *Anne Hutchinson, you must be reduced. . . . We will compel you to it. . . . You are banished from our jurisdiction as being a woman not fit for our society.*

Why am I banished? Mother had said.

Winthrop: *Say no more. The court knows wherefore and is satisfied.*

Katherine held out the gloves. I could not lift my hand. I would not pay respect to the man who had done this to my family.

"This invitation surely comes from Martha," Katherine said. "She meant the gesture to be kindly, I am certain. She pities your situation."

It did not come from Winthrop, who was dead now. It came from the woman he had been married to for only two years, the sad, uncertain woman whom Katherine had shown kindness. There it was again: I was an unfortunate girl to be pitied. Edward pitied me. John Cole, too. I could not reach out and take the gloves.

"I understand your feelings, sister." Katherine called me sister. She put her hand upon my arm. My throat went tight. "No one will force you to go. It is your decision to make."

Katherine put the note and gloves back into the box and set it on the cupboard by the hearth.

Chapter Fourteen

THE TRUNK IN THE ATTIC INVADED MY DREAMS THAT night—the lid open wide, revealing the white sheets of paper branded in black ink.

After chores, I climbed the steep stairs to the attic. Edward had gone to the docks. Katherine rested in her room while Elizabeth watched Anne. It felt as though Cotton's eyes bored into my back, his languid voice inside my head disapproving of me. "Blasphemous teachings of your mother," he said. "Poison." His voice grew louder as I lifted the lid. I shook my head to clear it.

The authorities were not here in the attic. They could not see me.

The papers and books lay in the same position as the last time I had looked in the trunk, beckoning and repelling me at once. What would I find as I read? Truth, surely. Truth had the power to burn whatever it touched, like a fire. Was it not better to know how things really were? Otherwise, how could I make sense of the now?

The slim volume Edward had shown me lay on top of the pile. The title read: *The Contract of Wit and Wisdom, 1579. Francis Marbury.* It appeared to be written as a play. My grandfather's name was also on the thick pamphlet: *The conference between me and the Bishop of London with many people standing by.* My grandfather's trial. I would read it another day.

I set the two books against the right side of the chest next to a dog-eared volume: *Acts and Monuments. John Foxe. 1596.* It seemed familiar. There were pictures of people tied to a stake amid flames. I set it down. What I needed was to acquaint myself with the circumstances that led to my mother's dismissal from Boston.

Beside it lay the black leather volume I had seen when Elizabeth and I came to retrieve the winter clothing. *John Winthrop, published in London, 1644.* More than five years ago and only one year following the death of my mother and siblings.

Inside the front cover I read:

A short story of the rise, reign, and ruin of the Antinomians, Familists and Libertines, that infected the churches of New England. And how they were confuted by the assembly of ministers there, as also of the Magistrates proceedings in Court against them. Together with God's strange and remarkable judgments from Heaven upon some of the chief fomenters of these opinions and the lamentable death of Mistress Hutchinson.

I struggled through the long words again. What did he mean? Judgments from Heaven. My mother's death and five of her children was the judgment of God? Pleasing to God?

The letters blurred, turning black to red like blood. How could one man know the mind of deity? John Winthrop was not a minister, who the people said had the proper authority to speak God's will. He was a public servant.

Why was this book he had written kept here? I wanted to throw it out the window into the snow, better yet take it to the shed behind the house where the cows were kept for milking and grind it beneath the dung. I understood Faith's bitterness toward our neighbor across the street and shared it. Cruelty could not be the will of God.

Ketanetuwit: the Indians called the Great Spirit, the Creator. He watched over and cared for the people. He was kind and loving. The God that John Winthrop worshipped seemed cruel, a being who would rejoice at death and suffering.

I set Winthrop's book on the opposite side of the chest from my grandfather's book, tucked beneath the other items so I could not see its blackness.

I picked up another volume: *Mercurius Americanus.* Strange words. *The Reverend John Wheelwright. London, published 1645,* one year after Winthrop's book. Faith had told me that John Wheelwright was my uncle. I was too young to remember him. I read the front page:

> *Being observations upon a Paper styled, Wherein some parties therein concerned are vindicated, and the truth generally cleared.*

Surely he had written this in defense of my mother? It may be valuable to read but not now.

I reached for the sheaf of papers bound together by thick brown twine, crossed t-shaped at the two sides and top to bottom: *The Examination of Mrs. Ann Hutchinson at the court at Newtown.*

November, 1637. I was not yet four years of age. Did I have any memories of that time? It would require dividing up the chapters of my life. My earliest years in Boston and in Aquidneck. My time with the Indians. The few months back in Boston. Like linen stretched from a bolt of cloth, I would need to fold them into segments until I came back to my early childhood spent in this house.

"Help me to remember," I said aloud to the floorboards and the walls. You are silent witnesses to all of the events of my family.

The Indians spoke of the soul of the trees and all of nature. Our home was built from them. Surely the things that happened here would be ingrained and preserved inside the wood?

A cart creaked on the road, a shouted greeting and a woman's answer in kind, the voice of John Winthrop's wife. Sounds of the present slashed through any sense of what was past. I held the sheaf of papers closer to my face. It held the stale odor of the passage of time.

The shaft of morning light from the nearest window would help me read. I sat on a flat-topped chest, the papers across my lap, and untied the string. The black ink letters swirled in someone's pen-writing, making it difficult to determine the words.

Mister Winthrop, Governor: Mrs. Hutchinson, you are called here as one of those that have troubled the peace of the common-wealth and the churches here. . . . I skimmed through the words. *We have thought good to send for you to understand how things are, that if you be in an erroneous way we may reduce you so that you may become a profitable member here among us, otherwise if you be obstinate in your course that then the court may take such course that you may trouble us no further. . . .*

Mother was trouble. What did Winthrop mean that he and the other authorities thought she should understand how things are? How things are, according to whom? The authorities? God? *That we may reduce you.* And if, as he warned, she should be found in an erroneous way? He hinted even then what her fate should be. *If you be obstinate . . . you may trouble us no further.*

I stood before some of the same authorities at the meeting-house, like Mother had. Reverend Wilson was shorter than I, and John Cotton tall like my brother Edward. Mother had been tall. She held her head high, shoulders straight. When the trial was held, the weather would have been cold. A cloak would have kept her warm.

The cold of the attic gripped my shoulders and I shuddered as I turned to the next page.

Winthrop declared that he was troubled by the weekly meetings held across the street from his door. He'd stood at the window, then, as he'd done up to his death, staring across the narrow road. He could observe every activity of our family, every person entering and leaving, how long they stayed. The governor seemed to feel that those meetings were not lawful.

A recollection stepped forward in my mind. A thrum of voices rising up the stairs from the meeting room that spanned the back of our house, benches placed facing the fireplace, a few chairs in front, Mother's Bible on the table beside her. The house hummed with a vigor that enveloped me as I had lain in my bed listening to the sounds from below.

I kept reading. Most of the written exchange was between Winthrop and Mother—he questioning, she answering. They spoke of covenants. A covenant of grace. A covenant of works. What did these phrases mean? It seemed from the record that Mother believed in the first.

He accused Mother of trying to persuade other people to her beliefs. She agreed that she held meetings once weekly in her house for the women to discuss scripture. Gossipings, they called them, a common practice in old and New England. Winthrop thought it to be much more than only a meeting between women. He claimed that she also taught men.

Reverend Wilson and Reverend Cotton had spoken to me of the proper place of women and that my mother defied it.

I read on. Another name appeared on the pages, one who bore the title of deputy governor. Thomas Dudley. He questioned Mother about her condemnation of many of the ministers. I followed the lines with my finger and stopped upon a familiar name. John Cotton. Winthrop called him forward to speak.

Mr. Cotton had been a friend of our family. They attended his church in England, where Cotton said that he and Mother worked together in the saving of souls. She trusted him above all other ministers. So, John Cotton defended her when the authorities brought her to trial? I tucked the page beneath the stack and peered down at the next.

The ministers questioned Cotton. *Do you remember that she said we were not sealed with the spirit of grace, therefore we could not preach a covenant of grace?*

I do not remember it, he said.

When I was in Old England . . . I went back. It was not Pastor Cotton's words that I read, but Mother's. In Old England. My birthplace. *When I was in Old England, God did discover unto me the unfaithfulness of the churches, and the danger of them, and that none of those ministers could preach the Lord aright.*

Mother's words. I touched the black letters. Someone had written down my mother's words. They could have been lost, remembered only if spoken aloud by someone who had been there and perhaps remembered wrong. Yet here they were on the page, penned in the very moment by witnesses to the scene.

The Indians did not write. Remembering the past came out of the stories told from the memories of others. My mother was on these pages. I found her here, lifted out of what was past.

I heard her voice in my mind as I read, the tone of it low and smooth as she spoke, sometimes quick, sometimes slow. *I had none to open the Scriptures to me but the Lord. . . . Ever since— bless the Lord—he has let me see which was the clear ministry and which was the wrong. . . . Now if you do condemn me for speaking what in my conscience I know to be truth, I must commit myself unto the Lord.*

How do you know this? they demanded.

By an immediate revelation, my mother said. *By the voice of God's own spirit to my soul.*

The words of my mother clanged like a church bell inside of my head. Louder than the clamoring of her accusers. She had no right to claim that God spoke directly to her, they yelled. That right belonged only to the preachers. *The revelation she brings forth is delusion,* John Winthrop said. *We all believe it,* the ministers cried.

Take heed how you proceed against me, she said. *You have power over my body, but the Lord Jesus hath power over my body and soul.*

Did they cower then before her, at her bold words? No. They asked Cotton what he thought.

That she may have some special providence of god to help her is a thing that I cannot bear witness against. Cotton defended her, or so it seemed.

Mother had a special providence from God. Reverend Cotton had believed it. So had Father.

The realization hit me then. These men at the trial were afraid of my mother.

John Winthrop: *This case is altered. The ground work of her revelations is the immediate revelation of the spirit and not by the ministry of the word. This is the means by which she has very much abused the country that they shall look for revelations and are not bound to the ministry of the word.*

Of what did they accuse her? I read it again. They claimed that she listened to her own conscience and not to the ministers who had the voice of authority. The rest of the people were to be bound to them.

John Winthrop: *This has been the ground of all these tumults and troubles. This is the thing that has been the root of all the mischief.* I could see his hard eyes as his finger pointed at my mother.

He said that my mother was a troublemaker.

John Cotton agreed with Winthrop's accusation that Mother thought herself to be above the preachers, that she heard the voice of the Holy Spirit for herself. In that moment my mother's friend turned his back on my mother as if he stepped from her side to the opposite end of the room where her detractors stood. How had she felt in that moment?

I could hear Winthrop shout his condemnation through the meetinghouse. *Mistress Anne Hutchinson. You are unfit for our society. If it be the mind of the court that she shall be banished out of our liberties and imprisoned till she be sent away let them hold up their hands.* Thirty magistrates raised their hands high in assent.

Mrs. Hutchinson, the sentence of the court you hear is that you are banished from out of our jurisdiction as being a woman not fit for our society and are to be imprisoned until the court shall send you away.

Father was in the meetinghouse. Edward told me. With other members of the family. They stood together against the forces, like the rocks of a seawall. But they could not stop the flood.

Not all the town would have condemned her. It could not be, or they would not have flocked to her house, seeking counsel and guidance. In that moment of time Mother's family and friends had been powerless against those who held authority.

My shaking spread through my middle and moved outward to my limbs. I could read no more. I tried unsuccessfully to tie the twine again around the bundle of papers. I threw the papers into the chest and shut the lid.

৯

I remember. I remember.

Mother could not live with us. She had to stay in the house of a minister in Roxbury. It was only two miles. During that long cold winter it felt as though she was a world away. We walked across the frozen water of the river. A stern-faced man opened the door with his arms folded across his chest. A name came to mind. Reverend Weld. Mother stood by the fire, thin and pale. She looked weary. Her belly was swollen. Father said she was going to bear another child. I wrapped my arms around her skirts that smelled of lavender. *Mother, why can you not come home?* She knelt beside me and put my cheek to hers. Hers were wet like mine. *I love you, my child,* she said. *Susanna, dear.*

I stared through the attic window to the house across the street. That man—that John Winthrop—was the one who had driven our family out of Boston. The trembling in my body ceased, crowded out by a hard rock around where my heart beat.

Chapter Fifteen

THE MORNING SUNLIGHT PIERCED THROUGH THE ATTIC window, painting the wood floor white. Tiny particles of dust danced in the light. I could not close the lid of the chest. How could I continue to read, and yet how could I not?

A few papers were folded together and tucked into the far corner. I picked up the bundle and opened it.

Reverend Thomas Weld. The same man who kept Mother in his house to punish her. *1643.* He wrote this the year that Mother died.

> *I never heard that the Indians in those parts did ever before this commit the like outrage upon any one family, and therefore God's hand is the more apparently seen herein, to pick out this woeful woman, to make her and those belonging to her an unheard-of heavy example of their cruelty above all others. Thus the Lord heard our groans to heaven, and freed us from this great and sore affliction.*

The man Weld rejoiced in the death of my family and claimed that God's hand was in it. The rock around my heart swelled even larger.

I turned to the next page.

> *John Winthrop, 1643: Thus it had pleased the Lord to have compassion of his poor churches here, and to discover this*

great imposter, an instrument of Satan so fitted and trained to his service for interrupting the passage of his kingdom in this part of the world, and poisoning the churches here—as no story records the like of a woman since that mentioned in the Revelation.

My mother a great imposter. An instrument of Satan.

A postscript was added at the bottom, written in another hand.

The verses in the Second Book of Revelation read: 'I have a few things against thee, because thou suffers that woman Jezebel, who calls herself a prophetess, to teach and to seduce my servants to commit fornication, and to eat things sacrificed unto idols. And I gave her space to repent of her fornication; and she repented not. And I will kill her children with death. . . .'

Jezebel. He called her Jezebel.

That was why Edward paled when Cotton and Wilson made me read the scripture about the wicked queen Jezebel.

These men wrote of the death of my family to be God's will and providence. Justice served for Mother's wickedness. The last words of the verse in Revelations enlarged on the page: *And I will kill her children . . .*

Anne Hutchinson's children. My brothers and sisters. Francis. Anne. William. Katherine. Mary. Zuriel. All of them dead with not even a grave to visit.

I was left alive. Why? Oh why?

❧

Four other papers were in the bundle, no doubt containing similar statements from other leaders of the colony. I dropped them onto my lap as though they were hot coals from the hearth, burning my fingers. My limbs tightened and then went weak. I slumped against the chest and buried my head in my arms.

Footsteps sounded on the steps, walking across the floor, a pair of boots appearing in the square of sun-painted floor in front of me.

"Susanna."

Edward. I could not look up.

He picked up the bundle. "You have been reading."

He sat down beside me. "You are young to know such things."

"I do not feel young." I touched my breast. "I feel old. In here."

"It is understandable. You have already lived two lives and now begin another."

I looked up at his face. "I cannot build a new life if I do not know what came before."

"I encouraged you to read these things. Seeing your sad countenance I wonder at the wisdom of it. If you settle into life here, you can move forward without the burden of the family's troubled past. Am I wrong?"

"Yes, brother."

He set the papers in the light so he could see. His lips tightened. "What else have you read?"

I lifted out the trial transcript.

"Any more?"

I pointed to John Winthrop's book.

A gull squawked, swooping low toward the window of the attic.

"I have been mistaken, sister. Perhaps more than all of your siblings, you have a right to know all, for you have suffered the most injustice of us all."

Was it more injustice to be robbed of life at such young ages? Or to continue to live?

"Not all of what is contained in this chest is full of the same hateful rhetoric. Our mother was not alone in the things she believed. Many friends stood with her. The families who came with us to Aquidneck Island and others who dared not speak for fear of the authorities."

That did not save Mother.

"You say that I have suffered more than my dead siblings? More than my mother?" Somehow his words brought anger.

"They are with God, their travails over. And you . . ." He trailed off and did not speak for a moment. "You still live. And I, and Faith and Bridget. Somehow we must go on."

The thought flew from my throat with the bitter taste of vomit. "Why did I not die with them?" Did I wish that I had died? Or did I feel remorse because I had survived while they had not?

"The answer to your question belongs only to God."

And I was left to wonder.

"I know a little of what you must feel, sister. I would have stayed in Aquidneck with Mother and Father. They wanted to make a place where people could be free to worship according to their own conscience, where it was not a crime to believe differently than someone else, a notion lost in Massachusetts. Katherine did not want to raise our children in a wilderness. I had to ask myself where my greatest loyalty lay: with my parents or with my wife and children. The Bible says to leave father and mother and cleave unto your wife. So, I chose my wife and children. It is still an open wound to feel so torn between those that I love. When my mother most needed me I was not there to protect her. I was safe here in Boston." He made a sound like a sob. I felt him trembling.

"Do you know why the Indians came that day to attack us?"

Edward sighed. "Perhaps it is best for you that we not dwell upon it. It is done now and in the past."

"Why?" I said again.

"You want to know all? Even if it may bring you pain?"

"Not knowing hurts more than the truth."

He put his hand over mine. "I will tell you. We heard the account from the Dutch settlers in New Amsterdam. After Dutch soldiers killed eighty of the Siwanoy they sought revenge. The Siwanoy chief sent a warning for the settlement to leave the area, that he would be coming to burn down every house. The Dutch warned Mother of the Indian threat and told her that she must leave. Mother told them that she saw no need to leave the property she had legally purchased. When they asked if she kept arms, she replied that she had always had good relations with the Indians and had no need of weapons."

The Siwanoy chief. Wampage had sent a warning that he was coming.

"The Dutch settlers fled. When the Indians came, they found only one family still in the settlement. Our family. They mistook them to be Dutch. If they had known Mother was English they would not have . . ."

He did not finish. When the Indians found me hiding in the split in the rock, they stared at my clothes, gesturing among themselves as though they were surprised I wore English clothing. When they took me to Wampage he did the same. That must have been why they spared me.

I heard again the screams of my family, the crackling of the house as the fire destroyed it. If Edward and his family were with us, they would surely have been killed, too.

If Mother had brought weapons, would they have died anyway? It could not be known. This tragedy did not have to happen, and yet it did.

I touched the papers Edward held. "John Winthrop and the other men. They said that it was the will of God that my family was killed."

"I do not believe that to be truth," Edward scoffed. "Some chose to believe that in order to justify their own actions in condemning our mother for her beliefs. They set themselves up to the stature of deity. That is the right of no man. Judge not, God said." I heard his anger in the tightness of his voice.

"Zuriel had no chance to become a man," he said. "Our brothers William and Francis could not marry and have children of their own, or our sisters Katherine and Mary. Our sister Anne and her husband William Collins could not grow old together."

"Yet I lived," I said.

"You lived, Susanna. The Indians spared you, and in that act you did not betray your family members who died. You need not feel guilt."

He put words to the feelings that had tortured me.

"The advice I give to you I have not afforded myself. I feel guilt. Daily I live with it. We have that in common, you and I."

I tightened my fingers on his. "Tell me more. I need to hear what you say."

"God has some plan of His own for you and for me and our sisters Faith and Bridget. He does not work in chaos. Only in perfect order. The Bible says that man cannot comprehend God's ways. We must trust that out of tragedy can come triumph. 'All things work together for the best unto them that love God,' it says in Romans 8."

"I will try," I said.

"And so will I."

Edward kept his hand upon mine. His warm touch made the screams in my head fade away. The square of sun on the floor grew smaller and smaller as the sun rose higher into the sky until no light was left. We sat together inside the shadows.

Chapter Sixteen

O N THE MORNING OF THE GOVERNOR'S FUNERAL, SUN-shine gave the appearance of a warm day. The breeze had a cold bite, as if the spring could not make up its mind whether to hold onto winter or give it up. The first bell toll had struck at dawn, sounding again every few moments. There would be sixty-one gongs, Katherine said, one for each year of John Winthrop's life.

No bells had tolled at Mother's death. Only the roaring of a burning fire to commemorate her life. Yet the man who had been so cruel to my family would have the funeral of an important man.

Faith and her husband Thomas Savage arrived from Mount Wollaston to attend the funeral. Bridget and John Sanford did not travel the forty-five miles from Aquidneck Island. Yet again, I would not see my sister Bridget. Faith and Thomas were to stay in the room where I slept. A bed had been set up for me in Elizabeth's room. Her happy chatter distracted me from my cobwebbed thoughts.

There had been no time to talk with Faith, as the house filled with family chatter and laughter from the children. Faith and Katherine worked together in the keeping room, their conversation full of Katherine's coming confinement and the month of lying-in afterward and the challenges of ensuring the other children were properly cared for. That part of life belonged only to married women and those privileged to bear children, not to me. I was not young, as Elizabeth was at age twelve, but I did not belong in a grown woman's knowing world. Not a girl, not a bride, not a mother.

John Cole had not spoken to me again. I pushed away the image of his soft eyes. It was only pity that had prompted his offer, not any kind of love. Not with the tender feelings I saw in Edward and Katherine or in Faith and Thomas. I could not abide pity. Pity looked down on an inferior from the puff of pride, a feeling not much different than contempt.

"Will you go to the funeral today?" Elizabeth said as we prepared for the day.

To pay homage to that man sickened me. Edward and Faith saw fit to go. If I attended, I could be with Faith. I reached in the cupboard for the dark gray waistcoat and skirt for Sabbath meeting. I put them on over my shift and petticoat, adding a white collar and coif.

"You are going then," Elizabeth said. "You must tell me all about it. And do not forget those beautiful gloves."

"I do not want them. You keep them, Elizabeth."

Katherine did not feel well enough to come. I followed behind Edward, Faith and her husband as we exited the house from the back door, turning the opposite way from the Winthrop house up Beacon Street, past the schoolhouse toward the burying ground. The church bell gonged every few moments—a hollow sound, the slow beat of it matching the mood of mourning.

Faith stepped back to walk beside me and tucked her hand beneath my elbow. "Are you well, Susanna?"

"I am well."

"Edward told me you read and write better than many Harvard scholars. The clergymen even admitted as much." She squeezed my arm. "I am proud of you. My little sister. You have become a woman, and a beautiful one."

A crowd thronged the road. Faith and I fell behind as people moved between us and Edward. It seemed that all the colony of Massachusetts had come, not just the wealthy and important. I recognized many from Sabbath meetings.

"Look, the Hutchinsons are come," hissed the woman who always turned to stare at me in church. "Obstinate family. Even the savage."

"Pay no mind," Faith whispered in my ear. "We belong here no matter what is said about us."

The burying ground was laid out square, gray headstones set in neat rows with space to walk between. We found an open spot to stand near the street.

The Indians did not bury their dead in the middle of the village. They picked a spot below the trees in the forest, where it was quiet. They lined the hole with bark and leaves and buried the body lying on its side, with the knees tucked close to the chest, putting in food and tools and *wampum* before covering it with dirt.

I was tall enough to see the long black coffin sitting atop a wooden bier in front of the gaping hole in the ground. Reverend Cotton stood beside the mound of brown dirt, wearing his funeral gloves, his silver hair curling over his shoulders, a stiff white collar at his neck. Reverend Wilson, Thomas Dudley and other leaders clustered behind him, along with a younger man who had Winthrop's long face and nose. This must be his eldest son. Martha stood next to him, holding her babe close against her breast. She looked lost and alone.

The steady gongs sounded from the church bell. The crowd kept swelling, filling the two cornered streets that faced the burying ground, standing in silence.

Reverend Cotton's languid voice carried across the living who stood above the buried dead, extolling the virtues of John Winthrop. The people must never forget the man who founded a place in a new world, he said, a city set upon a hill for all the world to see. Remember his greatness, his goodness.

I could not.

The coffin was lowered by ropes into the hole, the only sound the rhythmic thud as shovelfuls of dirt fell upon its top. The sound changed as the hole filled, from a hollow thump to a sound like heavy rain as soil met soil.

A gunshot rang out, then another, and another. I gripped Faith's arm. Sixty-one times. When the guns fell silent at last, the crowd stirred as though it took breath again.

"Well. The colony has not seen the likes of this funeral," someone said as we turned back to the street. I glanced behind me. It was Samuel Cole. John Cole walked behind his father.

"Good to see you, Edward, and you Faith, and your good husband. And you, young Susanna."

"Good to see you, Samuel, John," Edward said. "Your new wife is not with you, Samuel?"

"Margaret remains at home, for she bore a girl child a month past," Mr. Cole said. "At long last my son John has a sister." He slapped his hand on John's back and laughed.

"I am glad to hear this happy news," Edward said. We reached the corner. "Come into the house for a visit if you can."

"We would be happy to," Mr. Cole answered. "No need to return to the Inn just yet, for there will be few customers this hour."

"We have visitors, Katherine," Edward called as we entered the front door. He led the Coles into the front room.

Where could I go? I could slip out into the orchard. But crowds still passed the house, and I did not want to be seen. Faith went upstairs to the children. I would go with her.

"Susanna," Katherine called from the keeping room. "Come here. I need you." She handed me two cups of beer. "Take these to the men."

John Cole sat on the bench beside the table that held the Bible. He muttered a thanks as I handed him the cup. His boots were shined, with an edge of dirt from the road on the toes. I left the room and returned with the cups for the others.

Mr. Cole had a round, cheerful face, his hair cut short above the collar of his brown doublet. "New England has lost its leader right upon the heels of the death of the King of England." He slapped his knee. "What tumultuous times we live in. The king tried and beheaded! Sentenced to die by his own subjects. It has been the main talk at the Inn. They say he died with great dignity. One blow from the sword and his head was severed."

"Has the world ever seen the likes of these last years?" Edward said. "A civil war in our home country between king and Parliament. And Parliament has won. England must be a volatile place at present."

"And now England has a republic. The Commonwealth of England," Samuel Cole said. "Who knows what the future holds? Will Cromwell try to take power? It is the penchant of most men to seek to rule. New England seems the safest place. And now we have lost our leader." He took a long drink of the beer. "Enough of politics. I've not been in this house since your good parents dwelt here, Edward. Ten years now, is it?"

"Plus one year," Edward answered.

I turned to leave the room.

"Stay, Susanna." Edward patted the seat beside him on the bench by the hearth. I sat.

"So long ago, and yet not," Mr. Cole said. "I've always been sorry for the unfortunate events of that time. It cannot be brought back and set to rights."

"No. It cannot." I could not determine Edward's feelings as he answered in a flat tone.

"Like a river, life flows on," Samuel Cole said. "Mercifully, that troubled time has moved round the bend, with the colony in calmer waters. Your mother and father would be proud of their posterity." He looked over at me. "And happy, I am sure, for the miraculous preservation and return of their youngest daughter."

"Susanna is a great gift to us," Edward said. I felt my face growing scarlet and kept my eyes upon the braided rug.

Samuel Cole took another sip of beer and cleared his throat. "As we have been neighbors and friends for many years, if you will permit me, I wish to relay something which may bring comfort to your family. Indeed, I believe I would be remiss if I did not."

"You are a trusted friend, Samuel. What would you like to say?"

"During Governor Winthrop's last days of illness, as deputy governor, Thomas Dudley was left in charge of the affairs of the colony. Dudley takes his responsibilities most seriously, as we all know. On the most important matters, he sought out Governor Winthrop's permission. He recently came to his house with another order for banishment from Boston." He paused. "I tread upon matters most painful for your family."

Edward gestured for him to continue.

"Mr. Winthrop told Dudley he would not sign the order for banishment. That he had done too much of such work already."

Faith's husband, Thomas Savage, leaned forward in his chair. "Do you believe Winthrop regrets the harshness of his past actions? If so, it has taken him a very long time to do so."

"If indeed he regrets what he did to our mother," Edward said, "the news is most welcome."

"If this is so, one wonders if the change of heart came upon him suddenly or was a gradual one," Thomas Savage said.

"I heard the incident between the two men relayed at the Inn," Mr. Cole said. "I do not know from what source it came."

Katherine offered a plate of hot biscuits to the guests. "I have some knowledge of this," she said. "On the way to market a few weeks ago, we passed Mr. Dudley going into the Winthrop house. We encountered him again as he left, and he was most displeased. Martha relayed what happened. Her story matches the account that Mr. Cole heard."

"Dudley is a harsh man," Mr. Cole said. "Perhaps even more so than Winthrop. He keeps a poem he composed in his pocket. He showed it to me at the Inn one day over a pint of beer. Though full of high-sounding language, its message was clear. Men of God must watch that they do not tolerate heresy, for it is a cancerous poison."

Edward shifted on the bench. "What constitutes heresy depends upon the view of the one who accuses. Heresy to one may not be to another."

Katherine turned toward the doorway. "Come, Susanna. Leave the men to their talk."

"Let her stay, Katherine," Edward said. "If she wishes."

I wanted to hear what was said but also longed to leave the room, away from John Cole. I stayed in my seat.

"We speak of the dead," Samuel Cole said, "a delicate subject, since they can no longer answer for themselves. I have observed that seeing the face of your own death can soften even the hardest of men, if they will allow it."

John Cole spoke for the first time. "Unfortunately, the belated expression of remorse from Winthrop for his past decisions and actions cannot alter the events of the past. Or the consequences."

His words matched my own thoughts. I met his gaze. His eyes were kind. John Cole was right. Regretting one's actions could not change what happened. I had seen it before. Wampage had come to regret that he killed my family. It did not change the cost.

John Winthrop had declared my mother unfit to live in Boston society. He wrote that he rejoiced at my family's murder, even exulted in it as serving God's justice. His opinions were preserved in black ink in his book. Had John Cole or his father read it? Certainly so.

On the day I had talked with John Winthrop, he looked at me as if I were vermin. And yet, had there been some uncertainty in his eyes, guilt, even fear? If he did regret what he had done to my mother, his words to me gave no indication of it. Perhaps he felt he must continue to justify his past opinions and actions in order to keep on thinking himself right.

It was easy to keep thinking ill of John Winthrop, but had his heart changed?

"It raises a great debate, does it not?" Thomas Savage said. "Is a man the substance of all his actions? Or only a few?"

"And if some actions are better or wiser than others?" John Cole said. "And some worse? What then?"

"That is the sum of us all," Edward said. "No man is entirely evil or good."

"Does the good in a man have the power to outweigh the evil done?" I said my thought aloud. The men turned to me as though they had forgotten I was there.

"Only God knows. He is the supreme judge," John Cole said. "We must leave it to Him."

"Well spoken, son," Samuel Cole said. "Indeed, we mere mortals cannot know all, flawed as we are. It is not possible."

Some people acted as though they did. As though they were the supreme authority with everyone else beneath them. John Wilson. John Cotton. Thomas Dudley. Surely that offended God?

"Indeed," Edward answered. "We are fallen and flawed beings. Scripture speaks of making righteous judgments, so we are to reason. And in striving for understanding of a situation, can we excuse a person's evil or unwise behavior because of their good acts, as Susanna has pointed out? Or do we reason it out, determining that though an individual is exemplary in some respects, it does not take away the fact that certain actions were not right?"

The conversation confused me. Did Edward speak generally or was there something in his answer that referred to John Winthrop? Surely, he did not excuse the governor for banishing our family? Wampage had acknowledged his mistake in killing my family, not only to me but to the tribe. John Winthrop had punished my mother and forced her to leave, a punishment affecting our whole family. If he regretted doing so, then he admitted it only in private.

If he had not done these hateful things, my mother might still be living, and I never gone to the Indians.

&

I bolted from the house. The street was quiet, most of the people gone back to their homes from the funeral. I found the apple tree with the lowest hanging branches and sunk down upon a thick root rising from the ground. The bare branches of the tree looked tired and lonely. Tiny buds revealed the promise of the green to come.

I'd forgotten a shawl. The chill of the air felt good. I untied the string of my coif and took it off to let the breeze take my jumbled thoughts. The front door slammed shut, and John Cole and his father walked up the street. John looked toward the orchard. I sat motionless so he would not see me, and he turned back to his father. They disappeared around the corner.

"Susanna?"

Faith stood above me.

"The baby is sleeping, and I have a few moments of quiet. I wish to spend them with you."

She did not ask why I sat in the orchard.

"I have brought something for you, Susanna. Come." She reached down and took my hand. We walked to the furrowed plot near the woodpile.

"When I was here last, you remembered that our mother kept her herb garden here." Faith held up a small burlap bag. "I've brought you seeds from my garden at the farm. You can plant them here in remembrance of our mother."

She tugged at the string to open the bag. "Let me show you. The ginger seeds are the round ones, like tiny nuts. It is good for nausea. Here are the lemon balm seeds for melancholy. Sage. Garlic. Columbine and comfrey, myrtle, chamomile, jasmine."

On the ceiling of the *wigwam* hung bundles of plants and roots that Muh-teh-qway and I dried. I remember her pulling off a few of the leaves from the lemon balm plant, rubbing the soft, fuzzy leaves to release the mix of mint and lemon, a calming fragrance. She made me a tea of it to drink.

"This will lift your drooping spirits," she had said. She was teaching me the purpose of each of the plants. When the Dutchmen came, she had not yet finished.

Faith put a small brown leather book in my hand. "I brought you Mother's book of herbs. She learned the use of plants from her own mother, using them to care for the sick."

I opened the cover. Pictures of the plants were carefully drawn on the left page with instructions on the right. I recognized many of them from what Muh-teh-qway had taught me. A tingling went up from my finger through my arm as I touched the letters. Mother's handwriting. My mother had been a healer. I thought back to my vision quest and the voice I had heard in my heart. *You will be a healer.*

"I see from your face I have chosen right," Faith said. "Plant the seeds, Susanna. And see what will grow."

Chapter Seventeen

THE MORNING HELD THE PROMISE OF SPRING. ELIZA-
beth and I stood outside the back keeping room door with
Katherine and the housemaid. Today was soap-making day.

Two fires burned: one to boil the ashes from the hearth boiled
in rain water in the large black kettle, and a smaller kettle to melt
the lard. Katherine peered down to see if the ashes had all settled
to the bottom, the heat flushing her face and neck. She handed
an egg to Elizabeth.

Elizabeth grinned. "This is my favorite part of soap making."

"Drop it into the pot slowly so you do not break it," her mother
said.

We stared down into the ashy water. The egg sunk slowly to
the bottom.

Katherine handed me the ladle. "Now we must skim the lye
off the top into the barrel."

I dipped it into the pot and filled the ladle with the lye. As I
set it atop the cloth tied with a rope around the top of the barrel,
the ladle tipped sideways, and the lye sloshed onto Katherine's
skirt.

Katherine grabbed the ladle from me. "You have wasted it.
Now there will not be as much soap." She scooped the rest of the
lye out of the kettle, then squeezed hard to strain it through the
cloth. Again, I had displeased her.

"Let us help you, Mother," Elizabeth said. "You'll tire yourself."

"The child speaks truth," came a woman's voice behind us. "Let the girls do the work, Katherine. You must save your strength."

Katherine turned, hands across her swollen belly. "Alice Tilley!"

The woman walking toward us looked to be middle-aged, not young and not yet old, streaks of gray in her hair and neat smile lines around her eyes and mouth as though drawn there. Her rounded shoulders made her appear shorter than her medium height.

Katherine grasped Alice Tilley's hands in hers. "So, it is true you have been released."

"Yes. I am freed at last. That jail is not my favorite spot in this world. I can think of much finer places to spend my days."

"It took much too long," Katherine said.

"The magistrates could not prevail against the joined forces of the women in the county," Alice said. "And my husband's iron will."

She examined the group of us, stopping at me. "Who is this young woman? I feel as though I should know you. Your face is familiar to me."

"This is my husband's youngest sister. Susanna. She returned while you were imprisoned."

"Susanna lives with us now," Elizabeth offered.

Alice came closer until she stood directly in front of me, never taking her eyes from my face. "'Tis a wonder. Anne Hutchinson. My dear, dear friend. And you are her youngest daughter. We thought you to be lost forever. It is as though you have returned from the dead." I grew warm beneath her piercing gaze and direct words. "Your eyes are your mother's, and your hair and height. Praise the Lord. He works His miracles."

Alice Tilley dropped her grip around my arms and stepped back. "Let me help with the soap making, Katherine."

"You must need rest after your confinement, Alice," Katherine said.

"I am not with child as you are. I am too old for that. My months of confinement are precisely the reason I wish to help. It is a joy to do menial work when one has been robbed of the privilege. You go inside and put up your feet. Your daughter and niece can help me."

Katherine sighed, hands on her belly. "I would like to rest. I am most grateful to you, Alice." She gripped Alice Tilley's hands in hers. "I am glad you are returned."

When the door closed behind Katherine, Alice Tilley said, "Pay her harshness no mind. It is not meant to hurt you, Susanna. Her condition makes her testy. Someday when you are grown and about to give birth, you will understand."

Alice instructed us to help her lift the smaller kettle of lard and pour its contents into the bigger one. Elizabeth and I took turns stirring with a wooden paddle until the mixture was thick as mush. While we worked, we took bites of the bread and cheese the maid brought out from the kitchen. By midafternoon we had filled the greased wooden box molds.

My eyes and nose stung from the sharp tang of the lye. I had smelled these odors before, long ago. Mother was there.

In the village we did not use soap. We bathed in the streams each morning, scrubbing ourselves with the roots of a plant that formed a foam in the water. I had forgotten its name. It gave my skin the smell of the nature around me.

Alice straightened up, her hand on her back. She did not bend from the waist to stir the pot as the Indian women did. "We've done good work today. Elizabeth, it would be good for you to check on your mother." She washed her hands in the bucket of clean water and sat down on the back steps.

"Come sit beside me, Susanna. I would speak with you."

I lowered myself down onto the stoop. Alice Tilley gazed out at the trees in the orchard. What would she say to me? Would she be unkind like the women at the church who looked upon me as though I were less than the rest? Or an object to be pitied? I could not bear pity from this woman. Why, I did not know. Yes, I did. She had called Mother her friend.

Long moments passed before she turned to look at me. "You are returned at last to your own people. Tell me. Now that you are come back to your brother's house, do you feel as though you have come home?"

Her bluntness jolted. Yet there was something about her that calmed me. As though she saw the world in simple ways, absent of the added layers that complicated life. She reminded me of Muh-teh-qway. I recalled the conversation I had overheard months ago when Faith and Katherine discussed Alice Tilley's imprisonment. This woman who sat beside me knew well what it was to be falsely accused. To wait in captivity for justice to come. I did not see in her the edge that people wronged could carry upon their shoulders, a restlessness caused by anger. How had she come about her confidence? Her peace?

What did she see in me now? My confusion? My aloneness? I gripped the wood of the stoop.

"If you do not wish to talk, I will not compel you to it."

The question Alice Tilley asked waited for an answer. Did I feel I had come home? Home was a strange word: short, but long upon the tongue. I could hear its echo inside my head. Home.

I shook my head. "I do not know."

"Honest words," she said. "Tell me. What is it to feel that one is home?"

I shrugged.

"Home is where you are your true self. Have you yet found your true self, Susanna?" Her eyes were like two lamps lit for the darkness, so bright I had to look away. "Your mother, in all her wanderings, from Lincolnshire to Boston to Aquidneck, and south to the Dutch country, knew her true home. She carried it with her. Inside her heart."

What did this woman mean? I did not understand.

"You knew my mother."

"I knew her well. We spent much time together as we cared for the sick and helped at birthings. I knew your father, too."

"Can you tell me?"

"Would that be of help to you?"

A choking feeling in my throat kept me from answering. I nodded.

"I shall begin with William Hutchinson, your father. He was a kind man with a mild temper, always steady no matter the circumstances. None of the tumult around him stirred him to anger. He and Anne were in many ways opposites, for her moods could soar to the heights and then sink low. Your father's fire burned inside him, undetected from the outside. Your mother's shone for all to see. Which one is the better? One cannot say.

"Both were capable of great feeling. Each showed it differently. That is needed in a marriage. Two halves of a whole that are just alike does not make a good match. The differing characteristics of both husband and wife must blend together. That was the marriage of your parents.

"William suffered great criticism as he stood by your mother, all of it unjustified. 'More wholly a wife than a husband,' they said. Nonsense. To him, Anne was a dear saint and noble soul and he loved her dearly. He felt no need to be above her in any matter. That is a trait my husband has. When I was censured by the magistrates and imprisoned, he fought for me like a lion. Your father did the same for your mother."

I thought of Martha Winthrop and the way John Winthrop ordered her to do his bidding. She cowered in his presence. John Cotton and Reverend Wilson said women were below men. I recalled the words John Cotton said of Mother at her trial: "After all, she is a mere woman and more subject to error than a man."

It could not be all white men shared that opinion. Edward did not treat Katherine that way, and Alice Tilley did not feel her husband treated her as below him.

Indian women did not cower before the men. Opala did not, even as the wife of the chief Wampage. Muh-teh-qway, the eldest woman of the family, owned the *wigwam*, like the other women did in the village. She and the other wise women, the *lepwexkwe*, selected the male leaders of the tribe. That was how Wampage was chosen as *sachem*. The women determined who owned the land. They grew the crops, prepared the food, wove baskets and clothing and made the pottery. The men did the building and clearing the land. They hunted for food and protected the tribe. When there was war, the *lepwexkwe* chose the male warriors who would go to battle.

"William and Anne Hutchinson's marriage was one between equals," Alice said.

I was glad to hear it. Mother would not have had to cower before Father like Martha Winthrop did.

Alice looked out at the orchard. "How much do you remember of this place? Why your family had to leave here. How old were you then?"

"Four years."

"Do you have any memories of your life with your mother and father or has your time with the Indians taken them away?"

"I want to remember more."

"Even if one so young cannot recall the particulars, I believe the memories remain still, emblazoned on the mind. Embedded within the feelings."

"My brother has talked to me. I have read my mother's trial."

She raised her brows. "You do want to know." She stated it as fact so there was no need for me to answer. "Shall I talk now of the trial?"

I nodded. There was something about her that made me believe she would give me truth. Not some parceled-out, warped version like Mister Cotton and Mister Wilson, given out of their own bias. What motivated people to see a circumstance in one way or in another? It was to build up oneself, make one in the right. Some did that more than others. Alice Tilley would not, I thought.

"What a bitter November day it was. The governor ordered your mother's trial to be held in the meetinghouse across the river in Roxbury, not here in Boston where your mother had many supporters. The room was crowded with people who came either to deride or to support your mother. I watched your father's face during the proceedings: agony and sorrow in his usually tranquil countenance. On the first day, Anne was forced to stand before the magistrates for hours. In her expectant condition. Cruel. Cruel."

Alice Tilley's mouth pursed into a thin line and she shook her head. "When Anne fell to the floor in a faint, William was the first at her side to lift her up, give her water, demanding the governor allow her to sit upon a chair. On the second day, when she was banished, his face was gray as ash. A great injustice was done that day. This town is still poisoned with it," Alice said.

"William Hutchinson was made of the same iron as his wife. During those long winter months she spent imprisoned in

Reverend Weld's house in Roxbury, he labored hard to begin their life again in a new place. He built another home for your family. He was not able to be there at her second trial the next spring where they excommunicated her from the church. Your brother Edward stood beside her and Faith's husband, Thomas Savage."

Father. Father. I tried to picture his face, hear his voice, remember what it was like to be in his presence. Only feelings came, whispers from long ago. He was strong, never idle. He protected us. And then he was dead. A fresh grave with his name upon it.

"After your father's death, church authorities from Massachusetts came to your mother's house in Aquidneck and tried again to make her recant. John Winthrop had plans to add Rhode Island to Massachusetts. Anne knew she would never be free of the persecution. That is why she moved her family to New Amsterdam."

I saw the scene in my mind. We stood beside Mother at Father's grave set between the house and the Cove. The waves lapped against the shore. Her shoulders shook, and she whispered words I could not hear. I thought she was talking to Father. Then she lifted her head and walked to the wagon.

Alice Tilley's voice pulled me back. "Your mother's character can be summed up in few words. Anne Hutchinson was a healer. Of bodies and of souls. It was her gift from heaven."

I could hear her velvet voice in my ear as though she bent over me now, her breath against my cheek: "Susanna, dear."

"I worked by Anne's side as she helped to bring babes into this world," Alice said. "As the mothers labored, she comforted them with scripture that rolled off her tongue as easy as her daily conversation. She was a good woman. A great woman. No amount of lies and distortions of truth can alter that fact."

John Winthrop's written condemnations sliced through Alice Tilley's words. *Jezebel. We will reduce you.*

"Anne was many-faceted: fierce in her outspokenness one moment, soft and kind in another. No one born into this world is without fault. We are all fallen creatures. Best to keep that in mind. Your mother could be proud for she possessed extraordinary gifts of wisdom. Before her God, she was humble.

"At her second trial, she stood like the queen of Sheba in the Bible, even in her illness with another expectant child. She told the magistrates she had spoken rashly. 'It was never in my mind to slight ministers or scripture or anything set up by God,' she said. Governor Winthrop was triumphant. He thought he had won. And then she said: 'It was never in my heart to slight any man, only that man should be kept in his own place and not set in the room of God.'

"She told those men straight to their faces that they overstepped their authority. That was courage, majesty in the flesh. A woman with her head held high among those men wearing their black cloth and white collars, who called her an instrument of Satan.

"I've thought much upon this in the years since, especially as I sat in my own prison cell. Only God can know all. In scripture God declares man has not the right to judge. No one can know the heart of another. That belongs only to Him."

I did not want her to stop talking. "Why did John Winthrop hate my mother?"

Alice sighed and her mouth twitched. "Your mother's greatest enemy, John Winthrop. Four wives, and only one outlived him. His third wife, Margaret—everyone loved her—bore many children. Only one son survived. No daughter lived past childhood. Most of what he knew of childbirth and marriage was heartache and loss. The colony was his offspring, and he would have done anything to keep it alive. Including ousting anyone who disagreed with him. And he did plenty of that. At the end of the trial, when your mother predicted the doom of his beloved colony, Winthrop took personal offense. It is why he hated her so. She threatened his child."

I thought of Mother's statement written in the scribe's blotchy handwriting at the end of the trial transcript: *What you do to me will happen to Massachusetts.*

"Human nature will choose to fight when it feels it is threatened, like a cat caught in a corner lashes out with its claws. Remember this: what those men said about your mother did not make it true."

Alice Tilley's words swirled around me. I could not understand. Not yet. Perhaps never.

"I see you are troubled," Alice said. "Take comfort. The passing of time has a way of bringing truth to the fore."

"I want to know now."

Alice chuckled. "To the young, time seems to pass slowly. To those who are old, it rushes by." As if in answer to Alice, a group of birds passed overhead. "In the meantime, we wait."

I watched the seabirds until they became small specks over the water. If I could have the perspective of a bird, I would understand. They saw from above. That alone would turn what loomed large into something small. I was rooted to the ground like the trees, lost inside the leaves.

"Sometimes waiting means to sit in silence," Alice said. "Raging against injustice can sap our strength. I know a little of that." She put her hand over mine, warm and firm. "I cannot presume to know what you feel or everything you have gone through."

I waited for the nightmare to come, as it always did when I thought of the day my family died. Nothing flashed. I did not hear my family murdered. I did not see the flames burning their bodies inside the house. I did not feel the terror of being alone. As though a heavy curtain had been drawn across it.

Susanna, dear, I heard inside my mind. Mother.

Alice pulled herself up from the step. "I must go home now. My husband frets when I am too long out of his sight. Do not be troubled, young one. You have known much change and disruption in your young life. You have your mother's strength in you, and your father's. You have carried it within you all those long years away. It is there still. Rely on that strength and on the good Lord, for He will carry what you cannot."

Chapter Eighteen

AFTER ALICE TILLEY LEFT, I WALKED OVER TO THE garden plot. Soon the ground would warm, and it would be time to plant the seeds Faith brought me.

I wandered into the orchard, repeating Alice's words. *Home is where you are your true self. Leave judgment and understanding to God.* If I said them aloud, they would stay with me. On the apple trees, bees moved among the rose and white blossoms. It felt as though the things Alice told me became the buds, my mind like the bees passing one to the other, helping my memories to blossom.

Alice Tilley spoke of my true home. I was too young to remember Boston. Aquidneck Island, then. My years from four to nine were spent there. If I could tap into the place in my mind where my veiled memories lay, I would remember more of my life before the village.

My eyes shut against the present scene. I would think upon Aquidneck.

A picture appeared in the grayish-black screen of my eyelids. Water.

First, I heard the sounds, then the smells. And then I could see it.

We lived beside the water. I remember the sound of the waves lapping against the shore. I could smell its fresh scent, mixed with the earthen aroma of the red flowers that grew along the bank, and the green, grass-like reeds sprouting up on the bank. The curve of Great Cove wrapped gently around the land like a mother cradling her baby. The color of the water's calm surface mirrored the sky above: blue and gray, with patches of its glassy surface white like the clouds.

The front door of the house Father built for us faced the Cove, on the narrow neck of land that sat between two bodies of water: one tranquil, the other restless. To the east, the sea waves crashed, splashing against the low rock wall lining the opposite side of the road by the house, spraying water over the dirt tracks the wagons made.

I remember. I remember.

A few houses clustered around the western shore of the Cove, built by the small group that began the settlement. Names rushed back: Coddington. Coggshall. Aspinwall. Clarke. Dyer. Mary Dyer was my mother's best friend. She had hair the color of straw.

Six of us children lived with Mother and Father. My sister Bridget and her husband John Sanford dwelt nearby. They had two sons—Peleg and Endcome. My sister Anne lived in a small house near to us. She had married at age fifteen to William Collins. They came with us to New Amsterdam, where they died.

I pushed back against the memories that would block the scene of the Island.

I would think about the water in the Cove. Clear and clean and shining. The sun touched the tips of the gentle waves with light. I used to imagine an angel had done it. I told Father so and he smiled.

At dusk we crossed the road to watch the sun sinking into the western horizon, its rays spreading upward, firing the clouds orange and gold for a few precious moments before fading into gray. We saw two sunsets: the one in the sky and the one reflected on the water.

Father would stand silent beside me as we watched the sunset, his eyes fixed upon the horizon, as though he could see beyond the arch of the earth to somewhere far beyond. What had his thoughts been? He had not shared them. Had he longed for the place of his birth? Searching for memories as I did now?

Most of his life had been lived in a place far across the ocean. His childhood, his marriage to Mother, the births of his children. His memories must have remained vivid of the place of his birth. Alford, Lincolnshire. It was my birthplace, too. It must live somewhere within me, like Alice Tilley had said.

Memories were sights and sounds and smells, touch and taste, all blended into one.

What else could I recall? I kept my eyes shut, going deep into my mind.

Mother's garden.

It spread over the ground along the east side of the Aquidneck house to capture the morning sun. I remember the flowers. The colors. Clusters of yellow daffodils dancing among the reds and pinks and cream of the tulips that surrounded the house. Summer brought the white and purple wood lilies and sun-faced daisies, pink sweet peas and climbing red roses. I remember the ordered rows of vegetables: yellow and orange squashes, pale green and purple cabbages, deep green broccoli and kale. Waving stalks of maize.

Like the gardens in the Indian village where I spent many hours alongside Opala and Muh-teh-qway—planting the seeds, pulling the weeds, harvesting.

I pushed it from my mind. In this moment I needed to remember Aquidneck.

In the spring and summer, it would seem the garden was always green, freely giving of its abundance. Each autumn the leaves would color and fall, the plants bending limply to the earth, the supple green dying into brown. I helped Mother dig up the seeds in the dirt and stored them in bags to plant again in the spring and watch them come again to life.

I remember another garden. The one we planted in New Amsterdam. The vegetables and herbs were nearly ready to harvest on that hot day the Indians came. Again, I jerked my thoughts away. Back to Aquidneck Island when my parents still lived.

I remember the night noises of the frogs and the crickets as I lay in bed on the upper floor beside my siblings, drowsing into sleep. They blended with the lapping of the waves and my parents' voices as they sat on the porch in the twilight.

Could I recall Father's touch? Yes. I went to sleep with his kiss upon my forehead. He would squeeze my shoulder as he passed, bend down and put his arm around me. I wanted to feel that now.

A breeze rustled the leaves of the trees in the orchard, brushing my shoulders.

Father taught us to fish in the Cove with rods made of sticks and string. We took our catch triumphant to the kitchen and helped Mother to fry it on a black pan over the fire. In the evenings after supper, Father would sit in his chair by the hearth in the keeping room with the Bible upon his lap and read aloud to us, his round spectacles propped upon his nose.

Like Mother's, his presence was constant as the rising and setting of the sun.

What was the sound of his voice? During my time in the village, I could not bring it to mind. Chief Wampage's deep growl stood in front of my memory. Hearing the tenor of my brother's speech brought my father's back to me.

Father left us when I was nine. Little Zuriel must have been only three then. While we slept in the dark of night, his heart stopped. His still body lay upon the bed, Mother sitting beside him, holding his hand, whispering words to him as tears dripped from her trembling chin. Mother rarely wept, or we children did not see when she did. After that, Mother did not go out among people in her usual way. She kept to the house. Each dusk she still sat on the porch. Father was not there.

I sunk down upon a root rising up from the ground beneath one of the apple trees. I leaned my head against the trunk. A falling blossom touched my cheek and glided onto my lap: five white petals around a yellow center. Tender as a baby's skin.

Aquidneck. It had come back to me. There still, inside me. Mine to own always.

My thoughts took another turn.

If we had stayed in Aquidneck by Father's grave and not gone south to New Amsterdam, perhaps Mother and my siblings would still live. I would have grown up between the waters of the Cove and the sea with my family. My time with the Indians would never have been.

The Indians. The village.

Thoughts slammed me, like the sea waves splashing over the wall. Covering my memories of Aquidneck. Of Mother. Of Father.

❧

At the Big House ceremony, the year I turned fourteen, I saw another salt girl. She sat across the way. A babe lay in her arms, a boy who looked about three years leaning against her shoulder. She watched the man who stood by the center pole, talking of his vision quest.

"*Wanishi,*" he said. Thank you. To the Great Creator who gave him his children and his woman. When he finished speaking, he sat down beside her.

He was her husband.

I had to talk with her. The meeting that night went on and on. It did not end until the moon was high in the sky. The people left the house to find their places to sleep. The man lifted the boy in his arms and left the house.

I stood in front of her. Her babe sucked at her breast. She looked older than me. I guessed her age to be twenty years. She stared long at me and turned away. I did not leave.

"*Keku hach kata watu?*" she said. What do you want to know?

"*Laphala?*" You are adopted?

She nodded.

I pointed to my chest. "I am *laphala.*"

"Are you who they call the daughter of Anne-Hoeck?"

Was I Wampage's daughter? He called himself Anne-Hoeck. I lived in his wife Opala's *wigwam.* I had taken the place of his dead daughter.

"I am."

"They talk of you in the other villages."

"What do they say of me?"

She looked me over. "The salt girl's hair is red. She is a silent one."

I spoke in English. "Are you a wife?"

"*Wicheochi.*" She pointed to her chest. "*Ana.*" Mother. She kissed her baby's head.

"I have many questions," I said.

"Sit." The girl's fair hair was tied into two long braids that fell over her shoulders. Her babe grabbed one while it nursed. She brushed it onto her back.

"I was ten when I came to the Indians. I did not want to stay with them. I wanted my family, but they were dead. For a long time, I was angry. I missed my family. I grew up among the Indians. I came to feel myself to be one. My husband asked to marry me. He was kind to me. I had a child. My son," she said.

"Englishmen came to my village. They told me I must leave. My husband cried as they took me away. He was holding my son. They took me back to my old home. I did not remember it. My aunt did not want me. She was ashamed I was in her house. The people were not kind to me. I got very sick. My milk had nowhere to go. When I got well, I returned to the village. My aunt is not sorry, I am certain. I came back to my husband. To my child. Now I have another." She kissed the top of her baby's head again, cradling it tighter in her arms.

"Thank you for telling me," I said. *Manishi.*

"Stay here with the Indians. If the white men come to trade you, do not return. It is better for you. You will never belong again in the white world."

The man returned. She went with him. I did not see her again before the Dutchmen came.

&

Koch! "Why?" I said it aloud. A harsh word in either language. One sound strike, like the sharp cry of the seabirds that soared above the orchard, bringing me back from the past. I closed my eyes tight and tried to bring back Aquidneck. It was gone behind the curtain.

I had belonged once to Aquidneck, in the home of my father and mother. Then I came to feel I would always be in the village. In this place called Boston, I was different, just as the girl had said. Where did I turn now? Perhaps my home would be in Edward's house for the remainder of my life. A feeling inside told me it would not be so.

My true home, as Alice Tilley said. I did not know how to find it. How could I put the split pieces together? Was it even possible?

Mother and Father had found it in the places they lived. Edward had found it with Katherine. Faith and Bridget with their families. They could not do it for me. I must find it for myself.

Clouds moved overhead, heavy with unshed rain. A dark thought came. What if I did not find my home? If there was no place for me, what then?

Chapter Nineteen

M ID-MAY THE SOIL WAS WARM ENOUGH TO PLANT the rest of my seeds. The first shoots emerged from the soil, growing taller each day. By June I could see the blanket of green from the upstairs window.

I was on my knees in the dirt, a long apron covering my skirt. It had rained in the night, and the soil was dark and loose. I gently pushed aside the plants to tug the weeds free of the soil, their roots dangling, and tossed them into a pile.

The columbine I had planted along the side of the house already flowered, with blooms that looked like yellow and red and purple stars. Early spring, I had sown horehound seed into a large pot sitting at the garden's edge, the seeds buried just below the surface of dirt, just as Mother's herb book instructed. Its small, whitish stems resembled a piece of wood, with fuzzy leaves that smelled like strong molasses.

Rain drops from the early morning rain still clung to the wide round leaves of the lady's mantle plant, making them shimmer. They looked like the lily pads I remembered in the Cove. Their tiny yellow flowers were like bits of sunshine. Lemon balm, spearmint, and thyme grew side by side. I breathed in the scents mingling together in the air.

A cry came from the house, as though someone was in pain, and Elizabeth came running out from the back door. "Susanna, Mother's time has come. Fetch Alice Tilley. Quickly!"

I stood up, wiping the dirt from my hands on the apron. "I will go straightaway." I ran up High Street. The Tilley house was past the town dock at North End, next to Mill Field. At my knock, Alice came to the door.

"Have you come to help me in my garden, Susanna?" She looked down at the smudged apron I still wore.

"Katherine's time is come," I panted.

Alice took her shawl and bag from a peg beside the door and together we hurried back to the house.

"Mother is upstairs in her room," Elizabeth said.

"Take your siblings out of the house," Alice said. "Bring their meal out to the orchard and make certain they do not romp and yell. Your mother needs quiet." She turned to me. "Susanna, I will need a helper. You must have a strong heart and stomach like your mother did. I believe you have. Will you do it?"

I felt strange at the thought of attending a childbirth, both a pull and a revulsion in the same moment. That hallowed space of womanhood was not the domain of children or of men. Did I have the strength Alice saw in me?

Another cry came, a long moan of pain. Alice went up the stairs, and I followed.

Katherine stood at the end of the bed dressed only in a thin shift, holding onto the wooden rail, taking great, gasping breaths. Her skirt and waistcoat lay on the floor. Alice scooped them up and set them on a corner chair out of the way.

"There, there, dearest Katherine, I am come to help." Alice's voice was low and soft and soothing, as she smoothed Katherine's damp hair away from her face that glistened with sweat. "How close are the pains?"

"They come almost as soon as the last one ends," Katherine gasped. "This is much worse than last time. I fear something is wrong." She gripped Alice's hand as her lips tightened. She bent over, her hands stretching across her large belly.

Alice put an arm around her. "Your body knows what to do. Trust it will not be long now, and you will find yourself delivered. You are prepared, I see," Alice said. Beside the small fireplace sat the open-bottomed chair for the birthing, fresh straw beneath it. Alice turned back to me. "Drape the two windows with blankets, Susanna."

My fingers fumbled at the scratchy cloth. The daylight disappeared, making the room snug in shadow.

"Good, Susanna. The room must be dark like a mother's womb. Now fetch clean cloths, warm water and a drinking cup."

I ran down the stairs and filled a pitcher with water from the kettle hanging from a hook over the fire. I gathered the cloths and cup.

When I returned, Alice opened her bag. "Make a tea of the horehound leaves to ease Katherine's labor. Three leaves only and no more." I had taken too many leaves and returned them to the bag. "Crush them fine with your fingers and let them steep for a few moments," she instructed.

After I prepared the tea, Katherine drank a few sips, then pushed the cup away, her legs giving way beneath her. I grasped her elbow to keep her up. She let out a long, low moan.

"You have need to bear down?" Alice asked.

"I do," Katherine gasped, and bent with another pain.

"This is going very quickly," Alice said.

Together we moved Katherine to the corner and eased her down onto the seat. Alice frowned as she looked back at the trail of red blood on the floor. Katherine screamed when another pain struck her.

"Push. Gently now." Alice kept up a stream of soothing words. Three times Katherine bore down. Alice knelt on the floor and peered beneath Katherine's shift. "I see the head. Push gently, Katherine." She reached up and guided the baby out, holding a writhing infant firmly in both hands, connected to its mother by a thick, gray cord at its belly.

Alice snipped the cord with a knife and held the babe up for Katherine to see. "'Tis a girl child," she said.

Katherine opened her eyes. "A daughter. I have a daughter." She bent again with another pain.

"The afterbirth comes," Alice explained as she handed the babe to me. "Use a wet cloth to wipe the baby clean."

The baby was folded tight as a ball of yarn, her arms and legs and trunk covered with a thick whitish substance and red-streaked with Katherine's blood. She squealed, tiny lips scrunched, eyes shut. I set her atop the blanket on the bed and gently wiped her skin clean.

"Scrub more roughly, Susanna. 'Twill make her cry and clean out her lungs," said Alice. "Good," she added when the babe wailed. "Now swaddle her tight with the long cloth and set her in the basket by the hearth," Alice said. "Spread another cloth across the bed."

She cleaned Katherine up and, half-carrying her, laid her on the mattress, all the time murmuring soothing words. "Fetch the babe and bring her to her mother," she told me.

I held the babe close to Katherine's face as she touched its head. Her eyes closed and she sighed.

"Hold the baby, Susanna," Alice whispered. "I must get the bleeding to slow." She began to rub Katherine's belly with firm strokes of her hands, as though kneading bread.

I tucked the babe's head into the crook of my elbow, her tiny body resting along my forearm. She turned her face toward me and began to nuzzle, mewing like a kitten.

"Out of pain comes new life. 'Tis a wonder, is it not?"

I could not answer Alice for the lump in my throat.

"Take the babe to her father," Alice said, still kneading Katherine's stomach. "I am sorry for the discomfort, lovey," she said, as Katherine moaned. "'Tis a necessity."

When I opened the door, Edward stood outside with Elizabeth and the other children. I put the babe into his arms. "A female child," I said.

Edward bent his head and kissed the little forehead. "Thank the good Lord she is safely delivered. And all is well with Katherine?"

"I believe she is well," I answered.

"Susanna? Fetch linen rags and hot water," Alice called from up the stairs. "And wine."

When I returned to the dark room, Alice was still kneading Katherine's stomach. A stain of red covered the blankets on the bed. Katherine's eyes were closed, her body limp.

"She sleeps, poor thing, and that's a blessing after her ordeal. We need to lessen the bleeding. Soak the rags in the wine and give them to me."

I did so and watched as Alice stuffed them into the open cavern of Katherine's body, where the babe had come through.

"Now, heat more cloths over the fire until they steam."

I handed Alice the steaming hot cloths, and she placed them over Katherine's belly.

"Bring my bag," Alice directed.

She rummaged in it and lifted out a small jar. "Juice from the angelica root." She turned Katherine's head to the side, and spooned it into Katherine's mouth, turning her head back and holding her lips closed until she swallowed. The angelica had a sweet, pleasant smell that seemed to float above the heavy, musky smell of blood.

"Knead her belly, Susanna. Harder. Harder. It will shrink the uterus. Edward!" she called through the door. "Bring the babe in here to nurse. That will also help."

Edward laid the baby at Katherine's breast. His face turned white as he saw the blood.

After the babe nursed, Alice said: "Take the baby and leave the room now, Edward. You can do nothing here."

She left the bedside and examined the mess below the birthing chair. "Most of the afterbirth did not come," I heard her mutter beneath her breath.

We worked together without speaking, keeping the hot compresses on Katherine's stomach, replacing the blood-soaked rags, spooning angelica tea into Katherine's mouth. Her skin looked pasty and white.

Someone came into the room holding the baby. It was Martha Winthrop. She put the baby again to feed. Katherine did not notice.

Was this the common way of childbirth? From the set look on Alice Tilley's face, I did not think so.

The sunlight at the edges of the blanketed windows disappeared as the afternoon turned to night. While I waited for another cloth to steam, I peered out of the window. The moon had risen, a chalk-white ball in the sky. The color reminded me of Katherine's skin.

The stain on the bed covers grew larger. I had not known that blood had both a sweet and a sour smell.

"I cannot stop the bleeding." Alice straightened up from the bed, pressing her fingers against her shaking lips. "And there is naught more I can do. Fetch your brother, Susanna."

≈

Edward stayed all night by his wife's bedside while Alice kept up her nursing vigil.

"Go to bed, Susanna," she said. "There is naught you can do."

"I will stay here."

My aunt could not die. Katherine was needed by her husband, by her children.

Alice left the bedside and put her hand on my shoulder, speaking low. "It is certain. Katherine will be dead before morning."

A deep sob burst from Edward. "Katherine!"

He called out to her as though she were far away. She did not hear. She did not move. Her eyes stared. She was gone.

≈

Morning came. Edward remained upstairs with Katherine's body. Martha Winthrop brought a mother to nurse the crying baby; other women filled the keeping room, bringing food and whispering murmurs of sympathy. No one noticed me in the corner, listening. It was as though the women belonged in a separate world known only among their own sex, their spoken sentiments mingling together in a kind of rhythm.

"What a tragedy to die at only thirty-five years of age. This baby was Katherine's seventh child, and only the fourth to still live. We cannot cry against what is our lot in life. 'Tis the ordained way of things, the curse of Eve in Genesis, in travail thou shalt bear children. All expectant mothers stare into the face of death. For Katherine 'twas the seventh time that took her. Now there are four motherless children. Edward will need to marry soon."

My brother's next marriage spoken in the same breath as his wife's death. I slipped out of the room and up the stairs.

"Come, children," Alice came to the doorway of Katherine's room. "Bid your mother goodbye."

I backed away. This moment belonged only to them.

Afterward, Elisha and Anne came to Elizabeth's room. The three of them huddled together, weeping, at last falling into an exhausted sleep on the bed. I covered them with a blanket and lay down upon the floor.

When I woke, I went to Katherine's room. The blankets were taken down from the windows and sunlight flooded in, the windows open to air the stale room. Katherine lay in a fresh gown on clean bed covers, her eyes closed, hands crossed over her breast. So still. I watched for her chest to rise. It did not. Never would it again fill with the breath of life.

Alice walked to Edward and gently touched his shoulder. "Before I leave for home, there are things you must take care of. You'll need a wet nurse to nourish the baby for the first months. There is a young widow who had a son February last, a month after her poor husband died. Abigail Button. She has plenty of milk for both her own and your babe. I could speak with her if you wish. You will also need to hire a woman to care for the babe, for Mrs. Button must care for her other children. Elizabeth is too young for the responsibility."

The words came from me as soon as I thought them: "I will care for her."

"Susanna can take her to the wet nurse several times a day and care for her day and night. Do you wish it, Edward?"

He did not answer.

"Edward?" Alice said. "I do not mean to press you or interrupt your grief."

He raised his head. "Of course. Susanna will care for the child." His voice scratched.

The words echoed back to me. I could care for this helpless, motherless infant. I was motherless, too. In the cradle next to the fire, the baby squawked. I picked her up and held her upright on my shoulder, my hand behind her limp neck to hold it secure.

"Katherine worried but not for herself," Edward said. "She did not want to lose another child. I was not careful of her feelings. And now . . ." he trailed off. "She is gone." His shoulders shook.

Alice put her hand on Edward's shoulder. "For a woman to bear a child is to put herself in the hands of God. We must accept His will that is done. What else can we do?"

The baby settled into my shoulder, her soft, quick breaths like feathers on my cheek. Was death always God's will? Who lived and who died? A mother dead, and the babe she bore alive. The Indians killing my family was God's will? God's will was a mystery.

"Has the babe been named?" Alice asked.

Edward shook his head. "We did not speak of it before the birth, and at the last I could not ask Katherine her wishes."

Edward stood up from beside the bed, blinking as though it took a great effort to focus on his surroundings. He touched the baby's downy head, caressing her tiny cheek. He reached out, and I set her in his arms.

"How your mother wanted you, little babe." Edward looked at me. "Her hair is reddish. Like yours, my little sister." He kept his eyes on my face. "Susanna," he said. "She whose presence here is a miracle. The babe will be christened Susanna."

Chapter Twenty

A BIT OF MORNING MIST STILL CLUNG TO THE TREES, AS though the earth had not fully woken and still wished to sleep. I walked up High Street and north onto Sudbury to where the road split, and took the east fork. The lots were various sizes, most narrow and long with gardens in the back, the houses set close to the street.

One caught my notice: small and tidy looking, with only three windows and a door in the front, the steep roof higher at the back for the second story. Each window was white-framed, a pleasing contrast against the dark gray wood. Pink wood lilies grew along the east side of the house.

The yellow-painted door opened. It was John Cole. This must be his house, the one he had offered to me. I shrank back. There was no tree to hide me. He saw me standing in the street and walked toward me. I could not see his face clearly beneath his hat.

"Good morn, Miss Hutchinson. What brings you out so early and up this way?"

"I . . . must find the house where Mrs. Button lives." Alice Tilley had arranged for Mrs. Button to keep the baby throughout the night for ease of feeding. Every morning I was to fetch her.

"You've come in the right direction," he said. "It is two houses further east, on the opposite side. The one with green shutters."

I hurried past him, crossed the road, and knocked on the door.

"Come in," a woman called.

Mrs. Button sat in a chair by the hearth in the narrow keeping room, Katherine's baby at her breast. Her own baby boy lay sleeping in the cradle, as her three girls put bowls and spoons on the table. The oldest did not look more than seven. Slices of bread toasted on a grill above the fire. My stomach rumbled. I'd been in such a hurry to see baby I had not eaten.

"Help them with the porridge, will you, girl?" Mrs. Button asked me. "Hand her your bowls, children."

I dipped the ladle into the pot, filled it with the steaming gruel and poured the bowls full.

"Help them with the molasses, will you?" Mrs. Button said. "Not too much sweet, and a bit of the milk in the pail. And take the toast off the fire. That's a dear. I'm worn out this morning. The babe was a bit fussy during the early morning hours. At least my boy did not waken, too."

She was a big-boned, full-breasted woman, her eyes tiny in her full-cheeked face, with wisps of curly brown hair peeking beneath her white coif. She draped the baby over her lap while she covered her breast.

"Hold it upright against your shoulder and pat the bubbles out," she said as she handed the baby up to me. "She's a gassy one."

I tightened the blanket around Susanna and swayed back and forth to soothe her. She let out a loud burp and then calmed against my shoulder, her fast little breaths tickling my neck.

"You are good with children. That must be why Mister Hutchinson keeps you in his house. How old are you, girl?" Mrs. Button said. "Do you understand what I say?"

"I am sixteen years."

"So, you do understand me, though you are a silent one. I expect you feel strange here and miss your life among the savages. Your brother is too good to take you in. Perhaps it would have been better to leave you there."

Did she intend kindness with her words? I could not tell. It did not feel so.

"Sixteen years. Marriageable age." She stared at me. "You're pretty enough, with a fine figure. Your skin has seen far too much sun. A beautiful woman's skin is white, like mine. Use a washball in the morning and at night on your face and hands. The herbs and spices will help restore the skin, and then follow it with bran water. Scrub your face with cut lemons, too. You need a pomatum cream to soften it. Rice powder would work. I have some I brought from England, but I keep it for myself. Did your sister-in-law not instruct you in how to care for yourself?"

She shamed me.

"It would be better for Edward—Mister Hutchinson—if you married." She clucked her tongue. "Your time among the savages will make any man think twice to consider you. No, you will certainly never marry."

No one will want you, she meant. Cutting words. Yet she seemed unaware of her unkindness.

"I myself did not marry till nearly twenty-one, though I had my chances, mind you. Mr. Button was thirty when he asked for my hand. He had means, and Papa said I would be comfortable." She looked around at her room, with its hearth and ceiling beams painted a pale green, the plank floor polished so the wood grain stood out. The windows were paned glass like in Edward's house. "This house is a bit snug though, with four children come."

Baby Susan—that is what Edward called her. Her little body was warm and soft as she lay in the crook of my arm. A drip of white milk slipped from the corner of her little mouth.

"I thought my husband would last more years. Alas, he did not, and now I'm left a widow. I'm from Alford, you know, in Lincolnshire, where your family came from. Your brother Edward

is seven years my senior. Much closer to my age than Mr. Button."
Abigail laughed, three short bursts of sound that lifted her big
bosom up and down.

"You know of Alford?" I said. Perhaps she would tell me
something of it. Was the sky a bright blue or faded? Did it smell
of lavender in June as it did now in Boston? What did the house
look like where I was born?

"Of course, I know of Alford." Squawking came from the cradle, and Mrs. Button groaned. "Oh, don't waken yet, Samuel. I've
used up my milk till I get more nourishment. Hannah, hold your
brother while I get my gruel. With nursing two babes, I've got
such a thirst, and I am famished."

She drank from a big jar and ladled out a heaping of porridge
into her bowl while Samuel's cries filled the room. "Let him chew
your finger, Hannah, so he will not make such a racket."

Mrs. Button called to me above the din. "Take the baby home
now, girl, and don't forget to take the extra milk. It's in that covered jar on the table. It should be enough for the mid-morning
feed. Return here an hour after midday meal for her feeding.
Keep your finger in Samuel's mouth, Hannah!"

As I left the house, I shifted the blanket to keep Little Susan's
face from the sun. She sighed, the contented sound of a fed babe.
So helpless, completely dependent upon others to care for her
needs. Like a bowl of glass that might shatter. What if I tripped
on the stones and fell upon her? The thought made me shudder.
No harm must come to her.

Is this what a mother felt? This consuming love full of care
and worry? Yet I was not a mother to this child, merely an aunt.
If I did not marry, as Abigail Button said, I would never know
what it was to be a mother. I'd never feel new life grow within me
or labor in pain to deliver it, or feel the wonder of it as my own,
fashioned and nourished inside my own body. I peered into a

woman's world from the outside. It made me ache, like an empty cavern inside, never to be filled.

A girl did not have such feelings. A woman did.

à

When my first time came to bleed, I was thirteen years. It was Muh-teh-qway I ran to, terrified of what was happening. She was old and widowed and said she herself no longer had the time of women, or the need to stay in the moon house with the other women whose time it was to bleed.

"Do not be afraid. This is a day for you to rejoice, Sisika," she said to me. "A bleeding woman is holy, closer to the Creator, and blessed with wisdom. This is a fountain that makes you a woman." The blood that came from me had a musky odor, different than a cut or wound, and a darker red.

She took me to a small hut that stood alone among the trees outside the village. I remained there for four days, not to go out where others could see me. I had little to drink or eat and did not bathe. The women in the hut rested and talked together, laughing quietly. I sat in the corner and listened. A few of them whispered behind their hands.

After my bleeding stopped, Muh-teh-qway returned for me. She took me to the deepest part of the river and told me to walk into the water until it covered the top of my head. It was a ritual bath where I was immersed in water from my head to my feet. Never had I felt so clean, the musty smell of my moon blood cleansed from my loins. I was given new clothes: a longer skirt, a shawl of deerskin, and new moccasins.

"You are now a woman," Muh-teh-qway said, "ready soon for marriage."

Minsi married a warrior from another clan within the tribe. That was the custom. When the small villages gathered together for one of the Big House ceremonies, the man Talli asked to be Minsi's husband. There was no ceremony. They lived in Muh-teh-qway's *wigwam* with the rest of the family. Wampage had done the same when he came from the Turkey clan to be the husband of Opala.

Muh-teh-qway spoke to Chief Wampage. He told her he would search for a man to be my husband when the tribes met together next for the Nighthawk dance. Four warriors faced the singer, holding a rattle in their right hand and a fan of the wing of a nighthawk in their left. They jumped at the singer, leaping forward at him, swirling around him, moving back and lunging forward again.

The man he brought to meet me was one of the dancers. From the Turkey clan. I do not remember his name. His eyes were slits as he stared at me. He frightened me.

"I cannot do it," I told Wampage. He grunted and walked away without a word of anger or disappointment.

During the Big House ceremony the next fall, he brought another man. He had a handsome face and held himself well. He gave me a timid look as though he were afraid of me. He looked over at Wampage, a question in his eyes: *You want me to take the salt girl?* At least he did not say it aloud and shame me.

Again, I said I could not.

"You want children then you must choose a husband," Opala said.

Did I want to be a mother? Have children of my own? It seemed a distant dream. How could I be a mother when I was still in many ways a child? Longing for my own mother. That was the reason I turned away from the men Wampage brought to me.

"I will be another mother to Minsi's children," I answered.

Muh-teh-qway sighed. "Every woman wants children of her own," she said.

My mother, Anne Hutchinson, wanted children. She bore fifteen. So had my grandmother, Bridget Dryden.

The strange girl who had lived among the Indians would not marry in Boston. In the village I was the salt girl. Here I was a savage.

I had a place now in my brother's house. He needed me to care for his motherless babe.

ॐ

Through the morning, the baby slept in the cradle set up in my room. I weeded in the garden, leaving the window open so I could hear if she cried.

Inside the house, Anne began to wail. "Where is Mother? I want my mother!"

"She's gone to heaven, Anne," Elizabeth said to soothe her.

"Why does heaven need my mother more than I?"

Anne's question was also mine. Why did heaven need my own mother?

When Edward returned to the house that night, he took the baby from my arms and sat down in the chair by the hearth. He searched her face as though he would see Katherine in her features. When she began to fuss, he bounced her across his forearm to quiet her. Her cries grew louder.

"It is time for her evening meal," I said. "I must take her to Mrs. Button's to nurse." When he handed me Little Susan, his eyes were red.

Abigail Button met me on the doorstep, took the baby and shut the door without a word. My arms felt light as though they would float upward without something to weigh them down. Only two days and I was already accustomed to Little Susan's presence, as though she had always been here. It was as though a door had opened and she entered; and before the door closed again, her mother stepped out.

After I returned from Mrs. Button's, I waited outside the house, watching as the sun sunk down until I could not see it anymore. In a few moments, the long clouds fired red and gold, the sun still radiating its presence. The colors faded to gray and dusk settled on the town.

Dusk was a strange time, not yet dark but no longer light. Day caught in between night.

Was it that way for those who had died?

On the day of Little Susan's birth, death and life had arrived together, like the dusk that held light and dark.

What I had witnessed as I helped Alice Tilley would not leave my mind, both a marvel and a nightmare. I had not seen the midwife since the small funeral held at the burying ground for Katherine. How many mothers had Alice Tilley seen die? How many babes? Could something more have been done that Katherine might have lived?

Giving birth was a test of a woman's courage, Muh-teh-qway said.

Here in Boston a man was not present in the womb-like, darkened room during a birth—kept apart of the birthing process. Edward had waited downstairs and, at the last, sat at Katherine's bedside watching her take her last slow breath. He grieved her deeply. And loved the infant brought into the world by the very process that drained the lifeblood from the beloved woman he had called his wife.

Alice Tilley had been there for all of it, a powerful, comforting presence and help.

I remembered the conversation between Katherine and Faith, how Mother's skill and soothing presence had comforted many women in travail. Had Mother witnessed the death of a travailing woman as Alice Tilley had the day Katherine died? Or the death of a babe? What did a midwife feel at loss, to watch a life slip away as death took it?

The Book of Exodus in the Bible spoke of the Hebrew midwives in Egypt: Shiprah and Puah. The Pharaoh called them before him and commanded them to kill any male child born to a Hebrew woman and leave the females alive. The midwives would not do it. When the ruler confronted them, they said Hebrew women were so lively they often gave birth before the midwives came. Brave women to defy a ruler.

I wondered at Alice Tilley's imprisonment. She had displeased the authorities and suffered for it. Yet, like the Hebrew midwives, she had conquered.

The fading light clung at the edge of the horizon, gradually giving way as the darkening sky pushed it down to follow the sun out of sight. One by one the tiny white lights pierced the blackness.

Once again, I found the starry cluster. "Mother," I whispered, then the names of my dead siblings. "And Katherine."

ᴥ

I undressed in the darkness and pulled the nightdress over my head. The book of Mother's Faith had given me sat in a shaft of moonlight on the table beside my bed. I lit the candle and held it above the book and turned the pages.

Herbs for Childbirth written in neat letters across the top. Inside were three columns on each page: the left side a list of the herbs, in the center its purpose and, on the right, how it was to be prepared and administered. A decoction. A tea. A syrup. A clister. A pill. A vapor. Some were to be used externally: in a bath, or as an ointment, a plaster, or salve.

My mother was here upon these pages.

Betony or bishop's wort. To reduce the pains of labor. It is soothing to a woman's anxiety. I skimmed through the instructions and the list of herbs on the rest of the page.

At the bottom was an entry.

Black cohosh flower. From an Indian woman. For use in childbirth.

The candle sputtered and wax dropped on my hand. I swiped it off before it dried and licked my skin to cool the burn.

Besides the knowledge learned from her own mother in England, Mother had learned of herbs from the Indians. Like Muh-teh-qway, who also grew herbs and dried them and taught me what she knew of medicine.

The back of the book had empty pages. I took the pen and bottle of ink from the table and spread the book flat with my hands. I wrote the herbs I remembered from Muh-teh-qway's lessons:

Pekon. Use the roots and leaves for stomachache, vomiting, warts.

Sumac. Use the berries and leaves and bark and roots. For teas and dyes. To soothe sore throat, for toothache, and aching of the joints.

Ahpawi. Cattail. Leaves and roots to clean wounds, and poultice to soothe itching.

Sweetgrass. To repel insects. Keep a bundle above the bed.

Winakw. Sassafras. Use the oil to relieve pain. Make a bundle of bark and leaves to put among clothes to keep insects away.

Red cedar. For aching joints and itchy skin.

Hopefully more would come to me. I closed the book and held it against my breast. Something shifted inside me, as though two spheres touched.

I would learn to be a midwife. And a healer.

Chapter Twenty-One

EDWARD HELD LITTLE SUSAN OVER THE WOODEN BAP-
tismal font in the back corner of the meetinghouse. Wrapped
tight in the christening gown Katherine had stitched, Susan's
eyes squeezed tight, her tiny mouth opening into a square before
her cry echoed across the walls.

A small group crowded round. The baby's nurse, Mrs. Button, was there and Martha Winthrop. I stood beside Elizabeth,
Anne and Elisha. Ten days had passed since Katherine had been
placed in the burial ground.

Reverend Cotton, wearing a long wig of tight curls that covered his white collar, dipped his fingers into the font and sprinkled the water on the baby's forehead. "I baptize you in the name
of the Father and of the Son and of the Holy Spirit. Amen."

Little Susan quieted when her father pulled her back from
the font and held her in the crook of his arm, her downy head
against his coat.

Mrs. Button came forward, holding her baby boy on her
hip. Her white collar was stiff and clean, embroidered along
the edges as was her coif. "What a beautiful child she is, Mister
Hutchinson. Do you remember me from the days across the sea
in Alford? Abigail Fermayes, I was then."

"Life in England seems very dim now," Edward answered
without looking at Abigail. "I'm afraid I do not remember."

"Of course, you would not," Abigail said, "so much living in
between, with many changes." She reached out and touched

Little Susan's face. The baby turned and nuzzled against her hand, moving her mouth as though to suck. "She recognizes my scent. We have spent much time together of late."

Edward looked over at Mrs. Button. "You are the nurse Alice Tilley arranged for."

"I am. My son is still young, you see, and I have milk to give." Mrs. Button's cheeks reddened. "You are in great need with your poor wife dead."

Did Edward flinch at her blunt use of the word? His lip twitched.

"You have three other children in your care," Mrs. Button went on. "I share your circumstances. My own husband lies in his grave, and I've four fatherless children to raise."

Mrs. Button stood close to him, her hand still touching Little Susan, as though the baby belonged somehow to her. She did not. She belonged to my brother. She belonged to me.

"Prithee thanks for your aid," Edward said, "my wife . . . would be most grateful."

He backed away, and Mrs. Button's hand fell back from Little Susan. I followed Edward and the rest of the family out of the meetinghouse.

੩੩

The month of July passed, me caring for Little Susan during the day, taking trips to the Button house for nursing, and leaving the baby there to stay the night. That was the hardest moment, walking home in the dusk with my arms empty of her weight, retiring to bed with the cradle empty in the corner. I missed her fast, gentle breaths, the feel of her soft skin like the down of a new baby chick.

Baby Susan's face and arms and thighs fattened, and her colic lessened. Mrs. Button said she only woke once through the night. During her days with me, she remained awake for a longer time between napping, viewing her surroundings, her gaze upon my face as I held her.

One morning, as I took her from Mrs. Button's hold, Susan looked toward me, her mouth opened in a smile.

"'Tis gas bubbles," Mrs. Button said. "Though she is to the age where it could be more."

My heart leaped. Little Susan knew me. She loved me. I gathered her close and kissed her hair.

"How is your brother, girl?"

She never seemed to remember my name. "He is well enough. He mourns his wife deeply."

"Life moves forward," she said briskly. "I did not see him at Thursday meeting last. Is he at home this morn, perchance?"

"Aye. It is the day before Sabbath, when he does not go to his office at the wharf."

Mrs. Button adjusted her cap and smoothed her waistcoat. She lifted Susan out of my arms. "I will deliver the child to the house myself today. My mother is come to tend the children, and I can do with an outing. Run back alone; I will be there soon."

Little Susan began to wail. She spit curdled milk down Mrs. Button's bosom.

"Now I must change my gown!" She set the wailing baby in the cradle beside her own son. I moved to take her again.

"Go home, girl! Be quick about it. Make certain your brother does not leave before I come. Shut the door behind you."

I was dismissed. Baby Susan's cries followed me down the road.

I did not tell Edward of his expected visitor. He was out back with the children and their new game. He'd split a log from a fallen tree, turned it onto its side, and placed a plank longwise. Elizabeth sat on one end, legs straddled over the plank, her skirt tucked modestly around her. Elisha and little Anne sat together on the other to balance her weight. Elisha pushed his legs upward, Anne squealing, as they rose into the air. Elizabeth's legs bent as she neared the ground. As she pushed upward, Elisha and Anne moved down. Edward watched them.

Mrs. Button arrived on the front porch. I saw her through the window of the keeping room, Little Susan perched on her hip. The housemaid opened the door and showed her into the best room. Her skin looked fresh-scrubbed and white. She must have used her washball and pomatum and her precious rice powder. She bit her lips together and they reddened.

It was strange to see her in the house, holding Susan.

She saw me standing in the hall. "Girl. Tell your brother I am come."

"Edward," I said, as I went out the back door, "Little Susan is come."

"Where is she, Susanna?" He looked at me oddly.

"In the best room," I answered, "with Mrs. Button."

I stood outside the door where I could observe.

Mrs. Button sat in the chair by the hearth with Susan perched on her lap. "I have come to see how you fare in your unfortunate situation, Mister Hutchinson."

Edward took Susan from Mrs. Button. I could not see his face as he lowered himself down into the chair opposite. "That is most kind of you, Mrs. Button."

"How are your children? And yourself?" She breathed as though she had just run up the road from North End. She extended her hand and Edward took it. It shone on her face what she wanted: she a widow without a husband and he a widower without a wife.

In the village a woman mourned her husband for twelve moons, many longer. She then married her dead husband's brother, or another man chosen by the parents of her husband.

This woman was—a word came to mind, heard in a conversation between two women at the market—brazen.

I went outside with the children.

❧

A few days later, as I prepared to leave the house to take Little Susan up the road for the night, Edward said, "Rest yourself, sister. I will take the baby to Mrs. Button's."

Little Susan was sleeping through the night with no need for feeding, but still she remained at the Button house. Edward took her several times a week and did not return until after dusk, long past the time it would have taken me to walk.

After Sunday meeting, he spoke with Mrs. Button in the shade of the tree outside the meetinghouse. The August sky was cloudless, pale blue from the sticky moisture of the air, as though painted with a whitewash. Elisha began throwing pebbles against the wooden walls of the meetinghouse. Elizabeth scolded as she emptied his hands of his weapons.

"So," came a woman's voice behind us, "Mister Hutchinson courts the widow Button."

Elizabeth's eyes widened.

"That will make eight children between them," said another woman.

"And the sister also in the house," the first said. "I believe the task to recover the heathen is more burdensome than raising eight children."

"True that. Months back from the savages and still she looks as out of place as when she came. You cannot hide the Indian inside the calico."

"Seems more a mercy to leave children like that with the savages than bring them back."

They thought I did not understand what they said, that they could say whatever they wanted, and I would not know.

"Come away, Elizabeth." I took Elisha's hand and Anne's.

As we walked along the road toward home, it felt as though the women's words followed us like the hawking calls of pesky black crows.

Elizabeth's lips trembled. "Father courts Mrs. Button? What of Mother . . . ?" She trailed off.

"I want my mother," Anne wailed.

"We'll visit her grave," Elizabeth said, walking faster.

We passed the house and turned the corner onto School Street, headed toward the burying ground. The rounded headstone erected for John Winthrop rose above the rest of the stones as though he still held the power he had when he was alive.

Elizabeth stopped before Katherine's stone. I moved beside her and she grasped my fingers. "I will always miss my mother," she cried. Her chin trembled.

I thought of Katherine's waxy skin as her lifeblood drained from her. She would not know the child she had given her life for and that child would not know her. She would only be found in the stories from her family and friends. Susan would grow up and walk above the ground while her mother lay in a coffin below. Life was fragile. Uncertain.

A bird fell from the tree, lying on its side in the scraggly grass. A youngling. Its head was soft tan feathers, fading to white on its breast, the wings a rich brown, its eyes black and rimmed with white. Its legs were stiff and trembling, wings tucked tight against its body. It was dying.

An older bird flew down, walking awkwardly toward it. It remained at a distance, moving in close and then away again, hovering over the young bird. It moved no more, its tiny chest still. Like Katherine's had been as she lay upon the bed, clothed in her burial clothes, her empty arms folded across her breast.

Alice Tilley had been as that older bird, hovering, watching and waiting until death came. It seemed a holy thing to be a nurse: to aid in ushering in new life and watching over one who must leave.

The older bird walked closer, bent its head and touched its beak against the dead bird, as though bidding it goodbye. Then the bird spread its wings wide and flew away.

Chapter Twenty-Two

AFTER THE MIDDAY MEAL, LITTLE SUSAN WOULD TAKE a long nap. Elizabeth consented to watch her as I ran an errand. Sweat dripped down my back beneath my shift as I walked up High Street in the glaring sun. I passed the meeting-house and turned north onto the narrow road that led past the ugly stone Gaol, its few windows barred with iron.

The town was familiar to me now; walking about alone no longer filled me with angst. Alice Tilley's house lay beyond Reverend Cotton's on Tremont Street. She was out in her garden.

"Good morn to you, Susanna. What a shambles my garden is in. The lady's mantle and angelica are weeded over." She straightened, holding her hand against her back. "It is the end of the season. I can try again next spring."

"You can pick anything you need from my garden," I said.

"You have a garden, do you, Susanna?"

"My sister brought me seeds and I planted them."

"That is good. It is comforting to put your hands in the soil. Weeds are the bane of man, as it says in the Bible. Yet it is most satisfying to pull out the roots one by one and toss them away. One's efforts in life are rarely as evident as in a newly weeded garden." She looked up at the sky. "It will be a sweltering day. I'm going inside for a cup of cool water. Will you come?"

I nodded and followed her through the doorway into the keep-ing room. She did not seem to mind that I spoke little, as some did, as though it were an affront to them. Herbs hung upside down from a string attached to the ceiling above the fireplace, stems wrapped tight with twine. Lemon balm and lavender and thyme lay on the table. I rubbed the balm leaves and put my finger to my nose to inhale the clean, bright scent of it. It made me think of Muh-teh-qway. What was she doing now? Was she well?

"Those are garden leavings from some of the women in town," Alice said. She dipped a ladle into the bucket on the cupboard beside the hearth and poured two cups of water.

"Tastes a bit woody," she said. "Interesting how water has not its own taste and takes on the flavor of what it touches. Some people are like that, do you not think?" She sat down heavily on the bench and patted the place beside her. "You did not come here to talk of herbs and water and people who do not know who they are, did you? I sense that you have sommat else upon your mind."

My thoughts whirled too much to get them out.

Alice Tilley drained her cup and set it on the table. "It is all right, Susanna. You are with a friend. Say what you will."

I took a bit of cut twine and wrapped it around the stems of lavender. The action cleared my mind. "How did you come to be a midwife?"

She handed me some of the thyme, and I bundled it together with another piece of twine. "I have had two husbands, who between them gave me eight children and, thanks to the providence of God, all but one survived to adulthood. Most of the women who choose to become midwives are mothers. That makes them knowledgeable in the eyes of others."

She tied the herb bunches from the ceiling. "It is a service that earns money, but that alone is not enough. One must feel a call to it. I have felt that call. I do still." She took another drink. "Midwifery is not without its risks. The stone walls of the Gaol have a dank smell. It is in my nostrils still. I will not be cowed by the authorities incapable of understanding. I cannot say nay to a woman in need."

As I tied another bunch of lavender with the twine, I gathered the courage to speak. "I wish to be a midwife."

Alice Tilley turned, her eyes intent upon my face. "You are still young. How can the young know yet what they are to be?"

I should not have said it.

"And yet I should not be surprised. Your mother had the call. She learned to be a midwife from her own mother."

I had read my grandmother's name in the Bible: Bridget Dryden, married to Francis Marbury. My grandmother had not come to New England. Her death date was written below the names of her two husbands and her children: April 1645, her burial in a place called Surrey in England. She died two years after my mother. They would not have seen each other since William and Anne left in 1634. She must have held me as an infant in her arms. If only it were possible to remember her.

"Your grandmother gave birth sixteen times. The same as your mother. It is both a blessing and a wonder to have such a progeny. That alone gives a woman much authority."

Did that same desire stirring within me come from those two women? Something that called in my blood? Yet my sisters were not midwives. I kept my gaze upon the plants on the table. "My mother is not here for me to learn at her hand. Will you teach me, Mistress Tilley?"

"I am not certain. As I said, you are young. Not a wife or a mother. How can you know if you feel the call?"

I thought again of the bird in the burying ground, hovering over the dying baby bird. I would sound foolish if I tried to express what I felt, or speak of the voice on my vision quest: *You will be a healer.*

"I need to be a midwife."

"Do you know why?"

My hands played with the string around the lavender. "I cannot say."

"Does it have to do with your aunt's death?"

Was it that or something else? Was it because I needed to feel close to my mother? I had no answer; I remained silent.

"Let me speak plain. To be a midwife, you not only help to bring children into this world. You are nurse to the sick and the dying. Called out at all hours, day and night. You lose much sleep. You see people in their most difficult of moments. It requires an inner strength beyond what most people can, or are willing, to give." I could feel her eyes upon me. "Does that frighten you?"

I looked up. "It frightens me."

"Good. It should. You must learn many things: medicines, herbs, how and when to use them and when not. You must never have the arrogance to think you know all. You keep learning throughout your life. You must be both proud and humble, fearless and afraid."

The room grew warm, whether from the growing heat of the day or my own emotions. I took another sip of water. The smell of the lemon balm and the lavender made me want to breathe deep, again and again.

Alice fetched a plate of biscuits from the cupboard and set them in front of me, along with a crock of berry jam. I took one, though I did not feel hungry. The buttery, salty taste of the flour mixed with the jam tempted me to take another.

"There are many hazards to the profession. Most births occur without incident, nature running its natural course, the babe and the mother healthy. As you witnessed recently, it is not always so. A midwife must call upon her God for aid, drawing upon His strength. She must accept His will. She can use her efforts and skill and still fail. For He is the One who rules."

Alice looked fierce, her brows close together above her wrinkled nose. "I should not dwell only upon the hard things. Birth is a wondrous thing. There is naught to surpass it. It is blood and water and spirit. To witness the coming of life into the world brings great rejoicing. Also sorrow and pain. All of it mixed together, indistinguishable from the other. There cannot be joy without sorrow, for they come to mankind together. 'Tis the way of God, and we cannot change it." Alice's eyes shone like a burning lamp.

"I am done with my sermon. Now. After all I have said, do you still wish to be a midwife?"

I did not hesitate. "Aye. I do."

"Again, I ask. Why?"

"Again, I cannot say. Only that it is here." I touched my breast.

She reached across the table and squeezed my hand. "It is all right to not understand why. Someday you will discover why the desire is in you. Now it is enough to know it is there. You need patience, for there are many things to learn, and it cannot be done in a day or even a year. One must grow into the profession. Be a helper at first—a watcher, we call them. A watcher sits with patients, watching for changes in breathings, in color, in demeanor, perhaps turning them in bed, administering a tea or a rub or a plaster. She does not act except at the order of the midwife. That is what you did for me when Katherine's time came upon her."

"Will you let me be your watcher?"

"You will see hard things. Are you ready for it?"

She studied me. I lifted my chin and met her gaze. "I have seen hard things." Again, the roaring of the fire and my family's screams. The memory would never leave. It would stay with me even in my dying day.

"Truth spoken. You have seen more than I have in all my advanced years. I think it has made you strong."

I did not feel strong. Only lost and searching. "Did you work with my mother?" I asked her.

"I did."

"Tell me of the hardest birth you saw."

"It is not hard to pick that memory. It was in the autumn of 1637, only a few weeks before your mother's trial before the magistrates. My husband Thomas was alive then, and I was known as Mrs. Blower. Jane Hawkins was the main midwife in these parts. Both she and your mother aided in the birth of Mary Dyer's first child. I was also there. Such a tragic business. She began to labor two months before her time. She was in much pain and fainted clear away."

Alice stared at the glow of coals in the hearth. "The babe was so tiny. A girl. Horribly deformed. And dead."

Her voice went flat as she told me the story.

"I cannot forget the events of that night. 'What do we do?' Jane Hawkins said, 'for if this is known in the town, the Dyers will be accused of evil.' Anne Hutchinson said she would go to Reverend Cotton for guidance. She trusted him greatly. I kept the body of the babe on the far side of the room so Mary would not behold its deformities if she wakened. Her husband wept as he bent above the bed, grasping his dear wife's hand, kissing her brow.

"Your mother returned well after midnight. 'Conceal the child,' Cotton had instructed, 'though it be against English law. Bury it in secret in the darkness of this night.' So, we did. No one else knew, not even the women who had gathered below for the birth."

Alice clucked as she shook her head. "Poor Mary Dyer. Despite the difference in their ages, she and your mother were the greatest of friends. Every one of us in the room wept. It was one of the few times I saw Anne Hutchinson sobbing.

"Months later the governor learned of the incident and ordered the baby's body dug up from its grave. He exclaimed its monstrous appearance, claiming it had claws and horns and scales. Stuff and nonsense. He marveled how a young woman so comely as Mary Dyer could have borne it."

Alice Tilley's jaw tightened, and she grasped her hands together.

"As the head midwife, Jane Hawkins was summoned to court and accused of witchcraft. They could not get to your mother since she was already jailed. They did not know I had been there. Witnesses at the trial said Jane Hawkins gave oil of mandrakes to cause conception, consorted with the devil, and many other things. They called Jane a rank Familist, as they did your mother, a woman who had no morals.

"Mistress Hawkins was banished. Ordered to leave in the spring of 1638, the same year as your family. A few years later she returned to Boston and was expelled again. Jane Hawkins was a good midwife. She did no wrong. Still she suffered."

"Did they accuse my mother of witchcraft?"

"At Anne's trial some of the witnesses tried in a veiled manner to do so, but it did not carry. One man called her sayings 'witchlike.' To accuse a person of witchcraft there must be solid evidence. They did not have it."

"What of the midwife who was hanged? My sister and Katherine spoke of it."

"Dreadful business that. Both she and her husband were accused and imprisoned. It was she who was hung. Witnesses claimed she told them if they did not take her medicines, they would not get better. She was said to have a malignant touch. The witchfinder was ordered to watch her. He claimed her imp came in the night in the form of a child who then disappeared. Nonsense, all of it. The woman was no witch. Outspoken to a fault, for certain, and arrogant, but not with evil intent.

"There are the examples before you to prove my point. To be a midwife is to face possible peril." She watched me. "Do I frighten you with my bluntness?"

I thought of John Winthrop and John Cotton and John

Wilson and Thomas Dudley who held their authority close to their chests. An image of my mother standing in front of her accusers came to me, her head high. She did and said what she thought to be true, even in the face of conflict and danger.

"No. I am not afraid."

"To live is to be in peril. I will tell you another story. This one of your mother. The month after your family was driven from Boston, Anne went into labor two months too soon. It was her sixteenth child. She was ill and weakened from the trial and her forced separation from her family. She bled and bled after the birth. It was no babe, only a mass of tissue that had never grown into a human being. It is a rare condition. It was dangerous that she carried the pregnancy almost to term. She almost lost her life. Your family sent for a Doctor Clarke. He wrote to Reverend Cotton and said she would not live.

"Governor Winthrop heard the terrible news with great glee. He compared your mother's condition with that of Mary Dyer. They both gave birth to monsters, he said. 'See how the wisdom of God fitted this judgment to her sin. She brought forth a deformed monster.' Cotton put it into his Sabbath sermon: 'Mistress Hutchinson's unnatural birth.' God punishes the heretics, they said. The things they accused her of! I cannot think of it without rage.

"I have said too much. Enough of such talk," she said. "I make you suffer to speak of it. Pray forgive me."

"My mother was strong."

"As you are, Susanna Hutchinson. You have survived many hard things. You will continue to do so." She handed me another biscuit. "Have more jam," she said, and I did.

In five bites the biscuit was gone.

"You ask that I teach you midwifery, Susanna Hutchinson. I give you my answer. I will."

Chapter Twenty-Three

EDWARD WAS TO MARRY MRS. BUTTON THE FINAL WEEK of September, after he returned from his yearly eight day training with the militia. He set his musket and pistol against the window ledge in the keeping room and gathered Elizabeth and Elisha and Anne around him.

"I will return in a week. Be happy. Soon you will have a new mother to care for you."

Elizabeth had tears in her eyes. "We lost Mother only three months ago. I am almost grown. I can care for my siblings. Susanna is here, too." She pointed to where I stood holding Little Susan.

The baby reached up and tugged at the hair beneath my coif, a laugh bubbling up out of her. Every movement she made seemed new, as though it had never been done before. Her skin was new, too, and soft, especially beneath her chin and the dimples of her elbows and knees. I kissed the downy top of her head.

"That is noble of you, Elizabeth. I would not put that burden upon you when you are so young, nor upon your aunt. It will not be long before you are grown and become a mother yourself with your own household to keep, as your good mother did. Let yourself be cared for now by Mrs. Button . . . by Abigail . . ." He trailed off. "To marry her is a logical choice. She is a widow and needs protection and support from a husband. Her four children need a father. Would you deprive them of that?"

Elizabeth wiped away tears with the back of her hand. "No, Father. I would not."

Did he speak the words aloud in order to convince himself this was the right thing to do? Abigail Button was not like Katherine. She put herself above others; she did not like to give. Did Edward see that?

"My marrying Abigail will not change much in this house," he said. "We will still be a family like we are now—you children and Susanna. Only larger."

Edward kissed each of us and held Little Susan close. He set the baby back in my arms, gathered his weapons, and left the house.

ᓱ

With Alice Tilley's help, I harvested my garden. She showed me which plants to cut down to the ground, leaving a bit of stalk, and how to save seeds to replant in the spring. She helped me hang the plants upside down to dry from the beams in the attic.

In the hours I did not watch over Little Susan, we studied Mother's herb book together.

"You are no novice to medicine, Susanna. The things you learned from your Indian friend are most valuable. I look forward to including them on my visits to the sick."

A letter came from Faith. I broke open the seal. She would arrive a few days before the wedding to help with the preparations, leaving her husband with his chores, and the children to come later. She included a list of foodstuffs for me to purchase at the market for the dinner following the ceremony.

Another letter came from Bridget in Aquidneck addressed to me. Tucked into the folds of the paper were dried flowers, pressed flat: a stem of red bleeding heart, purple sage, and the greenish-white, tiny blooms of lady's mantle. Too easily crushed in their dryness, I removed them carefully with the ends of my fingers and set them on the windowsill.

> *I heard from Edward about your garden. I wish with all my heart I could come to Edward's wedding,* Bridget wrote in a straight, flowing script. *How I wish to see my little sister Susanna! But I am with child and the babe is due to be born only two months hence. My husband thinks it not safe for me to travel. I have sent something to remind you of your old home here—flowers that grow between the Great Cove and Mount Hope Bay.*

The Great Cove. Mount Hope Bay. The names clanged inside my head: three gongs each.

I could almost feel and smell the breeze that caressed the plants as they grew along the bank beside the water, basking in the sun. I set them on the table beside my bed. When baby Susan cried out in the night, I paced the floor to hush her. In the moon-filled light from the window, the flowers seemed to glow.

❧

Edward returned from training, and Faith arrived from Mount Wollaston.

Faith read Bridget's letter and set it back on the shelf in the cupboard. "Of course, she should not travel. She's borne a passel of sons and one daughter, her eldest. Eliphal must be thirteen years now. John Sanford had two sons from his first marriage, and she's borne six more. There are ten children in her house." Faith laughed. "I could not keep up with such noise. And her husband is as serious and studious as Bridget is lively. You can see his solemn nature in the names he gave two of his sons: End-come and Restcome. They were born just before Mother moved south to New Amsterdam."

"I remember them," I said. "Eliphal. Peleg. Endcome. Restcome." I tasted the names on my tongue.

"Oh, I do wish you could see Bridget. Her buoyant spirits lift everyone around her. She has the endless energy needed to raise all those children. I do hope she has a girl this time round to keep her and Eliphal company."

We set about making the preparations for the wedding. We cut up the pumpkins Faith brought from Mount Wollaston, roasted them over the fire and sprinkled the pieces with spices to make the sops. Elizabeth and I helped to knead what Faith called the thirded bread: made with equal parts of rye, wheat and corn, and baked in the two ovens on the side of the hearth. Chatter and laughter filled the room as we worked.

Opala had said a woman must never be angry when she prepares food, or her bad feelings will drip into the meal and hurt the family. "Pray to the Great Creator that those who eat your food will be strengthened and happy," she had told me.

Faith and I mixed up pans of gingerbread. The warm, yeasty smell of the bread mixed with the savor of molasses and sugar filled the house with a wonderful aroma, even up into the attic. I knew this smell. Mother made gingerbread. Had I helped her?

"Of course, we must sample some to see it is fit for company," Faith said. She cut a loaf of the bread, slathered the thick slices with butter, and cut small squares from a pan of gingerbread for all of us to taste.

We went to market and bought spices and ale to make the sack posset for drinking at the dinner after the ceremony; also, mussels, salted fish, and mutton. From the cellar, we brought up pickled eggs stored in straw and potatoes, carrots and cabbages for the stews. We made sugared almonds, a jam of plums to spread on the bread, and syllabub—a custard of cream and wine with a sprinkle of nutmeg on top. We took everything down to the cellar to stay fresh.

"I forbid you children to sneak down for a taste," Faith said, laughing.

We spent a morning scrubbing down the walls and floors in the best room. Elizabeth and I took down the curtains and washed them in hot water in a tub in the back yard, along with the white embroidered cloth on the table that held the Bible. We used the heavy sad irons to press them flat and smooth.

Faith surveyed the best room with hands on hips. "It needs flowers. Shall we collect some, my sister?"

She called me sister. That made me feel as content as the smell of the warm bread still lingering in the air.

A chilly wind came off the sea. We gathered silvery stems of sage, purple astor, and yellow tickseed that grew along the road. Faith helped me arrange them in earthenware pots. They made the house smell fresh as the outdoors.

After the children were put to bed, Edward, Faith, Elizabeth and I sat at the keeping room table.

Edward took a leather-bound volume from the cupboard and handed it to Faith. "I encountered John Woodbridge today, back from his years in Old England. He told me a curious thing."

"What is it?" The book was not much bigger than Faith's outstretched hand.

"It is a book of poetry written by his sister-in-law Anne Bradstreet."

"Anne Dudley, Thomas Dudley's daughter? Bridget and I knew her when we attended John Cotton's church in Lincolnshire. Before the family moved north to Andover, they lived down the road from here. She was five years older than I. She writes poetry?"

"Aye, besides being the wife of a magistrate and a mother. John Woodbridge speaks very highly of her literary abilities. He took her poems to England and had them published July last. They are selling briskly on both sides of the ocean."

Faith opened the cover and held it close to the lighted candle. "*The Tenth Muse Lately Sprung Up In America*," she read aloud, "*By a Gentlewoman of these parts. Several poems compiled with great variety of wit and learning, full of delight.* I am filled with wonder. A learned book, written by a woman. Look, Susanna. Elizabeth."

I stared at the tiny, black type—short lines that left much of the page still bare. Even without yet knowing the meaning, the words beat their rhythm in my mind.

"Governor Winthrop would not have approved," Faith said. "He believed women who put themselves to much study would descend into madness, for women's minds cannot do what a man's can. What nonsense. What would our mother think if she were here to see this book?"

"She would highly approve," Edward answered. "Then she would recite from memory the ballads of Mary in the New Testament, and Hannah and Deborah in the Old."

I resolved to find those verses in scripture and read them.

"Well," Faith said, "I will purchase my own copy at the market before I return home. It will be a delight to read. Anne Bradstreet: the first published woman poet in New England."

Faith set the book back on the cupboard. "And now we must go to bed, to wake early for the wedding tomorrow." She put her arm around Elizabeth. "You do a wise thing, brother. Your children will have a mother and you a wife to care for you. Of course, you will always mourn Katherine, but she would not want you to continue life alone. If I die, I would want my Thomas to do the same."

Elizabeth's eyes glinted with tears. Edward gave a solemn nod. I thought he looked sad, too.

❧

The ceremony was done almost before it began.

The couple stood side by side before Reverend Cotton near the hearth in the best room. Only family was present. Edward's four children, Mrs. Button's four. Her father and mother, and Faith and me.

Before the ceremony, Mrs. Button took Little Susan out of my arms and gave her to Elizabeth to hold. "That is better," she said.

Reverend Cotton asked a single question. "Edward Hutchinson. Do you wish to enter into the contract of marriage with this woman?"

"Yes," Edward answered, looking at Cotton.

"Abigail Fermayes Button. Do you wish to enter into the contract of marriage with this man?"

"Yes." Abigail's shoulders and bosom shook beneath her blue gown and embroidered white collar. She looked pleased and relieved, her gaze on Edward's profile. She had gotten what she wanted. Another husband.

Reverend Cotton handed Edward the register to sign, and it was done.

I stood near the table holding the Bible, its spine open to the first page. Beneath Edward's marriage to Katherine Hamby and the names of their children was already recorded in black ink: *September 1650, Edward Hutchinson joined in marriage to Abigail Fermayes Button.*

"We will now sing the psalm chosen by the bride," Cotton said. "Psalm One Hundred and Eighteen." He squinted at his psalm book as he sang the first line: "I will love thee dearly, oh Lord, my strength."

I had not sung this one before in meeting, so I only listened to those around me as they repeated the line. *The Lord is my rock, and my fortress, and he that delivereth me, my God and my strength.* The metre was the same as the first line, and I added my voice to the others. *In Him will I trust. . . .*

Did this ancient poetry inspire Mrs. Bradstreet to compose her own verse? *And he rode upon a cherub and did fly, and he came flying upon the wings of the wind.* The singing around me continued. I listened no more, hearing only the same line. *He came flying upon the wings of the wind.* Did the psalmist speak of God? Or man?

Soaring above the earth like my spirit animal, the seabird, going wherever it wished.

The psalm ended, and so did my reverie.

The house filled with neighbors, come to drink the sack posset and taste the dishes spread across the table in the keeping room and in the long meeting room at the back of the house. The people moved past Edward and Abigail, offering hearty good wishes and then filled with food the plates they had brought from their own homes.

I took a few cranberries and a pickled egg, some of the squash and pumpkin sop, then took Little Susan from Elizabeth's arms. "I will feed her," I said.

I set the plate on the round table set in the corner next to the window, out of the way of the guests. With a cloth around Susan's little neck to keep her dress clean, I dipped some of the bread in a cup of milk and fed it to her, crumbling the egg, giving her bits at a time along with the sop.

Samuel Cole's booming voice sounded across the keeping room. "Greetings, Susanna," he called. His son would be with him. I pretended not to hear.

Little Susan turned away, shaking her head no to more food, and the spoonful of sop smudged on her mouth; I wiped her face clean. She settled against me and fell asleep. Both doorways were blocked, and I could not get out. From the best room, Abigail's chatter sounded like a bluejay.

I stared out the window at the breeze ruffling the golden leaves still clinging to the trees. The house was stuffy and noisy. When would the festivities end?

&

When the day at last was done, I lay in the darkness, Faith's even breathing beside me in the bed. In the cradle, Little Susan stirred. I slipped out from the coverlet and put my hand on her back, and she quieted. What would life be like with Mrs. Button moved in? Mrs. Hutchinson now, as the neighbors called her. Something would change. What would be my place?

The caw of a seabird came in the quiet night. I could imagine it soaring on the air in the moonlight. Lifting up its wings like the eagles, as the biblical Isaiah wrote. Riding upon the wings of the wind.

Chapter Twenty-Four

THE HOURGLASS SITTING UPON THE WOODEN PULPIT showed the sand in equal parts of the top and bottom, meaning Reverend Wilson was not done with his sermon. I pulled Mother's cloak closer against the chill of the meetinghouse. Abigail Button wore her new white coif and collar. She smoothed her skirt, tucked her feet beneath the bench and stretched them out again, glancing Edward's way. Katherine had always sat motionless in the pew. Edward did not turn to look at her.

"My sermon is complete," Reverend Wilson said. At last the meeting would end. "The Reverend John Eliot from Roxbury wishes to speak to us."

Another sermon. My back ached.

John Eliot. That name was in the transcript of Mother's trial. He had testified under oath of the things Mother had said against some of the preachers. "We much fear her spirit," he had told the court at her trial. He did not approve of Mother.

John Eliot rose and took his place behind the pulpit. He looked older than my brother Edward, his face round and fair-skinned, dark hairs above his lip and on his chin, thick brown hair waving down to his white collar. He had a gentle look that belied his testimony against Mother at the trial.

"I have come here today to speak of the Indians."

Abigail turned her head and looked at me. I did not meet her gaze, keeping my eyes on the pulpit.

"Four years past, our assembly passed the propagation that the gospel is to be preached amongst the native tribes. I felt then a strong call to do so. In the beginning of my efforts, I preached without success. Then God's hand stretched out to the Chief Waban, and he embraced our Christian faith. The truth is spreading among them. There are now above fifty Indian souls who have accepted their Lord and changed their heathen ways. Our efforts of conversion have recently raised interest in Old England."

Mr. Eliot seemed to grow taller as he spoke of his success. "With an act of the long Parliament to assist us, twelve thousand pounds have been raised." He looked around the quiet room. "I am come here today to convince the good people of Boston of the need for these converted Indians from the nearby Massachusett and Nipmuc tribes to have a place of their own. A town to dwell in and schools for their children. They should have the Bible in their own language. With the assistance of the Indian Cokenoe and a few other of the Indians, I have begun a translation of the tenets of our faith."

He held something up: a large piece of parchment attached to four sticks, with two white feathers and a small wooden cross at the top. I could see "The Lord's Prayer," written in English across it, and below, Indian words. In his other hand, John Eliot held up a different paper. "Allow me to read the declaration of faith from these Indians, written in our English."

We are the sons of Adam. We and our fathers have a long time been lost in our sins; but now the mercy of the Lord beginneth to find us out again. Therefore, the grace of Christ helping us, we do give ourselves and our children to God, to be his people. The Lord is our judge; the Lord is our law-giver; the Lord is our king: he will save us. The wisdom which God hath taught us in his book shall guide us, and direct us in the way.

John Eliot shook the paper. "My good brethren, these people must have a place of their own in which to dwell where they may worship the Lord as we do," he boomed. "I envision not only one, but many towns surrounding Boston and the other settlements. Filled with Indians who have come into the light of Christian faith. The situation of these towns will also help provide protection for our own communities.

"The first of these towns will be named Natick. A most fitting name, for it means 'place of searching.' I expect it to be established soon after the first of the next year. The land we have determined upon is twenty-three miles east of the town of Boston. We will need teachers and preachers from among you to work with Indians. Look to your own hearts to see if you feel that call."

John Eliot raised his head higher. It seemed he looked into every eye. People in the room shifted in their seats, murmuring among themselves. Abigail Button stared at me.

"Come and talk to me after the meeting is over. I wish to speak of one thing more. The Negroes among us. I have seen some of the people of Boston treat them as they do their horses and oxen. This is not pleasing to our God. God instructs us that all creatures, no matter their status, be treated with dignity. It is so with the Negroes. It is so with the Indians."

Abigail's gaze was still fixed on me. The woman sitting in the pew ahead turned her head to stare, too. If I did not move, perhaps my presence would be forgotten. I kept my eyes on the parchment John Eliot still held high and the black English letters: *The Lord's Prayer*.

I would ever be an oddity. An outsider. A heathen.

❧

Abigail tucked her hand into the crook of Edward's elbow, nodding to all the women as they walked across the churchyard.

"Our first Sabbath meeting together as husband and wife," she said.

I followed behind Elisha as he kicked the fallen chestnuts with his boots. Elizabeth had stayed at home with the children: Anne, Little Susan and Abigail's four. We turned onto High Street.

Edward looked down at his new wife. "I hope you enjoyed it, my dear."

"I am proud to be the wife of Edward Hutchinson," she gushed. "Although the pew was so crowded, I was hardly comfortable. When the rest of the children come with us to church, there will not be enough space in it." Abigail kept on. "Eight children fill your house, even with my three girls sharing a room with your Elizabeth. Surely, we will need more room, especially if God sends us our own babes." She giggled. "You must get Mr. Button's house sold soon, so we will have the funds to expand."

"I am making inquiries," Edward answered. "With fewer people coming over from England now, there is not the demand for housing to buy or to let. It will take some time."

"Well, then," Abigail gave a big sigh, "I suppose we shall have to make do for the present time. There is the chamber where Susanna stays with the baby. The babe can soon be installed in the room with her sisters. And surely Susanna will not need her room much longer."

She never called Little Susan by her name. It struck me as curious. What did Abigail Button mean I would not need the room? Where would I go if I did not live with my brother?

"John Eliot's sermon was most interesting," Abigail prattled on. "And his request for people to help the heathens. What did you think of it?"

"He is earnest in his desires to better the lives of the Indians," Edward said. "Many in the tribes have died of disease and live in want. I believe his motives are above reproach. The Indians love him for it."

"His request for teachers," Abigail repeated. "Surely there must be some in the town peculiarly suited for such a task. People who have experienced considerable interaction with the heathens."

She looked behind at me. I turned away. Edward did not answer.

≈

Elizabeth waited on the front porch.

"A messenger has come for you, Susanna," she said. "He waits in the keeping room."

The boy looked about ten years, his breeches and hose smudged with mud from the road.

"Mistress Tilley inquires for Susanna Hutchinson," he said in a small voice, his lower lip trembling, "and asks that she come to help my grandfather. He has taken a fit and lays uncomprehending."

"I will come," I said.

"Mistress Tilley says for you to bring your herbs."

I cut a slice of bread and took the cheese wheel wrapped in cloth from the cupboard and cut a thick wedge.

"Are you hungry?" I held them out. The boy finished it in a few bites and took the other wedge of cheese from my hand.

I went upstairs and put Mother's shawl around my shoulders. Little Susan lay sleeping in her cradle. I bent and kissed her cheek. I took the small box that Alice had helped me to prepare and returned to the keeping room.

"Where do you go in such a hurry, girl?" Abigail said.

"Mrs. Tilley asks for me."

"What have you to do with the midwife?" Abigail said.

I had told no one about my arrangement with Alice Tilley.

"I expected your help for supper," Abigail said. "Surely that is more important than whatever Alice Tilley wants."

"Alice Tilley sent for you, Susanna?" Edward asked.

"She . . . needs . . . she gave . . . her permission for me to assist her."

"For what purpose?" Abigail demanded.

Why would it matter to Abigail Button what I did? Her comments to Edward seemed to indicate she considered me to be in the way and yet she relied upon me to help in the house.

"Do you wish to become a midwife, sister?" Edward's eyes were kind. "You are young for such a difficult duty."

Since I could not speak my feelings before Abigail, I did not answer. Surely Edward would not keep me from it. The words I wanted to say churned inside my head.

He put his hand on my shoulder. "We can speak of this another day. Go along with the boy and help Mrs. Tilley."

"Very well, if you must do it," Abigail snapped. "When will you return? I need help with the children."

"It is fine, Abigail," Edward said. "I am here, and Elizabeth. Susanna will return when Mrs. Tilley does not need her any longer."

The boy and I walked quickly up High Street and turned south toward the small bay called Bendall's Cove. He pushed open the door of one of the small houses that sat along the wharf.

The grandfather lay on a bed set in the narrow room at the back of the house, Alice Tilley beside him. His right leg and arm twitched, his head bent to the side, eyes closed, mouth slack. The fire in the hearth did little to keep out the chill. Alice placed a blanket atop the patchwork quilt and tucked it beneath the man's chin, wiping his drool with a cloth.

"So, there is naught to be done for my father?" asked a younger woman. Beneath her skirt her belly swelled with child. "Is he going to die?"

"It cannot be determined now," Alice answered. "He may rally. Time will tell. We can give him broth and wine to keep fluids in his body, and administer herbs that may help. His limbs must be moved every two hours. You have not long before your baby's birth, and other children to care for." She looked toward the woman's husband. "And you must be out early tomorrow for your fish catch to sell. Susanna and I will watch him through the night."

"You are the Hutchinson girl?" the woman asked me. "I have seen you at meeting. You are most kind to help us." She stood up from the chair, her hand against her back. "I will get the supper."

When I saw the meager meal she prepared, a thin soup with no meat and hard bread, I wished I had brought the bread and cheese to share. When we finished the meal, dusk had fallen, the dying fire the only light in the small room.

The woman kissed her father's forehead and stroked his thin gray hair.

"Go upstairs and rest, Ruth," Alice said. "I will call you if there is any change in his condition."

Ruth followed her children up the stairs, leaving Alice and I alone with the grandfather.

"It is apoplexy," Alice said. "I am glad you brought your box. Get out the garlic, the mustard, black cohosh and bilberry." She took a candle out of her bag and set it into the holder. "I always bring a light when the family is poor," she whispered. She added a log from the box to the fire. "Now we can see to work."

I lifted out the small bottles and set them on the table. She showed me how to make a tea from the garlic, cohosh and bilberry. We took turns spooning in broth, wine, and the teas, turning the man's sagging head to the side, only to have it spill out onto the cloth placed beneath his chin.

"His breathing is labored. We must make a mustard plaster to put on his chest."

We mixed water and flour with the dried mustard to make a paste. "Do not put this directly on the skin or it will burn from the heat." Alice took a towel and spread the paste on one side with a knife and folded the other part of the towel over it.

"Set it on his chest," she instructed. "Keep it on no longer than twenty minutes and watch for blistering. If his skin grows deep red, take it off."

After some moments, the man began to breathe easier. Alice took off the towel, washed the skin, and smoothed lard across his chest. She taught me how to turn him to the side, remove the soiled sheet and replace it, and how to massage his limbs. She opened a window to freshen the fetid air.

The waves lapped in rhythm against the wharf poles. The moon rose higher in the black sky. The breeze grew into a wind that whistled against the doors of the house. The single candle burned low and sputtered out. We kept the fire burning with the cut logs in the copper kettle.

The man's breathing grew deep and rattling.

"Give him no more liquids." Alice whispered. "That rattle you hear is the sound of the dying."

As the night hours passed, the rattle increased in volume. The man's breaths came with more space in between, long moments when it seemed as though his chest would not rise again and then a gasp. His jaw slackened, hollowing his face.

I had seen death in the village, but never close to it until Katherine died.

I did not see my mother and siblings as they lay dead, so in my memories they were still standing tall, fully alive. They dwelt beyond, perhaps in the place with the cluster of stars as the Indians believed. They were in a room with a door that did not open to me.

In the early hours, Alice climbed the narrow staircase to wake Ruth and her husband. The boy followed them down the stairs. They surrounded his bedside as the man left this world, his daughter quietly weeping while she held his limp hand tight in hers, her husband standing behind with his hand resting on her shoulder. The boy followed his father's example and put his hand upon his mother's other shoulder.

"Go with our love, Father," Ruth whispered.

The grandfather gave one long sigh and went still. I did not need Alice to tell me the signs. The face of death was unmistakable. One moment life and then only a shell. Amid the quiet weeping, Alice closed the man's eyes.

I felt the terrible sadness, yet mingled with it was joy. The joy of loving and being loved. Woven together like the strips of cloth on the loom that sat in the far corner of the room.

এ

Alice and I walked home. In the place where the sky met the ocean, the rising sun's rose-colored rays swept upward. The night darkness yielded to the light.

"You did well, Susanna," Alice said. "A family was comforted in their time of sorrow by your service."

"I did not say much," I answered.

"That can be a gift to others. Some people talk to drown out the silence when silence is what is most needed. Comfort is offered best with action more than words. A look. A touch. An ear that listens."

The night wind died down. A morning mist settled on the trees and grasses.

"'Tis certain, Susanna Hutchinson. You have the gift to be a midwife."

Chapter Twenty-Five

IN THE MARKETPLACE, I SAW HER SLUMPED AGAINST the cart of vegetables. An Indian girl. Thin and gangly, with long limbs, she looked to be about eight or nine years. She wiped tears with her fingers and rubbed it into her deerskin skirt, staring around her, terrified.

Abigail stood at the meat cart, her basket slung over her arm. "Girl," she called to me, "go across the way and buy a wheel of cheese. With so many mouths to feed, I cannot keep up with the making of it." She handed me a few coins. "Fetch it quick and return to help me carry the meat."

I did as she said.

The Indian girl was sobbing now, her shoulders shaking, making the beads around her neck rattle. I was her age when I was taken by Wampage and brought to the village. I was frightened, too.

Indians were not often seen in the town. Why was she here? Was she alone? I walked to her, Little Susan on my hip and the wheel of cheese under my other arm.

I searched in my mind for the words. "*Ktaonkel hach?*" Are you lost?

"*Nitka*," she murmured. She stared at my clothes, her gaze puzzled. "*Nitka!*" she cried louder and shoved me away.

"Mother?" I asked.

"*Nitka!*"

A voice spoke behind me. The language sounded similar to what I had learned, yet different. An Indian woman wrapped her arms around the girl, cradling her head close to her chest as she rocked back and forth. She did not kneel, bending from the waist like the Indian women did when they cooked at the fire.

Muh-teh-qway had held me just that way when I was frightened.

The woman searched my face, looked in my eyes. She decided that I had no wish to harm her daughter. She looked toward Little Susan, pointing with her lips instead of a finger. "*Nitka?*"

I knew what she meant. I shook my head side to side. "I am not her mother."

The woman reached out and touched Susan's cheek, and Susan grabbed her fingers. "*Kekhitahola,*" she said, and touched her hand against her heart and then to my chest. I knew that word. You love her.

"*E-e.*" Yes.

"*Kuliteha,*" I answered. You are kind.

Perhaps they were in the market because they were hungry. I took one of the coins that Abigail had given me and pressed it into the woman's palm.

"*Mhala,*" I said. Buy. "*Michewakan.*"

She looked puzzled. "Food." I put my fingers to my mouth.

"What are you doing?" Abigail cried from behind me. "What did you give them?" She pried open the woman's fist and retrieved the coin, then wiped her hand on her sleeve as though she had touched something dirty. "You give these savages money? Foolish girl!" She slapped my face. Little Susan wailed.

The woman held something up: the same kind of parchment John Eliot had shown at meeting, with the words 'The Lord's Prayer' on it.

"You think that matters to me? You are no Christian, you heathen!" Abigail cried. She grabbed my arm and hurried away from the woman. "I forbid you to do that again!"

She took the cheese from me and shoved the heavy basket full of meat under my free arm. "Supper will be late for my husband, and you are to blame."

My cheek felt hot from her slap. People were staring. I heard a woman laugh.

Abigail walked ahead of me up the street. When we reached the house, she barked: "Give the baby to Elizabeth, girl. You are confined to your room without supper."

❦

Next morning, Abigail did not look once toward me, as though I were not sitting at table with the rest of the family. Her silent anger was more tolerable than her words. I would need to stay out of her way today.

I took Susan up to the attic where she sat on a blanket, chewing on a bit of clean rag to soothe her sore gums from a protruding tooth. I went to the chest and lifted the lid. Mother's trial transcript pages were dog-eared from my reading. I picked up John Winthrop's book and opened to the first page. His words beat in heavy rhythm upon my heart.

I shut the book and picked up my Uncle John Wheelwright's defense of Mother. A discussion of the same events, only from an opposing point of view. The words blurred, the dim light of the attic making my head ache.

I would never know what had happened. How could one ever fully comprehend the past? Was that why Edward had pushed the chest full of books and papers into the corner to not look at again? I set the book back into the chest and lowered the lid.

Susan dropped the rag and began to cry, lifting her arms for me to take her.

I must look forward from now on. Not backward. Future days flowed ahead, round the bend of the river. What would be there I did not know, could not know. I must look to it.

ﷺ

While Susan took her afternoon nap in her cradle, I raked the soil in the garden smooth to ready it for planting in the spring. The breeze was cool and sharp and smelt of the coming winter.

Edward did not come for supper. I wiped Susan's mouth clean of the bits of soaked bread and boiled pumpkin and helped her drink a cup of milk.

Abigail said, "Elizabeth, take Susan and put her to bed. Move the cradle to your room. You are to watch her through the night."

Elizabeth looked at me, puzzled, and obeyed her stepmother. What Abigail's purpose was I could not determine. It was clear I was in disgrace. I kissed Susan's soft hair and handed her to Elizabeth. Susan stretched out her arms to me and wailed.

"Take her upstairs, Elizabeth," Abigail snapped. "I will not tell you again."

A knock came at the door. It was a note from Alice Tilley. She was detained on other business, she said, and asked if I would go to the Culpepper house on Sudbury Lane. Their son had cut his leg. She would come when she could. "Do not worry. It will come to you what to do."

Abigail said nothing as I gathered my box and left the house.

"Where is Alice Tilley?" the mother said when she opened the door.

"The midwife sent me on ahead," I explained, "and will be here when she can."

Mrs. Culpepper stared at me. "You are the Hutchinson girl. Does Alice Tilley trust you?"

"She calls me her helper," was all I could think to answer.

She stepped back. "Well, I know not what to do for my boy. You may as well try, and we'll see how you do."

The boy's right lower leg was badly cut, his hose stained with blood. I asked for a bucket of fresh water, clean rags, and a knife. As gently as I could, I cut away his pant leg and hose. He winced and cried out.

"You are a brave boy," I said. "What is your name?"

"John."

"How old are you?"

He held up five fingers.

I pulled back the bloody clothing. The layers of muscle were sliced almost to the bone, so deep that blood no longer seeped from the wound. It made me think of raw chicken meat. His whole body shuddered. He did not cry out again, even as I set the wet cloth against his skin and wiped away the dirt.

At first it felt as though my own leg was sliced, as though the boy's pain was also mine. My limbs went weak. I must not allow it, or I would not be able to help him. His wound was not mine. My calmness could be transferred to him only if I disciplined my thoughts.

I pulled Mother's herb book out of my box. *Make a poultice of yarrow to cover the wound, then smear with honey. Repeat the procedure after a few hours.*

I mixed the yarrow with water and covered the cut. Muh-teh-qway used *ahpawi* to kill the impurities. Cattail. I made a paste from the roots and leaves I'd collected.

"This will hurt but it will help to make you well," I said. I dabbed it on the wound as gently as I could. His face clenched. He did not scream.

"You are a brave boy."

"I'm a brave boy," he repeated to himself.

"I need some honey," I said to the mother. I dripped the honey she gave me from a spoon over the wound and covered it with a clean cloth.

A strange feeling came. Mother was beside me. Muh-teh-qway, too.

Alice sent a note. She could not come. A Mrs. Pratt had need of her. "You have the knowledge to do this," she wrote.

The boy's cheeks were flushed. I felt his forehead with the back of my hand. I did not have to look in the book, for I'd already read the instructions for fever. "I need boiling water."

The mother sat nursing her babe and pointed to a cup on the table. I took some from the pot hanging over the fire. I put three pinches of dried feverfew leaves into it and let it soak until the water darkened to a rich brown hue. When the mixture cooled enough, I spooned it into his mouth. He relaxed into sleep.

"I have done what I can for now," I told her. "In a few hours he will need more herbs for the fever, and the wound will need another poultice."

"Can you stay through the night?" she asked. "You seem a competent girl. I want you to care for him. I've extra eggs and a butt of ham to give you in payment. You'll have to sleep on the floor by the fire, for I've not an extra bed."

"I will stay."

She took the baby from her breast and set it in the cradle in the corner. "You must be hungry." She ladled out a bowl of stew from the pot over the fire and cut a hunk of bread. She stood with her arms folded while I ate. "You've steady hands and a calmness about you that I like. I feel more at ease with you here. Besides, you cannot walk home past the curfew. There is evil in the dark."

I remained through the night, sleeping a little on the blankets, rising to change the dressing and give the boy more feverfew, and a little of the broth from the stew. When the moon was high overhead, his forehead cooled. He fell into a deep, tranquil sleep.

I walked home in the pink of dawn with the butt of ham and a basket of eggs, and the woman's words of thanks to warm me.

~

Abigail's voice carried up the stairs. "It is midday, Edward, and still your sister sleeps. She squanders time. Shameful."

I sat up, my mind fuzzy. Sunlight seeped into the room through the curtains, outlining the square of the window on the floorboards and across the end of the bed. The door to the room was open. I could hear their conversation.

"It is not yet midday, dear wife, and Susanna did not return until morning. She must be very weary."

Edward was still home. It must be Saturday.

"That is twice these past two weeks she has been out all night. Why do you tolerate her assisting the midwife?"

"Susanna is doing a good thing," Edward said.

Abigail's tone grew pouty. "I could use another helper, especially for the cooking. If I cannot use the girl, could you not do as the widow Winthrop, and bring one of your young female slaves from the farm to help with the chores?"

"My family keeps no slaves."

"Odd you do not, for you are well enough off."

"I'm sure there is another girl I can engage to help you with the cooking, if that is what you wish, wife. And Elizabeth is a great help with the children. Susanna cares for Little Susan, for she dearly loves the child, and her love is returned."

"Elizabeth is old enough to care for her little sister, so I have instructed her to do so. Susanna is no longer to take charge of the baby. Besides, it was I who nursed the babe from her infancy in the absence of her mother, not your sister. It is a hard business to nurse two babes at once, and the good Lord knows I was run ragged because of it."

"I know that, wife, and am most grateful. The babes take food and milk now, so your strength need no longer be taxed."

"It is I who have sacrificed most," Abigail persisted.

"I do not discount what you have done. Do try to understand my sister and have compassion for all she has suffered."

"It has made her odd. And her silence unnerves me. It is like the savages I pass in the street who say nothing, only pierce you with their black eyes. Why must they be allowed in the town?"

She was going to speak of what happened at the market. I knew it.

"We went to market, and she . . . she spoke with the Indians! Went right up and spoke to a filthy woman and the child with her. What makes matters worse, she was holding your child! In her recklessness, she endangered Little Susan. What if they had grabbed her and taken the babe?"

"The Indians here are not of the tribes from the south where Susanna was taken. They are some of the Praying Indians converted by John Eliot."

"Let them go to their own town. They do not belong here. How can a savage be converted to the true faith? They are not capable of it. I am suspicious of those unlike myself and you must be also. That is the wisest and safest course."

"I am not certain of your reasoning, Abigail. Let me . . ."

"Your sister is marked," Abigail interrupted, her voice shrill. "As though she still wore the greasy skins of an Indian. You yourself must see it. She will carry that mark with her the rest of her days."

"Lower your voice, Abigail. Get to know Susanna and you will love her as I do."

"I have not time to try and penetrate her dreadful silence or to love her. It is you I am to love and care for, not your lost sister."

"See how your own girls flock to her. They do not see her as strange."

"And what heathen ways might she be teaching my girls when my back is turned?"

He took a breath so loud I could hear it. "I have not been aware you felt so, Abigail."

"Well, I do. You should, too. You are wrong to trust her. She is not the sister you knew. She is a stranger. A savage."

Silence from Edward. Finally, he responded. "Susanna is not what you say. To return to your earlier complaint, you should not mind the time Susanna spends helping Alice Tilley."

"Humph," Abigail said.

"If she feels the call to follow in the footsteps of our mother to care for the sick and afflicted, I find no fault in it."

My brother understood my need, and it warmed me as though I stood in the sun's rays. Abigail's words were as chilly as the fall air.

"In the footsteps of your mother, Edward? Is that not a dangerous thing? Be careful who you say that sentiment to in this town."

Edward did not answer for some moments. "Yes, I see that now. Even here in my own house."

"What is to be done with her?" Abigail paid no heed to Edward's statement. "She is of age to marry but what are the chances of that? No man wants a girl who has dwelt with the heathens. She will be a thornback, mark my words."

I'd heard that cruel phrase used for women past the age of thirty and unmarried.

"My youngest sister has returned at last to the bosom of her family." His tone was flat and measured. "There is naught to be done about or worried over concerning Susanna. Only to love her."

"You have buried your head in the sand refusing to see the truth, Edward. Something must be done with her. Why can she not go to teach in the Praying Towns John Eliot spoke of? She is uniquely qualified. She could live in the family of one of the ministers."

"If you were listening closely, wife, you would know Reverend Eliot meant only men to teach and preach in those towns. That lessens Susanna's qualifications considerably."

"Well, then," Abigail said. "We'll find another solution. You have many siblings, husband. She can go to live with one or other of your sisters. It is best that she be out of Boston. Then we could avoid such distressing interactions as what happened at the market."

"Distressing to whom, Abigail? To you?"

She continued, "And our meetinghouse pew would not be so crowded."

What would Edward say? The silence from downstairs stretched on.

"I would never part from my sister."

Abigail's voice softened. "My dear husband. You have a new wife now to care for and make happy. Surely that should take up all your time and exertion. A wife takes higher rank than a sister. It was said by the minister in our wedding vows. I am your wife. Your first duty. Not her."

The back door slammed, and the squealing of the children drowned out any answer from Edward.

Chapter Twenty-Six

CHRISTMAS PASSED AND TIME CREPT SLOWLY TOWARD the New Year on March twenty-fifth. Abigail either ignored me or cast mean looks upon me. She made certain I did not have care of Susan. My days were long and empty. Alice Tilley had not called for me in a few weeks. There was no garden to care for, and with the orchard trees bare of leaves it no longer provided a sanctuary in which to be alone. The attic was cold as ice. The chest in the corner remained shut.

White clouds lazed in a blue sky, with no wind. The day would be mild. I packed some food in a bag and walked down Summer Street to where the path ended. No one would miss me at the house, or notice if I spent the day on the beach.

The hollow feeling inside me was familiar—I had felt it in the village when I first arrived and for months afterward. As though an essential part of me was missing. Why must I feel it again? Katherine had been distrustful of my presence at first but came to accept me. I had almost belonged. Now it was snatched away. Perhaps Faith or Bridget would take me in. They had husbands and children to love and care for. I would be a burden.

I did not belong. In any place.

Would it have been better if I had remained in the village? An Indian maiden, yet not. Living between two worlds. Even now, returned to the life I had known as a child, I was still wedged in a place between, like the split in the rock where I had hidden on that fateful day of my family's death.

ॐ

Living in the village, I became used to the brown faces of the Indians. I did not look at my reflection in the still pools of water when I bathed and no longer thought of my own white skin. I remember the shock of seeing the Dutchmen's pale skin as they walked into the village. It made me think of a deer I had once seen with no pigment to its skin: stark white with no brown and white spots, pale pink eyes and nose. The hair of one of the men had white streaks above his ears when he removed his hat. So strange. They frightened me. I stepped backward. Muh-teh-qway and Opala took my hands and held me close to them. They were shaking.

The white men stared at me, pointing in a rude manner. People in the village did not point with their fingers. They used their lips and looked in the direction of the thing they wanted.

"*Ashentisi*," one of the men said. "The salt woman."

Wampage moved to stand between me and the white men.

"Trade the white woman," they said. "Give the white woman to us as part of your peace pact." They took bundles from their horses and piled furs and beads and hatchets on the ground.

"Give us the white woman and we will not attack."

Wampage stared at the piles of goods for a long time. No one spoke. He stepped aside and gestured toward me. Muh-teh-qway and Opala began to wail.

"*Chitkwesi*," Wampage said. Be quiet. He walked to his wife and her mother and softened his tone. "We will give Sisika back to her people."

"*Ku!*" Opala cried. "She is our daughter. Yours and mine. The white men killed our daughter Gela. Sisika belongs to us. Not to the white men."

"I hear what you say," he answered.

Wampage looked long at me. He looked back at the white men. He did not look again at the pile of goods on the ground. He stared up into the sky. I did not know if he would speak.

"I must right a wrong done long ago. The Great Spirit tells me to do it." Wampage put his hands upon my shoulders and pushed me toward the white men.

"*Ikali wachi*. Go. You are no longer the daughter of Anne-Hoeck."

In that moment I belonged to the village no more.

❧

And now, I was no longer wanted in my brother's house. A lump in my throat grew. It made my heart pound. I put my hand against my chest and tried to take a deep breath.

Hope deferred maketh the heart sick, I had read in the book of Proverbs, *But when the desire cometh, it is a tree of life.* I understood the beginning of the verse, for it described my feelings now. The second part eluded me, though it had a haunting beauty as I whispered it aloud. The breeze blew my words away. What was my desire?

To belong.

The choking feeling subsided, letting me draw in great breaths of air. I undid the clasp on the neck of Mother's cloak, laying it across a low rock near the edge of the water to sit on. I removed my coif, taking out the pins behind my ears that kept my hair in a narrow plait behind my back. The breeze caressed me.

A lone seabird landed on the beach, yellow feet in the wet sand, walking awkwardly. It belonged in the air, not on earth. It opened its wings again and flew low, settling down upon a wave that drew it back toward the shore.

"Miss Hutchinson?"

I jumped to my feet. It was John Cole.

My thoughts had been so lost in the past that I started at his pale skin. The coif would not sit again upon my head. I fumbled for the strings. The breeze took the coif with it down the sand. John ran and scooped it up and handed it to me.

"I am sorry to startle you. I usually walk this beach at this hour and encounter no one for they are all at their midday meal." He backed up a few steps. "If you would prefer to be alone, I will leave you."

I shivered and put Mother's cloak around me again, leaving the coif in my hands. Abigail would shame me as improper. She was not here to see.

I had not spoken alone to John since that awkward day outside the church. Only a moment in the street in front of the house he owned. The house he had offered to me. My face went hot.

The seabird lifted its wings and soared away. I had thought escaping here would bring me calmness. It had not. Perhaps I needed to talk with someone else, escape the prison of my own thoughts churning inside my head. He stood waiting for me to answer. His eyes seemed kind.

"I do not wish to be alone." I revealed my weakness. He would pity me.

"I will stay then. I have long wanted to visit with you."

I stared out at the Cove. He did not speak, as though he waited for me.

The sounds of men shouting came across the water. I could see the tall masts of a ship far down the pier, tiny figures climbing the masts. With the white sails folded, the ship looked bony and naked.

"What is that ship? I see it there often," I asked.

"It is a slave ship, the *Desire*. Come from Barbados. Strange name, I've always thought. It performs a grim business. It takes captured Indian men, women and children to trade for black slaves."

Captured Indians to be traded. Snatched from their native land. It could be Muh-teh-qway or Opala or Minsi. Any of the laughing, happy children who played with me in the village, hiding our tokens in the woods for the Mesingw to find, huddled around the fire listening to stories. The village was much farther south, and the people aboard that ship would likely not be those I knew. It did not matter. Below the deck huddled suffering human beings. It made me ill.

John Cole cleared his throat. He looked ill at ease. "I saw . . . what happened to you in the market. With the Indian child and Mrs. Button—er, Mrs. Hutchinson."

I looked away from him, out at the waves. He would express his pity and leave. I would be glad of it.

"I am more of the sentiment expressed in meeting by the missionary John Eliot," he said. "The Indians have already suffered much, many of them killed by the diseases our people brought to this land. They need our compassion. Our acknowledgment of their equality. Your mother felt that way, as I remember."

The mention of Mother jolted me.

"I recall your mother and father spoke against the war with the Pequots. Governor Winthrop did not like that." He was silent for a moment. "Before the fighting broke out, Governor Henry Vane, a great friend and ally of your mother's, brought the chief of the Narragansetts, Miantonomi, to dine at my father's inn. Twenty Indians sat upon the floor in a circle to eat. I was thirteen then. I remember every one of their faces. Chief Miantonomi wished to show his support of the English."

"What happened to the chief?"

"Miantonomi sided with us when the war with the Pequot tribe broke out. He was disgusted by the English soldiers, who brutally slaughtered Indian women and children. The chief was captured and killed by another of the chiefs. In 1643."

I took a step back, staring at him. "The year my family died."

"I have offended you. I did not mean to talk of things that cause you pain."

I shook my head. "No. It . . . is better to speak."

John nodded. "Perhaps it hurts more not to speak of hard things. Shall we walk a bit? The air is fresh. I can smell the coming spring. Yet it still holds the cold of winter, as though it cannot forget."

"We are caught between the seasons." I did not hold my thought back. That surprised me. Usually I did not say what I was thinking. His openness made me feel I could.

"Well put, Miss Hutchinson. You have given a better voice to my sentiment."

We walked around the curve of the beach. Without my coif, my hair blew out behind me. John took off his hat and held it in his hands. The roof of clouds broke as the wind parted them, making room for the shafts of sunlight that streamed down to touch the earth.

John pointed south out in the bay. "See the island farthest out? Centered between the ones closer to us. The one with a great hump upon its back. Indians once dwelt there. A few years ago, my father purchased it and dubbed it Hog Island." He laughed. "Why that name, I do not know, for he keeps no pigs there. I think he meant he is a hog for land and property."

I saw something in the distance, a blue hump almost lost in the mist.

"Words do not have the ability to describe what one can feel there on the island. 'Tis a wondrous place."

We did not speak for a while, staring out across the water.

This time it was I who broke the silence. "I was born in England and have no memory of it. I was only two when my family left."

"And I only six when my father came with Winthrop's fleet. My memories are more of the journey on the ship than of my homeland. I remember climbing far up the rigging before my father hollered at me to come down and forbade me to climb again. After that, the journey was not so enjoyable."

When he smiled, the outer corners of his eyes slanted up toward his brows. He twisted his hat in his hands, the silver buckle flashing in the sunlight.

"Week next I will take one of the boats out to the island. My father wants me to check things there." He looked down at me. "Would you like to see it? I could take you with me. Forgive me if you think me too forward." His pupils darkened. He seemed nervous of what I would answer.

A longing to see the island filled me. I thought of the scripture about desire. *When the desire cometh, it is a tree of life.* "I must first ask my brother."

"Of course, you must. Perhaps your niece Elizabeth would like to come with you for company. If he grants his permission, you can tell me at Sabbath meeting."

What would Abigail Button say? Would she allow me to go? She would not need to know. I could ask Edward out of her hearing. I stared out toward the island. A mist of clouds hung above it.

"I will return to my workday and leave you to enjoy the beauty of the day," John said. "Prithee thanks for the visit. My day is brighter now."

He set his hat back on his head. I watched him as he walked through the sand and turned onto the path back toward the road.

৪▲

I remained at the beach until the sun had traveled across the sky, now a glowing ball above the western horizon. I followed the trail to the streets of the town. The family was gathered in the keeping room, sitting down to supper.

Abigail looked at me from the end of the table. "Where have you been? As you have been gone all day, I did not expect you for the meal."

Elizabeth rose from the table. "I cooked you a potato," she whispered, swiping the ashes off the paper wrapping. She unfolded it and scooped the soft potato onto a plate. "There is cod and biscuits."

"Susanna can fend for herself, Elizabeth. Finish your meal," Abigail said. Elizabeth moved over to make room for me at the end of the bench.

"Edward, did you not receive a letter from your sister Bridget today?" Abigail said.

Edward looked toward me as he answered. "I did receive a letter from Aquidneck. Bridget reports that John Sanford was elected chief magistrate there. You may read it after supper, Susanna."

"That will keep him much away from home, do you not think?" Abigail said. "All those boys to raise, including two from her husband's first marriage, you told me. What a burden she has upon her shoulders. Elizabeth informed me that Bridget lost a male child two years past. Is that not correct, Elizabeth?"

"No," Elizabeth answered. "Her son Francis is two years, and well."

"She is with child once again." Abigail's voice raised. "That is why she did not attend our wedding." She gave Edward a simpering look.

"Her babe might have been born since we received her letter," Edward said. "It is most kind of you to have compassion for my sister, Abigail."

"I inform myself on all your family, dearest husband."

The fish was cold, and the biscuits stuck in my throat.

"Susanna could go to help Bridget." Abigail did not look at me. "She would be needed for months, I should think."

Elizabeth put her hand on my arm. "Susanna is needed here, Father. Is she not?"

Edward set down his knife. "I think it would be up to Susanna. What would you wish, sister?"

"I have my work here with Mrs. Tilley."

"Family takes precedence," Abigail snapped. She did not speak out of care for Bridget or for any of the family. She only wanted me gone from the house.

"Alice Tilley does not need you to help her," she kept on. "Doubtless she would rather do it herself, so she knows it is done right. The neighbors do not want you. Mrs. Pratt told me that herself at the market."

"You forget the time of year, Abigail," Edward answered. "The winter is not done with the snows. Aquidneck is a long journey of sixty-two miles. It would not be wise for Susanna to travel until spring has come."

Abigail's sigh came down the table. "Leave the table, children. Go play in the orchard while it is still light. Take them, Elizabeth. Susanna, there must be some chore you have upstairs. I have things I wish to discuss with my husband."

Whatever she had to say to Edward, I had no desire to hear.

I went to my room, closed the door, and knelt to retrieve the bag I kept beneath the bed. The *wampum* belt that Muh-teh-qway made for me. I put it around my waist. There were two rows of purple beads. Three rows of white.

"These mean friendship," she said. "They mean respect. They mean peace. That is what I feel for you, Sisika."

Muh-teh-qway wanted me. She loved me. I had come to belong there. I put the necklace over my head. The white and purple whelk shells stood for friendship, too. They had been rolled on a grinding stone and rubbed with water and sand till smooth. I rubbed them in my palm.

I could return to the village. The women would welcome me. Wampage would not make me go back to Boston.

It would be easier for Edward if I were not here. My sisters said they loved me. If I went to them, it would be the same as in Edward's house. Their husbands would not want me. I would be in the way. And I could not see Susan grow. She had learned how to stand and walk along the furniture and babble nonsense words.

The village was south of Boston. South of Aquidneck. The Indians called the place *Sewanacky*. Or I could ask where the fort at New Amsterdam was. I did not remember the way. I could go to the market tomorrow. Perhaps one of the Indians would be there to ask where it was and tell me how to get there. *Ku.* I could not tomorrow. It was the Sabbath. The next day, then.

I could show them the necklace. I put it down the neck of my dress, the shells cool against my chest. I folded the belt back into the bag and bent to return it to its place. My hand knocked against the medicine box. What of my training as a midwife? I could learn from Muh-teh-qway. She had begun to teach me. I could be a healer in the tribe. A *kikehwet*.

I would tell Alice Tilley. She could explain to Edward after I had gone.

Through the closed door, I could hear Abigail's voice below but not Edward's. I dared not return downstairs.

The stairs creaked as I climbed up to the attic. Outside the window, the sun had already disappeared below the horizon.

There were no clouds for its light to paint them gold. Shadows gathered in the cold room. I shivered.

The chest seemed to mock me. My mother was told she did not belong in Boston. She was not wanted. They thrust her from them.

Abigail was determined. One way or another, she would have me out.

The herbs drying stem down from the rafters emitted a musty odor, black in the growing shadows. Rootless. Like me.

Chapter Twenty-Seven

I WOKE TO A BITTER COLD SABBATH MORNING. LITTLE Susan and Abigail's youngest son remained at home from meeting with the maid Edward had hired to help Abigail.

Reverend Wilson droned on and on. The cold kept me wakeful, and the feel of the shell necklace against my skin. This day would never end. I would be caught forever in it.

Reverend Wilson coughed, his throat raw from speaking long. Across the aisle, Edward looked toward me. Our eyes met, his troubled and sad. His gaze turned to Abigail and back to me and dropped to the floor.

Reverend Wilson went into another fit of coughing, which ended his sermon. Reverend Cotton stood and faced the congregation to lead the psalm singing. His languid gaze flickered over the congregation, resting upon me. His mouth tightened. He had not acknowledged me since the long-ago day when I stood before them to defend my education and prove my right to remain in my brother's house. What would he think if he knew of my circumstances now? Would he secretly be pleased? Perhaps Abigail had spoken to him already of her feelings about me, or with Reverend Wilson.

I closed my mouth against the words of the song. The rhythm of the music could not move me as it usually did. Elizabeth glanced sideways at me. Edward's head bent above Elisha's as they sang together, his arm across Elisha's shoulders.

Abigail spoke truth that my brother's first obligation was to his children and his new wife. What place did a sister have?

My heartbeat thudded up into my throat. Those who had loved me most were dead or lived far away. If Katherine were still alive, perhaps I would still be welcome in my brother's house.

I was alone, like the islands dotting the bay.

※

John Cole stood outside the door where the women exited from the meetinghouse.

"Good day, Miss Hutchinson."

"Good day." I did not look at him.

"Are you ready to see the island?" he asked in a pleasant voice.

The ache inside me swelled until I felt faint. My eyes stung. "I cannot come."

"Did your brother say you could not?"

"I did not ask."

"If you would rather not go, I honor that."

Last night I dreamed of it. A green hill in the distance surrounded by the blue water, enveloped in morning mist. If I opened my mouth to speak, my voice would crack.

John backed up several steps. "Very well, then. I will not impose upon you again." His mouth a thin, straight line, he bowed and walked away.

Abigail walked briskly past. "Come at once, Susanna. After supper, your brother wishes to speak with you."

※

"Will you walk with me a bit, sister? Before night falls."

I set my bowl and spoon in the bucket for washing. "I will get my shawl."

As I put it around my shoulders, Edward's mouth twisted. "Our mother's shawl," he said. "Wear it always."

We walked up Cornhill Road and turned northward, the late afternoon sun a white ball in the azure sky. At the base of the northernmost of the three small hills called Trimount, Edward stopped.

"Father owned this field," he said. I almost did not hear him, his voice carried away in the breeze.

The earth had been turned, revealing its rich brown hue. Dried stalks from the corn crop stuck up in the soil. A few seabirds walked along the rows, picking at the stalks with their beaks.

"It will be spring soon. Time again for planting," I answered.

"Aye. It has been a cold winter. It will be good to see the green come again." He slipped his arm beneath my elbow and pulled me close to his side, the edge of the buckle on his belt hard against my ribs. He sighed. "I find myself to be in a most trying situation."

I would answer for him. "Your wife does not want me."

He glanced at me, then out again at the field. "It is plain to you, then?"

"Aye."

"What she feels toward you, Susanna, . . . I was not aware of until after our marriage. Abigail can be a dear, and she is good to my children. But she is headstrong to have her own way. I know not what to do. I do not want you to go." His shoulders sagged. "I failed in my promise to you. You have suffered much, and now it is by my actions."

"Not by your hand, brother."

Abigail would be pleased to have more room in the house. I would miss Elizabeth. Little Susan would grow up. I would not be here to see. She would forget me. My training from Alice Tilley would end. I would not be a midwife in Boston as Mother had been.

The shells of the necklace warmed my skin beneath my dress.

"Faith would take you in at the farm. She wanted you to come before, she said."

He would not know of my plan to go south. Let him think I would go to Mount Wollaston.

"I think Mother and Father would think it best," he said.

A neighbor was traveling the next week to his farm in Mount Wollaston, taking his wife and children to spend the summer months. Edward arranged for me to go with them.

The seeds I had planted were coming up in the garden. Every morning I pulled the weeds growing alongside the slender shoots. Watching, waiting. Now I would not see the harvest.

There was no one else besides the family I wished to bid farewell except Alice Tilley. She was not in her garden. I knocked upon the door. It did not open.

A neighbor woman called out: "You seek Mistress Tilley?" She came closer. "The midwife reports to me where she goes that I may tell it to those who seek her." The woman looked most pleased with her status. "She has gone to Cole's Inn. She knew not when she will return."

I followed the lane that led past the small bay. On the north side stood a three-storied building: *Cole's Inn. All Welcome.*

The long, dark-paneled room inside the front door was lined with wooden tables and benches. It smelled of hot bread and yeasty beer and the sharp tang of smoked meat. John Cole stood behind the counter. When he saw me in the doorway, he came across the tables to greet me.

"What brings you to my father's inn, Miss Hutchinson? Father feels poorly today so I take his place at the counter." He lowered his voice so others would not hear. "Is your mind changed to see the island?"

I looked down at the knots in the oak planks of the floor. "Where is Goodwife Tilley? I am told she is here."

"She is at the house tending to my father. I will take you there."

As John weaved through the tables, I kept my eyes upon the back of his coat to avoid the stares of the men. The house was in the lot behind the inn. John opened the gate and walked beside me across the yard.

"I have heard you are learning the midwife trade from Mrs. Tilley."

I nodded.

"It is most commendable to seek such a profession. It says much for your character."

He opened the back door and stepped to the side to let me enter the house first. Mister Cole sat in a chair by the hearth in the best room, Alice Tilley beside him. A woman who looked much younger than Mister Cole stood behind him, a babe on her hip.

"How is my father?" John asked.

"Well enough now," Alice said. "Still a shortness of breath and fatigue. He must rest until he feels better. Make certain he does, Margaret." She handed the woman a small bag. "He will require another tea made from this borage at suppertime. It will calm his heart."

"Getting my father to rest will not be an easy matter," John chuckled. "Will you do as Alice Tilley says, Father?"

Samuel Cole grunted. His face was flushed and his breaths quick and shallow. "I've not time nor desire to rest."

"You will suffer for it," Alice said firmly. "So will your poor wife, for she will have to bear the brunt of your complaining. Do not take any of his nonsense, Margaret. Be firm."

Alice turned and saw me standing behind John Cole. "Susanna. What brings you here?"

"She has come to see you, Mistress Tilley," John said.

Alice set the mug of medicine on the table. "I have done what I can. The rest is up to your father. Are you comfortable here, Samuel Cole, or would you prefer your bed?"

"Not in my bed in the middle of the day," Mister Cole snapped. "I can sleep sitting upright like the cows and birds do."

"Very well, then." Alice tucked the blanket around his shoulders. "Then best you do it. Report to me, John, Margaret, if he still ails in the morning."

John walked with us to the door. "Prithee thanks for your attendance, Mistress Tilley." He turned and bowed to me. "It was good to see you, Mistress Hutchinson. I will return to my business at the inn."

I wanted to call out: "I am leaving this place and will not see you more." I kept silent.

ع♠

A rhododendron bush stood on the side of the house. Its deep scarlet blossoms smelled like sweet honey. Alice and I turned up the road toward the Tilley house.

"I do love the scents of spring," she said. "The lilac bush outside my window has the loveliest fragrance that lulls me into sleep. It reminds me how this land can be soft as well as harsh." Alice stopped walking. "You have sought me out for a purpose, Susanna. It is not to talk of blossoms or springtime. I see it in your countenance."

"I . . . am come to bid you farewell."

"What is this, Susanna? You are leaving Boston?"

"Aye. I am going to live with my sister Faith." I did not say what I had determined to do instead. That I would go back to the village.

"Where does she live? I do not remember all your siblings."

"In Mount Wollaston."

She looked intent at me. "This seems unexpected. Why do you leave? Do you wish to?"

What to answer? "It will help to ease my brother's situation."

"Ah, I believe I understand. Is it Edward's marriage?"

I looked down.

"It is his new wife, then. I will not say what I think of her. I am saddened to hear this, for you have proved a most capable assistant to me."

"I want to be as you are, a midwife."

"Like your mother and your grandmother and perhaps her mother before her. It binds you to them. To the past. To your family."

Alice understood me without me having to search for the words that gave voice to things too deep inside to say.

"Tell me, Susanna. Do you wish to leave?"

"I wish . . . to belong. Somewhere."

I looked toward the ocean where the island that belonged to the Coles would be: a space that lay between two worlds.

That would ever be my place.

"Do you recall our conversation a few months ago when first we met, Susanna? We spoke of home. I told you that your mother was unjustly ripped from her home, not once but twice. Yet she chose to carry the sense of home within her own heart. As her daughter, that is also your choice to make."

"I go only to my sister's home, not my own."

"Believe that your true home will find you. God gathers to us what we need."

I could not see the island. Gray clouds moved in, low upon the water. Yet it was there, out of my sight.

"You feel now that you step into darkness, the future uncertain. God requires it of His children and, like or not, we must accept it. Take just one step forward at a time when you cannot see and wait for light to come. Then take another and another."

She put her hand upon my arm and turned to look at me. "Child, I warn you. 'Despair maketh the heart sick,' scripture says. Do not choose that path. Take the opposite which is hope. All will not be dark as it seems now. Life will be full of light. Believe it."

"I will try," I answered.

"To try is sufficient." Alice put her hand beneath my elbow. "I will miss you sorely, Susanna. Come. Walk this old woman the rest of the way home."

ᐧᐧ

Every day I visited the market. No Indians were there to ask the way south. Did I want to return to the Indians? I did not know. Only that my heart felt sick.

I took the journey to Mount Wollaston in a two-sailed shallop that cut swiftly through the water, leaving white waves in its wake. The family I traveled with—the Stowells—were quiet people who did not feel the need to make up talk. Like me. Goodwife Stowell was kept busy keeping her two sons from climbing the rail.

Sitting near the bow I could watch the changing curve of the shoreline. The wind whipped at my hair and clothing, taking my thoughts and blowing them away, sweeping the inside of me clean.

We pulled into the dock and Goodman Stowell hired a wagon to carry us the rest of the way.

"The Hutchinson land lies on the edge of the Dorchester line," he said as he clicked the reins to drive the horse, pointing as he talked. "That land just yonder belonged first to William Coddington. He sold it to a wealthy merchant named Tyng before he moved to Aquidneck. Beyond that is land that belongs to Benjamin Keane, and Mister Quincy, and Mister Hough. They dwell in Boston and have servants to work the fields. It is on Mister Keane's land that I work until the harvest."

He pulled the wagon to a stop in front of a narrow lane. "The house of Thomas Savage is yonder," he said. He handed the reins to his son, telling him to hold it tight, and lifted my small chest from the back of the wagon to set on the road. My shoe caught on the top of the wheel as I climbed out of the wagon. I stumbled, falling onto my knees. Goodman Stowell helped me up.

Goodwife Stowell nodded solemnly to me from the wagon bench. "Give your sister Faith our good will. Be a good help to her."

"I will try," I answered. The weight on my shoulders that had plagued me since my farewell to Edward came upon me once more. I needed the sea breeze to clear away my fears.

"We will see you in meeting." Goodman Stowell climbed back up into the wagon, and it clattered away.

Faith ran up the lane. "Susanna!" She wrapped me in her arms. "You are come to us."

"I do not wish to be a burden to you, sister."

"How could you be a burden, Susanna?"

We walked up the lane, carrying my chest between us. "Edward sent me a letter explaining what happened. I must say I've a hard heart against his new wife. But it brought you to us and for that I rejoice."

I could not answer. My throat was too tight.

"You seem older since I saw you, sister. A woman grown. You look more like our mother every day. What fun we will have."

She chattered on, telling me of the children and the things we would do together.

When night came, the house drenched with sleep, I slipped out into the darkness, taking my Indian bag with me. The starry cluster shone bright against the black sky. Each star glittered like sunlight on water.

I shouted the names of my family inside my head. It was not enough. The Indians chose their way of mourning. I must choose mine. Speaking their names would help me remember. I said them aloud. Each name clanging against the air: *William Hutchinson. Father. Anne Hutchinson. Mother. Francis. William my brother. Zuriel my brother. Anne my sister. Mary my sister. Katherine my sister.*

"Mother. What would you have me do?"

Faint inside my mind: *Susanna, dear.* Like Mother called me. *Open your heart to love and be loved.*

Here in Faith's house? I should stay?

Your family.

I reached inside the neck of my nightdress and gripped the necklace. Mother and Father would not want me to return to the Indians. The shells were cool in my hand as I lifted it over my head and set it back into the bag.

Chapter Twenty-Eight

I DID NOT KNOW HOW MUCH I WOULD MISS THE SEA.
Though it lay only a few miles east of the gray clapboard
house where Faith and her family lived, I could not smell it, see
it, nor hear it.

In the weeks since I had come, the fledgling green shoots in
the furrowed fields of Thomas Savage grew taller, spreading out
around the house. Six hundred acres of wheat, barley, oats and
corn, and grass to dry for hay to feed the thirty head of cattle.
Unlike the town, the houses stood far apart, at the ends of the
narrow lanes in the center of their fields.

Long-necked geese and goats walked the lanes with the ducks
and hens, their squawks and bleating taking the place of the
town's chatter. Only a few seabirds flew high overhead, white
wings stretched wide, dipping with the wind currents, touching
ground to feed on the insects. Always they returned to the sea.

They were my spirit animal. Muh-teh-qway said seabirds
knew how to survive. They brought healing. Now they were far
away.

Above the fields and houses rose the big bowl of the sky, each
hour of the day a different hue. Without the sounds of the town
around me, I was aware of the sky more: the pink of dawn turning to brilliant blue in midmorning, paling to a hazy blue as
the sun climbed high overhead, then blazing gold and red and
orange after the sun set below the fields.

The highest point of the land was the hill they called Mount Wollaston, named after the first settler. From the top, the fields looked like the patchwork quilt Faith was piecing together. When the wind blew, it played the stalks in a steady rhythm. It made me think of the waves of the sea upon the sands. The rote singing of Psalms in church. The Indian chants in the village.

It was difficult at first to determine which grain grew in the field. As they matured, I noted how the oat plants developed pods reminding me of an insect wing. The barley tops drooped as though they each bowed to some superior, while the corn stood erect like royalty. Thomas Savage told me that the darnel weed grew up indistinguishable from the wheat stalks. It was allowed to remain until the plants came to ear and the farmer could determine the difference. The poisonous ones would be removed, and the life-giving wheat left to flourish.

Is that what the magistrates like John Winthrop and Thomas Dudley did in the colony before they determined what persons should be plucked up and cast out? Abigail Button had done this with me. I was not worthy and must be cast out. I thought of asking Faith what she thought of that analogy but did not want to talk of it aloud. It made me weary.

When they were not at the school, Faith's oldest sons, Habijah and Thomas, twelve years and ten, helped their father and his servants in the fields, five-year-old Ephraim following behind. Mary, three, and one-year-old Dyonisia toddled about the house. She made me think of Little Susan and it pressed at my heart. When Dyonisia decided to let go of the walls and chairs and walk on her own, the whole family cheered.

Susan walked, too. Elizabeth told me so in one of her letters included in a packet with Edward's. They missed my presence, they said, and said my garden flourished and would make a good harvest. Edward promised to send me some of the plants to dry to keep in my box. I wondered how they fared with Abigail ruling the house.

I slept upon a cot in one of the two tiny upstairs rooms with the girls, the three boys in the other. Faith and Thomas slept in the room they had added behind the keeping room.

"The house is small for us," Faith told me as we took our usual walk after supper before dusk fell. "Father built it, so it means much to me. Mother stayed a few weeks here when she was released after her church trial that spring while she waited for Father to fetch the family to Aquidneck. Do you remember this place, Susanna?"

"No." I shook my head.

"I am sorry to ask," she said. "Perhaps it is just as well. I do not recall many things as a small child in Alford. It is what we have now that is most important. Time slips too quickly by, and in a moment, it is gone."

The days were busy. We worked in the garden together, made cider from the apples on the trees in the orchard, dipped the wax to make candles to light the night, and mixed lye soap to scrub bodies and clothing clean. She taught me more of cooking and how to bank the fire in the evening so there would be live coals the next morn. There were no ovens built onto the side of the fireplace, as in the Boston house, only a single one at the back of the hearth. Faith showed me how to keep my skirts from catching fire.

In the evenings after supper, the family gathered at the table, two candles lit, and we each took turns reading in the Bible. As the summer lengthened, we did not need the candles, for the sun set later. The corn stalks were topped with yellow and the green wheat turned to gold.

ॐ

In the village, it would soon be time for the Gamwing, the Big House ceremony.

Tribes from all around gathered together after the harvest in a time of rejoicing and thanksgiving for the Great Creator. We traveled three days to attend.

The Gamwing had a ceiling and four walls made of bark. The four walls represented the four quarters of the earth. The ceiling was the dome of sky where the Great Creator resides. The floor, the earth. The pole in the center, the staff of the Creator. On the floor was an oval dancing path—the starry cluster—the white path of life leading to the spirit world. It led to the twelfth heaven. There we would be reunited with our loved ones who had gone before. In that place the sun was not needed, for a brighter light created by the Great Spirit shone on those who dwelt there.

The people entered through the east door. East for the sunrise. For a new beginning.

The *sachem* would begin with a prayer of thanks using the twelve prayer sticks. A prayer for safety. He was the first to recite his vision. A bear would give its life, its hide tied to the center pole to replace the one from the year before, its meat eaten in thanksgiving.

I looked forward to the Gamwing. I danced across the starry cluster painted on the floor and imagined myself greeting Mother and Father and my siblings.

"When you dance, you shine like one of the stars," Opala told me. Minsi frowned.

Muh-teh-qway said, "I knew you would dance." Because they said this, I danced more.

For twelve days the tortoise shell would pass from hand to hand as the people who received a vision recited them, often late into the night. There would be drums and singing. It was a time to search for your guardian spirits and try to reach toward them. At times as I sang and danced, I could feel them near.

On the tenth day, the ashes of the old fire would be thrown out of the west door and a New Fire built. For unity. For rebirth. For new life.

On the twelfth day, the ceremony completed for another year, the people would raise their hands in a prayer chant. *Hoo. Hoo. Hoo. Hoo. Hoo.* Twelve times, we would say it. We moved out of the west door one by one. Gone symbolically from the beginning to the end of the world.

The Puritans had no special house in which to celebrate. True, they had their meetinghouses, cramped and too hot or too cold. No ceremony to celebrate life and death, separation and reunion. No dancing. I felt sad to think of it.

ﺰ

Faith's herb garden needed weeding. The apron she'd given me had not kept the dirt from streaking my skirt. The late August air was thick with moisture and my clothing stuck to me. The strings of my cap came loose, and I took it off, the midday sun hot on my hair. Months and months away from life among the Indians and it still felt strange to cover my head.

"Susanna?" Faith called.

"I am here, sister," I called up through the row of tall angelica.

"Someone is here to see you."

The family in Boston had not written of a visit. I stood up, only my head visible above the plants.

"There you are. Come and greet your visitor. I must return to the house before Dyonisia overturns the sack of flour I left on the floor."

I replaced my cap and wiped my hands on the apron as I stepped out from the row. I first saw a pair of boots, a black hat in a man's hands.

"Greetings, Susanna Hutchinson." It was the voice and the face of John Cole.

I felt anger like a rock in my middle. "Why do you come here?"

His fingers gripped his hat. He cleared his throat. "I could say that on my fishing expedition, my shallop was blown too far by the winds and I lost my way, or that I had business in Mount Wollaston. Both would be a falsehood. The truth is I have come to see you."

"Why?" I repeated. Blood rushed to my head.

"When last I saw you at my father's house, I did not know you were leaving Boston. Your brother told me later you had gone."

He still fumbled with his hat. I wanted to snatch it from him and throw it on the dirt.

"You are not pleased to see me. I am sorry for it. I will answer your question and tell you why I came. I promised to show you Hog Island, and I have come to keep my promise."

"Because you feel pity for me. The girl who does not belong." I spat out the words.

"It is not pity I feel."

"Duty, then."

"Not duty. It would mean a great deal to me to keep the promise I made to you."

I did not answer. The rock in my middle churned. My face reddened.

"Those things do not bring me here to Mount Wollaston. Duty. Pity. Whatever it is you have come to expect from others."

I could not quell my anger. At him. At all of them. "You look at me with scorn as they do. You only feign kindness and then spit upon me when my back is turned."

"I do not." He seemed as though he, too, fought for control. Sweat dripped down his neck. "You do not know what I think and feel, for you do not allow me to show it."

Was that what I was doing, heaping rejection from others onto this man who stood in front of me? But he was one of them.

He bowed toward me. "I have brought distress to you when I wanted the opposite. I should have written and sought for your permission to come after your brother Edward encouraged me."

"Edward told you to come?"

"Aye. He did."

Now I was angry at Edward, too.

What did I feel? I could not tell. Only that now he was here, I did not want him to leave.

I walked past him. "The sun is hot, and I thirst. You may have a drink before you leave."

I turned my back on him. His footsteps sounded behind me on the path.

Faith waited in the doorway at the back of the house. She looked from me to John Cole and back again, her brows furrowed. "Are you well, Susanna? You have not seen too much sun? I am happy you have come, John Cole. Come inside the house. Sit down at the table."

I set the basket by the door. John lowered himself down on the bench.

"The Coles were our near neighbors in Boston, Susanna. I remember your family well, John." Faith set mugs of cider on the table. "You both must be hungry. Susanna, sit beside John." She put two plates with hunks of bread and dried meat before us. "Have you lately seen our brother Edward and his family? Are they well?"

"They were when I spoke with them last Sabbath." He gave me a sheepish look. "I did not . . . think to ask your brother if he wished me to bring a letter."

"So, he knew you were coming, then," Faith said.

John's face flushed red.

"'Tis no matter," Faith spoke quickly. "We had a letter only last week. Will your business keep you here long?"

"I do not know." He looked at me. "I want to sail the shallop before foul weather."

"True," Faith said. "When the snow comes the roads are impassable, and the sea route too bitter cold for a ship journey. You are right to come now while the weather is mild."

"My father wants me to check on his island. Hog Island. It is four miles south and east."

"I've heard of it," Faith said. "You would not have time today to get there and back before dark. Of course, you must stay the night here. If you do not mind sleeping upstairs in the same room with my rowdy boys."

John looked toward me. "If your sister has no objection, I would be happy to accept your invitation and go to the island on the morrow."

His eyes asked what I would have him do. Why would he want to stay when I had been so rude?

"Perhaps Susanna would wish to accompany you to the island," Faith said. "She is too much in the house."

"If you can spare her, I would be happy for the company."

"I can. There is no one to go with you. The boys should not miss a day of schooling. Dyonisia has the sniffles, so I must stay with her and Mary."

"Do not fear," John said. "I will make certain I return your sister back to you safely."

"I know you will." Faith looked from John to me and smiled.

So, it would happen. I would see the island. John should not know how much the place had occupied my thoughts.

"In return for your generosity in allowing me to stay, I could help your husband this afternoon in the fields."

"No need for that," Faith said. "He has sufficient helpers and I do not know what field he harvests today."

That was odd. Faith's husband always told his wife where he worked. My anger passed and left me with shame.

Faith peered out the window. "The children are returning from school. Do you like to play games, Mister Cole? My boys are keen for them."

"I do like games."

"What was your favorite as a boy?"

"Outside games, I assume?" he asked.

"Both," Faith grinned.

"Town ball."

"That is also my boy's favorite game. I will get out the stick and ball, and there shall be a spirited game of town ball after supper."

I stole a glance at John Cole. He grinned as big as Faith.

෯

While we ate a supper of mutton stew and bread, clouds rolled in. A drizzling rain prevented the town ball game, much to Habijah and Thomas' disappointment. Faith took out the flat, checkered board for draughts, and the boys took turns playing against their guest. I watched as John maneuvered the game with five-year-old Ephraim to make himself lose. Ephraim giggled at his triumph.

They set aside the draughts and played hop frog on the rug in the best room. While John was on his hands and knees waiting his turn to leap over Habijah, little Mary climbed up onto John's back. Keeping her secure with one hand, he reared upward and whinnied like a horse.

"My, the house rafters will fall down from the noise," Faith laughed.

"We must play All Hid!" Thomas cried. "Now Father is come, he can play with us!"

"It is almost time for bed," Faith said.

"Just one game, then!" Thomas said. "Cover your eyes, Susanna, for you must find us."

I heard them scatter. It became quiet. Ephraim was easy to find beneath the table in the best room. I snuck behind and touched his shoulder, putting him out of the game. He helped me to find Habijah, who had flattened himself behind the cupboard, and then Thomas, crouched by the pile of wood beside the hearth.

"Now we must find Mister Cole!" they shouted.

Faith and Thomas Savage sat upon the bench in front of the fire in the long room behind the kitchen. "We have not seen Mister Cole," they said.

A blanket covered the bench. I saw the shape of a boot. Faith shoved it beneath the bench with her shoe.

"We know where he is, Susanna!" Habijah called, pointing. Together the boys pulled John's legs from beneath the bench amid shouts and laughter.

"I think we have had enough of games for the evening," Faith said and dismissed their protests.

"Now you are all here together," Faith's husband said, "we will read scripture and then you children are off to bed. As our guest, John Cole, will you pick the passage for reading?"

The children settled on the rug as John turned the pages of the Bible. Dyonisia crawled to him and stood up, holding onto his chair. He patted her hair.

"First Samuel chapter sixteen, verse seven: *God seeth not as man seeth; for man looketh on the outward appearance, but the Lord beholdeth the heart.*"

"What are your reflections upon this passage?" Thomas Savage asked.

John Cole raised his eyes from the book and found mine. "It is what is hidden within the heart that matters."

Chapter Twenty-Nine

I SLEPT LITTLE, WAKING IN THE DAWN. IN MY DREAM, I was alone in a boat sailing toward the island in the distance. I could not reach it.

I dressed quiet as I could, to not disturb little Mary and Dyonisia, and climbed down the steep staircase. John was already in the keeping room with Faith.

"Good morn, Mistress Hutchinson," he greeted me.

Faith handed me a basket. "For your journey. You can get an early start before the heat of the day. There is enough here for your morning and midday meal." She turned a stern look on John Cole. "Mister Cole, I trust you with one of my most precious possessions, and that is my sister."

John bowed. "You will have no reason to believe your trust has been misplaced."

"I take you at your word. Now go, before the children awake and demand more games." Faith laughed and kissed my cheek.

~

As the wagon rounded a bend of the narrow road, the sea spread out across my view, the water a vivid blue reflected off the cloudless sky.

"See how the sun lights the sea?" John said.

Sunlight sparked the ripples the breeze made on the water. I answered without first deliberating. "The stars left over from the night are fallen and sit upon the waters."

He gave me a solemn look. "Indeed, it looks just so."

I studied his face as he looked out at the water. He turned and saw my stare before my eyes darted away.

"You have a most unique view of the world, Susanna Hutchinson."

My anger flared again. "You mock me."

I could feel his gaze, so intent it felt as though he touched me. "There is no one here who scorns you. You can speak what you think and feel."

The sparkles on the water seemed to make a path toward the island. Did he mean what he said? He looked as though he awaited an answer from me.

"I . . . have been taught two ways of viewing the world: in my childhood with my family, and my time in the Indian village."

"To possess the knowledge of two different cultures seems a wondrous thing to me."

I shook my head. "It makes me strange." To Abigail. To the magistrates. The ministers. The people at church meetings.

"You are not strange. Many people in Boston do not like to feel discomfited. They prefer to see their own ideas and scorn the views they do not see or think themselves. They look with fear and suspicion at the Indians. It is a hard thing to open our minds to new ways and ideas. It is the nature of mankind to be narrow. I think you already know that."

John gave a gentle flick of his whip, and the horse moved forward, the wagon following the road. We did not speak, although the silence did not strain. He reined the horse to a stop in front of a stable, telling the man he would return that evening for the horse and wagon.

He took my hand and helped me down from the wagon seat. I followed behind him through the tall grasses and then onto the sand toward the dock. The air clung about us, thick with salt. I could taste it on my mouth. We walked above the water lapping against the poles, our shoes clunking on the wood of the dock. He stopped before a small shallop—one mast, its single sail like a seabird's white wing—and stretched out his hand to help me step over the side. His palm was warm and smooth.

"You may wish to remove your cap before the wind takes it." I removed my cap and kept the pins in place to keep the hair out of my face. He gave me his hat to hold.

After John unhooked the rope that kept the boat tied to the dock, he took a seat beside me in the stern, his hand upon the tiller. The sail swelled as the boat turned in the direction of the island, the wind whipping at our clothes and hair. I clutched John's hat and my cap close so they would not blow away.

John pointed up at the seabirds overhead. "Upon the water we feel a little of what it is to fly," he shouted. I caught his words before they blew away from me.

A phrase from the Bible came to mind. "God flies upon the wings of the wind," I shouted back.

"Aye. That He does."

He pointed out toward the island, much closer now. The ground rose to a peak in the center, sloping downward at each end, making it resemble a water tortoise. It grew larger and larger. Soon we would reach it. I trembled with the anticipation of it.

The boat pulled beside the small dock, and John looped the rope around the post to secure it. We stepped onto the wooden planks, weathered gray by wind and rain. The air smelled of the pungent odor of the brown seaweed that lined the beach and the tang of the scrubby pines growing up among the brush.

"I told you before there is something wondrous about being on the island. We are in between," he said. "This affords a most interesting perspective. I can look across this way," he pointed toward the mainland, "and see where I spend my days. Then I can walk only half an hour to the other side and look across the sea toward the mother country."

John turned and pointed back across the bay. "This is your first view. There. Our present life."

I dwelt on that thick strip of land and, in this moment, viewed it from a distance. I stared past the beaches and the fields and the tall trees toward where Faith's house must be, and then northward toward Boston Bay, and Edward's house and Alice Tilley's.

"It seems as though no person dwells there," I said.

"And yet it teems with people with their concerns and worries, disappointments and triumphs. All of it matters," he said, "and yet not, in the long view of things. It puts our lives in perspective, does it not?"

"It does," I said.

"Look there." I pointed with my lips like the Indian women did. To the south. John looked puzzled. I lifted my arm and pointed with my finger. "My mother's last home was there. At New Amsterdam."

From the vantage point of the island, it felt close. Just beyond the curve of the land, beyond the dark green of the trees.

"When we walked from the village to the winter place, we passed through it," I said. "The house was rubble. Grasses grew against the foundation. The stones of the fireplace were still piled."

"Did it make you sorrowful?"

"*E-e.*" I had answered in Indian. "Yes." I could not speak. John was silent. I felt his eyes on my face.

The memory flashed. I felt as if I lived that time again. It forced its way out of me. "Opala saw me weeping. She asked me why. 'That was my house,' I told her. 'Not your house,' she said. She was angry. She thought I would not love her if I mourned my old home and my family.

"I did not want Opala to be angry. She only said those things because she loved me as a daughter." I felt like I was again that child, walking through the graves of my mother and my siblings. "The wood lilies Mother planted. They still grew in the garden.

I could not stop my weeping. Opala tried to pull me up but I could not. My grief went too deep. Muh-teh-qway put something into my hand. A wood lily. The round bulb had roots that spread out. 'Plant it when we return to the village,' she said."

The memory receded into a back corner of my mind. Yet I'd said it aloud. My face flushed hot. Why did I tell this to John Cole? Perhaps because he did not speak ill of the Indians. I did not want him to speak. He must not. There was nothing he could say.

I turned my back on the view of the south and looked at Hog Island. "Show me this place."

"The house is through the path there. Shall we see it first?"

I nodded. As we moved through the trees, the sense of being on an island vanished. We could have been on the mainland again. The house stood in a small clearing, a single-story dwelling with a small porch covering the front door, pieces of wood for a fire stacked on one side. The windows were cut with more height and width than many houses. I liked that. It let in more of the wild. Pink blossoms covered the bushes lining the sides of the house.

"My mother loved to come here. She called it her escape. She planted the wild rose bushes. They don't require constant care in order to flourish."

At John's effort, the front door creaked open. There were two square rooms with a hearth in the center to warm both spaces: a parlor for sitting and sleeping and a keeping room with a table and bench. No need for a staircase, for there was no upper floor.

The house felt both empty and full, as though it waited for something. I thought of saying my thought aloud but did not.

"Everything looks in fine shape, though it can use a good scrubbing," he said.

I picked up the broom by the hearth and began to sweep the floor.

"You are my guest and should not do the work," he chuckled.

I kept sweeping. John went out to the well and returned with a bucket of water, wiping down the table and chairs. He began to work on cleaning the windows in the keeping room. After finishing the floor, I removed the spider webs from the corners with the broom, then found another rag and scrubbed the grime off the panes in the window by the door.

"Your mother would like it to be clean," I said when we had finished.

"That she would." When he smiled, a dimple showed at the side of his mouth. He started to close the door.

"Wait," I said. "One thing more. Have you a knife?"

From the bushes along the side of the house I cut a few of the roses, leaving the stems long. I set them in a cup of water on the table.

"Lovely," John said. "That is what my mother did."

In a few days, the flowers would shrivel and die. The petals would dry, showing a different beauty. No one would be here to see them.

"I have worked up an appetite," John said. "Are you hungry? Would you like to eat?"

❧

We took the path back to the boat to retrieve the food basket, walking further along the curve of the beach. Other islands dotted the bay, blue-gray in the mist, like whales rising above the surface of the water.

When we turned at the curve, the mainland disappeared. John pointed toward the far horizon. "Now we look toward the place of our past. The old world from where our people came."

The present and the past was in this place, depending on where I stood.

"And what of the future? Can we see it?" I said.

"Alas, that we cannot see."

I pointed up to the sky. "Perhaps it is there."

"Surely you must be right."

"Or from the top of a high mountain," I answered. "As the prophet Daniel saw in the Bible. There are no mountains here."

Speaking freely felt peculiar. It was like eating a food I had not tasted before, sweet, not bitter. This would not last. John Cole would soon see only that I was different and turn away from me.

"Perhaps one day it will be our privilege to see from a mountaintop," he said.

John brushed a spot of dry sand clear of seaweed for us to sit, a few clouds overhead providing shade. In the basket, Faith had included a square cloth to put the food on. I spread it out and set out the bread, salted turkey and mug of cider and a pumpkin pudding.

The waves crept toward us, then receded. The rhythm of it soothed me.

"Look," John pointed. A tortoise crept slowly along the beach.

"Have you heard the story the Indians tell of how the earth was created?" I asked.

"Tell me."

"The Indians call God the Great Creator. He-who-creates-us-by-thought. The Creator saw in a vision the moon and the stars and the sun. He saw the earth and everything in it: the forests, the waters, the animals. Four spirit beings helped the Creator make what he had dreamed. The Creator made laws for the balance and order and harmony between all things."

I sat again in front of the fire in the village and heard the *sachem* tell the stories. "The Indians say before earth was formed, the heavens were inhabited by men. The Indians descended from them.

"The good and evil spirits fought so hard that the earth filled up with water. The animals and the trees and the people drowned in the great waters. Nanapush, the Strong Pure One, decided a new earth should be made. He did so by the power of the Great Creator. The new earth he made was beautiful. A slender, shining tree grew up and from its roots a man was formed. The tree touched its top to the ground. From it was formed a woman. From the first man and first woman all men and women came."

John Cole listened to every word, so still he did not move.

"There is another version of the story, too." I picked up a stick and etched an oval shape in the sand. "This is a tortoise." I drew a head and a tail and four feet. "There was water all around the tortoise. After a long time, it raised up out of the water and the water fell away from it and it became dry."

I picked up a thin reed and placed it in the middle of the circle I had drawn. "A tree grew up on the tortoise. Its roots sent forth a sprout that grew into a man. The first man. He was alone. The tree bent over until its top touched the earth and another root formed. From it a woman grew. Henceforth, all men came from them."

John sat back on his heels, staring into the sky. "It reminds me of the story of the creation in the Bible."

"Tell me the story in the Bible," I said.

John closed his eyes. *And God said, let the waters under the heaven be gathered into one place and let the dry land appear.*

"The tortoise," I said.

His deep, rich voice made the words sound like honey. *God called the dry land, Earth, and he called the gathering together of the waters, Seas. Then God said, Let the earth bud forth the bud of the herb the fruitful tree . . . .* He pointed to the tree above us. *And God saw that it was good.*

Birds called overhead, wings spread wide, flying with the breeze that ruffled the tree leaves and the brush. The grasses tickled my palm as I touched them. A wave hit the shore, spreading white foam across the sand, and then receded back into the sea.

"What does the Bible say about the first people?" I'd read the story but I wanted to hear him speak aloud the words.

The Lord God made the man of dust of the ground and breathed in his face breath of life. And the man was a living soul. And God said: It is not good that the man should be left alone. He looked over at me. *I will make an helpmeet for him. Then God caused a deep sleep to come upon the man and took one of his ribs. And the rib which God took from the man, made he a woman. And brought her to the man. And the man said, This now is bone of my bones and flesh of my flesh.*

"Words of great beauty," I said.

"And so is the story the Indians tell," John said. "Pastor Eliot tells the Indians that the God of the Christians and their Great Creator are the same."

John did not think it odd for me to talk of the Indians. Something inside me relaxed as though I had taken a deep breath and slowly let it out.

"They do believe so," I said. "I should like to see the Bible written in their language when it is finished."

"You should have one of your own. And would you like to see Natick when it is established?"

"I would."

John settled onto his back, arms beneath his head. "Tell me of the people you knew in your village."

I told him of Muh-teh-qway. Of Opala and Minsi. Of Chief Wampage.

"I was adopted into their family. They treated me as one of their own. The people in the village called me the daughter of Anne-Hoeck."

"Anne-Hoeck?"

"It was the name the people gave to Wampage. After he killed my mother."

I expected to hear the screaming in my head and the roaring fire, as I always did when I thought of the day my family died. It did not come. A bird descended, landing on its feet a small distance away. It turned its black eyes upon me, staring as one of its kind had done on the day of my vision quest. I kept still so it would not fly away.

"Wampage told me that killing my family was a wrong he had done. We were not Dutch. We were English. They saw that my clothes were different from the Dutch when they found me hiding in the rock. The day that he traded me to the Dutchman, my Indian family wept. They did not want me to go. But Wampage said he must right the wrong. That I must return to live with my own people."

The bird kept its eye on me as I talked. I threw pieces of the leftover bread on the sand. Three more seabirds joined it. The four gobbled the pieces and spread their white wings, lifting into the air. I watched them until they disappeared into the sunlight.

"What was your Indian name?"

"Sisika. Bird."

"Sisika. Susanna." John smiled.

I gathered the leftover food and put it back in the basket.

John walked toward the edge of the water, bent and picked something up. He sat down beside me and opened his hand, revealing sea shells, the tiny animals that had inhabited them gone and leaving them empty.

"Set it to your ear," he said, as he held out the largest one. "You will hear the sound of the sea."

His fingers were warm as he placed the shell in my palm. It was cool and damp, wet sand clinging to it. I raised it to my ear. A rushing sound came from the hollow place within it, like an echo of something that had been and was no more.

I had not wept since I left the village. I turned my head so he would not see my tears.

"Susanna?" He said my given name, the sound of it sweet upon my ears. He touched my sleeve and drew his hand back. "Let us find shade. The sun is hot."

A cooling breeze fluttered the leaves of the tree, cooling the damp on the back of my neck. John handed me the mug and I drank. The cider soothed my throat. My breaths slowed.

"To feel is not weakness for it was God who made us thus," he said. "What I do not care for is when the feelings come upon me unawares and overwhelm me. Is it so with you now?"

My hand went to my throat. I could not look at him. "You show me kindness and I have answered you with anger."

"Anger is only a mask for the other things we are feeling. Sadness. Loss. Shame. We Puritans live on shame. What is it that angers you most?"

The sharp edge of the shells cut into my hand and I loosened my grip. I leaned my forehead against the tree. What did I feel at this moment?

"I want . . . I want my mother and my father and they are dead. And now my Indian family is also dead to me."

My voice did not sound like my own. Why should I tell what I felt to this man? I did not know him. Yet it felt that I did.

On the trunk of the tree, the bark was torn away, leaving deep gashes. An extra thickness formed at the edges around the wound where the tree had sought to protect itself.

"Our lives are filled with gaps and holes like these." He touched the gash in the tree. "The prophet Isaiah called them breaches. Like this one."

Breach. A fitting word.

"You are a woman of great strength, Susanna Hutchinson. It is healing that you seek, is it not? To close the breaches life has brought to you."

Muh-teh-qway said to me as we collected bark for medicinal use: "Strip the bark only from the east side of the tree where the morning sun hits first." This tree's wound was on the east side where the sun could infuse its healing. The Bible said that God made the sun.

I dropped my hand from the tree. "Yet we cannot change what is past," I said.

"No. We cannot. But we can heal. I think you have done much of that even now. More than you know."

Chapter Thirty

JOHN AND I COMMENCED WALKING AGAIN. SOON WE would circle the island and end where we began.

The seabirds flew so low I could see their feathered underbellies and gaping beaks, perhaps hoping for more bread. As we rounded the bend, I stopped and looked out at the sea on the far side of the island, pressing the memory into my mind.

The white-bluish color of the sky and the water faded in the distance to a muted gray. More of the world lay beyond what I could see and that knowledge comforted me. I did not need to see it to know it was there.

"You do not speak like Mister Wilson or the other preachers," I said.

"Indeed, I hope I do not. I do not find God to be the harsh, punishing God they speak of, who doles out justice without regard to mercy. We find that in much of humanity, always so quick to judge and condemn. That is not God's way."

"Like John Winthrop did to my mother."

"He and others like Thomas Dudley cannot tolerate others who think differently from them. Puritans wrangle over ideologies. A covenant of grace. A covenant of works. The battle rages around us. Men will always try to compel. It is in our nature, and not the better part of it.

"Word has come across the ocean of a rising group called the Quakers. I am sure we will soon hear its precepts preached in this new land. Most in Massachusetts will not welcome it. They believe in liberty only for those who believe as they do. It is a great irony. The oppressed in old England have become the oppressors in the new land.

"That is a depressing view of human nature, I admit. I must also remember it is in men's nature to seek diligently for truth. It will ever be so."

"Like my mother and father."

"Your good mother dared to speak what she believed. She looked for her God in holy Word and found Him. As a young boy, I felt her words to be true: that God can speak to our hearts through His Spirit. The gospel she preached was simple. My father remembers her saying she cared not for graces or promises or meditation and duties, but only to seek for Christ."

"The authorities did not like her views or that she dared to express them. I have read my mother's trial. 'We will reduce you', they said. 'We will compel you.'"

I turned my face away from him.

"Your parents had many friends and admirers," John said. "They decried her treatment by those in authority. And yet, good came even from that great injustice. The government formed in Aquidneck by your parents and others did not establish a church of the state in Rhode Island. Men and women are free to believe and to worship as they choose. I would dwell there if I could."

The narrow strip of land where my parents' house stood reached out to me, set between the calm waters of the bay and the crashing waves of the sea. Longing clogged my throat.

"As I read my mother's words at her trial," I said, "I felt of her strength."

"Her descendants will read them," John said, "and many more. She will be remembered and honored for her courage. Her suffering has brought good and will continue to do so."

His words flowed over me like cooling water. "You speak wisdom, John Cole. Tell me more of what you think of God."

John stared out at the gray-blue water ruffled by the breeze. Sun rays turned the tips of the waves into lanterns, as though each was touched by a divine hand. It must be so, for God had made it.

"I have not heard the preachers speak of this, but in my heart I feel it." John spoke softly. "In scripture we read that God sees all things at once: past, present and future. This world and all things in it. That includes each of the children that He created. He sees where you have been and where you are and knows what will come to pass in your life. I believe that a part of His great mercy is to, in His own time, make the circumstances of our life as they always should have been."

I shook my head. "How can that be so?"

"We read in Isaiah that God's arm is stretched out always to His children. His patience and long suffering are infinite. 'You shall remember the shame of your youth no more,' he said. God has the power to do this and more. Turn things for our good. That includes the bad. This is the God I believe in."

"How? To work both rearward and forward to make all things right? It cannot be so."

"Is that not what Heaven is?" He smiled at me. "The sour and the sweet of life blended by God until only the good remains."

I could not hold onto the thought; as though the tide gave it to me, only to pull it away.

꙳

Our shadows lengthened as the sun moved from high overhead to hang slanted in the afternoon sky. We had covered the circle of the island and back to the boat.

"I am glad to have seen this place," I said. "It is all that you say. Prithee thanks."

"I am glad to have shown you."

At the edge of the dock, John stopped. "I would say one thing more."

He took a deep breath and blew it out. "I am drawn to you. You are strong and you are good. And beautiful," he added. "I came to Mount Wollaston to see you again, for I have missed you sorely." He gave a low chuckle. "And not just to play games with your family."

I looked up at him. The white of his eyes caught the sunlight, so bright I had to look away.

"When we return to the house, they will make you play more."

"I will not mind it," he laughed.

"Yesterday, you said I feel only pity for you. It was not pity which drove me to speak to you that day outside the church. Nor was it duty or obligation, though I can see how you would have taken my words that way. I spoke too soon and too blunt and am most sorry for it."

He took a step closer to me and reached for my hand, his grip warm and firm.

"I . . . would marry you, Susanna. If you would consent to have me to be a husband."

I snatched my hand away. "You cannot mean what you say. No man will want the girl who lived among the Indians. I will never marry. Abigail Button told me so."

I pushed past him onto the dock, startling a seabird who squawked and flew upward. The boat rocked as I stepped into it. I lost my footing and slapped down hard on the wooden seat. The boat lowered with John's weight as he stepped in and sat down across from me.

"Abigail Button told you a lie. She is a cruel, selfish woman." His eyes flashed. So, he, too, could anger. "But it is not her opinions that make you reject me. I am distasteful to you and you will not say it. That is why you spurn me."

I folded my arms across my waist. "It is I who will become distasteful to you. Others will scorn you as they do me, because you join yourself to the girl who lived among the savages."

"You suppose I think of you as Winthrop and Cotton and Wilson do? Or the women I've watched scorn you at meeting? What reason do you have to think that?"

I hugged my arms tighter against me. His gaze burned.

He leaned toward me. "Hear me, Susanna. You are more than what has happened to you. More than how you have been treated. Will you continue to see yourself only as that?"

"I do not. I will not. You judge me." I stuck my chin out. "You said yourself the people of Boston do not want anyone who is not like they are. I will never belong."

"You do not need to belong! Can you not see it?" his voice lowered, pleading. "We can make our own place. Together. Is that not what marriage is?" He flung his hand out. "Like this island."

"It is not possible. Return me to my sister's house. We have been gone too long. She will worry."

He unhooked the rope from the post and pushed against it, the boat moving backward in the water.

I turned back to the island. The house was hidden in the trees. John's mouth set in a tight line, eyes toward the mainland, hand firm on the tiller. How could I blame him for his anger? I had taken all his words and thrown them into his face.

When we had traveled halfway between the island and the mainland, the wind calmed. The sail drooped. We sat still in the water.

John removed his coat, got out the oars and moved to the middle of the boat to row. "It will take me longer to return you back to your sister. I am sorry for it." He did not look at me. The boat moved slowly forward at his pull on the oars.

To the east, I saw a sliver of pallid moon, bright enough to show in the daytime sky.

He kept up his steady rowing, his shoulders and arms moving back and forth in a steady measure. The paddles made small splashes in the water.

John must mean what he said, or he would not be so angry. Anger, he had said, masked the things one really felt. Like hurt or rejection or pain. I lashed out at this man who had only shown me kindness and understanding.

"Do you . . ." I could not finish.

"Do I what?"

I wanted him to look at me.

"Do you mean what you have said to me this day?"

"I have said many things," he answered without stopping his rowing. "Which do you question?"

"That . . . that you . . . would have me . . . for your wife."

He ceased rowing, his grip still tight on the oars. The boat rocked on the gentle waves. His face softened.

"I wish to care for you. To make certain you are safe and contented. I bear a great love for you, Susanna Hutchinson. If you do not want it, I will honor your desires." His eyes looked flat, resigned to my rebuff.

John would not ask me again. Two times refused was too much. He would return to Boston and be lost to me. He would choose another wife to live in the house at Sudbury End with its view of the cove and room for a garden. He would be good and kind to her.

I stared up at the chalky sliver of moon showing in the bright light of the day. A seabird flew high above, moving across it.

Open your heart to love and to be loved, Mother had said. It would take all my courage to do it.

I need not doubt this man. There was no need for fear.

I reached across the distance between us and touched the back of his hand. He startled.

"I could care for you, John Cole." There. I said my words aloud.

His gaze turned to me, eyes wide.

I put both my hands atop his hand that clutched the oar, his warmth flowing into me. "I do."

Joy lit his face.

Alice Tilley said I would find my true home. I knew it now. It would be with John Cole.

Together, like the island, like the seabirds, we would find our place between.

Epilogue

WARWICK, RHODE ISLAND, 1713

When we are young, we are meant to believe life will last always. Days and years stretch out before our view and we cannot foresee there will be an end to it. Though the young die as well as the old, we feel it will not be so for ourselves. I believe this serves a purpose for it helps us to move forward and have courage to do what is needful.

My beloved husband John has been six years buried on the knoll in the woods not far from the house he built for us. We were married for sixty-two years.

At eighty years, I am come to old age. Though I understand the wisdom of the blind view of the young, I no longer have need of it. My days to walk on the earth will soon come to a close. I know more than ever that life is short, even for those who grow old and bent and wrinkled. The road ahead leads to the burial of my body beside John. It will be a joyous reunion in heaven.

Until that day, I have only to look backward now.

❧

When John and I reentered Faith's house that long-ago day at Hog Island, we told my sister of our plan to marry. Faith threw her arms around us both together, exclaiming her joy: "How proud Mother and Father would be to see you wed such a fine man, Susanna! Come and see, children, for you will soon have a new uncle." They cheered.

John took me back to Boston with him on his shallop. I stayed with Alice Tilley until our wedding three months later. Now that I was a betrothed woman, Abigail had a change of heart toward me and threw herself into plans for the ceremony to be held in the best room of Edward's house. The last day of December, the year sixteen hundred and fifty-one. A winter storm covered the world in white.

We moved into John's snug house in Sudbury End. In the spring, I planted my herb garden and more wood lilies along the sides of the house. When the weather cleared, we went to the island and spent three days and nights in the little cabin on Hog Island. The bowl of his mother's roses I had left on the table had dried, the red and yellow petals perfectly preserved.

Alice Tilley continued to train me to be a midwife. I worked alongside her, attending many births. The women I served trusted me. "Your hands and your words are gentle," an old woman said to me as I tended her. "Like your mother."

When I attended a birthing, in that shuttered room away from the world, I felt . . . how do I express it . . . a comforting, instructing presence beside me. Mother. My grandmother. My midwife work tied me to them.

My beloved sister Faith bore a son in February of 1652. I could not be with her at her birth. The heavy snows made the roads not passable. Three days later she died. My laughing, beautiful sister. Grief overwhelmed me. Her death brought back every grief at the loss of my family on that long-ago day in New Amsterdam.

I could not sleep. I stood out in the bitter cold, staring at the starry cluster as Faith made her way to join Mother and Father and all my siblings. John wrapped us both tight in a blanket and held me as I wailed.

A year after Faith's death, I first felt the signs within my body that I would have my own babe. Muh-teh-qway's words came back to me: "Every woman longs to be an *ana.*"

Alice Tilley put my girl babe into my arms. "What shall we name her?" I asked John. John touched her downy head. "Susanna," he said, "for her hair is red like her beautiful mother."

The authorities in Massachusetts grew more and more rigid. As John had foreseen, the Quaker movement came across the ocean from the old land. No person who professed themselves a Quaker was allowed to live in the colony. My mother's staunch friend, Mary Dyer, joined that faith. Two times she returned to Boston, was jailed and cast out. The third time Mary returned, they hung her at Boston Neck. The first day of June, in the year sixteen hundred and sixty.

On that day, inside the shuttered windows of our house on Sudbury End, I felt the darkness of her death. It came to me: my mother also cried for her friend Mary Dyer. She cried for all of those who suffered when men used their pretended authority to try to act in the place of God and, in doing so, offended Him.

For a dozen years we lived in the house at Sudbury End. I bore three children. My sister Bridget's husband died suddenly at age fifty-four while serving as the governor of Portsmouth. Soon after she married a Major William Phillips and brought her three sons and one daughter to live in Boston, where she bore three more sons. We had a glorious reunion and lived near each other for only a few years before that time came to an end.

In 1663, three years following Mary Dyer's hanging, came our opportunity to leave Boston.

My brother Edward approached us with an opportunity. The six hundred acres he had purchased in Narragansett country needed tending. John and I recalled our conversation years before of our desire to live where people were free to worship as they wished. It was possible because of my mother and father—Anne and William Hutchinson.

We settled on the land in Warwick, Rhode Island, sixty-three long miles south of the city of Boston and twelve miles northwest of Aquidneck. To the south and west is New Amsterdam and the Indian village.

In Warwick, the two-storied, planked house I still live in sits inside the peak of land set in the center of the cove. John built it and painted the plank wood the color of sunshine, with white-trimmed windows cut wide to let in the light. In the cove, the water is blue and green, the hue dependent upon where one stands. Below the pale sky, green is everywhere: the dark green of the tree leaves, and the lighter green of the grasses that spread to the white edge of the beach.

Four years of great contentment passed for us, and we determined we would stay in Rhode Island. We sent Edward instructions to sell our properties in Boston: the house at Sudbury End and another deeded to me by Samuel Cole in Bendall's Cove.

Narragansett territory grew. Only a few of the settlers who came learned I was the daughter of Anne Hutchinson. They knew me only as Susanna Cole, wife of John Cole. Midwife: the tender of the sick and dying, a comforting and guiding presence when their children were born.

Connecticut and Rhode Island each staked a claim to Edward's Warwick land. John and I joked that God had heard our talk of building a space between for ourselves and literally granted it. Five years after we settled there, my husband John was elected magistrate for Connecticut. Rhode Island contested the action. A sergeant threw John into the local prison, demanding from me twenty pounds for his release, which I promptly gave. His incarceration was only a few days but the divisive matter hung over our colony for two decades. John and others sent a petition across the sea to the King, appealing for resolution. In the end, John was fittingly appointed Conservator of the Peace for the area of Rhode Island.

In the year 1675, we received a letter. *Captain Edward Hutchinson received a wound from the Indians in a treacherous assault when he was marching to a peaceful meeting with them, of which he died on August 19th.* My brother was only sixty-two. Yet another of my family was dead.

I followed in my own mother's footsteps and bore many children. Eleven children: six sons and five daughters. My fourth child, John, died young. In honor of that boy, we bestowed the name again to our sixth child and third son. That John grew to manhood. Parenting is a curious thing. I came to feel that our children are only borrowed for a short while. They quickly grow to adulthood and then we give them away in marriage. As it says in Genesis: *And the man shall leave his father and mother and cleave unto his wife.* Yet John and I have tucked in our minds and hearts the memories of each of them as babes, then grown knee high, waist high, until they looked us in our eyes as adults.

In a corner of the attic sits the chest my brother Edward passed to me with the books and papers containing my family's past. As each of the children matured, I opened the chest and told them of their grandmother and grandfather: William and Anne Hutchinson.

I told them my story.

"You lived among the Indians, Mother?" they asked, eyes wide.

I told them of the woman Muh-teh-qway and Opala and the warrior chief Wampage. I told them of Gela the Indian girl who was killed, and how, for a while, I took her place.

I showed them my *wampum* belts and told them the stories in the beads—of my coming to the Indians and my leaving. They held my necklace of purple mollusk shells, and my Indian skirt with the porcupine design that looked like lace. I showed them how to pluck the quills off a porcupine, how to soften them in water and dye them white, and how to sew them onto a skirt of deerskin.

In the night sky, I pointed out the starry cluster that Muh-teh-qway showed to me. We said aloud the names of my father and mother and my siblings: William, my father. Anne, my mother. Francis and William and Zuriel, my brothers. Anne, Mary, Katherine, my sisters. Faith. My eldest brother Edward and his wife Katherine. Muh-teh-qway and the dead girl Gela.

As they drifted into sleep at night, I played songs for them on my river cane flute. I told them of the Great Spirit Kishelemu-kong who is the same God we find in our Bible.

Along the crooked paths my life has taken, I found my place between. With John.

He helped me to accept all the parts of life, the good and the bad, and learn from them. Many times over the years I have returned to John's sentiment that Heaven works in a circle, both in past and present, mixing the good and bad of life together, forming one path to heaven.

The union of husband and wife is truly an island. Now one of us is gone. Though surrounded by children and grandchildren, I live on that island alone.

After John's last breath came, I closed his eyes and kissed his mouth. His body lies beneath the earth in the graveyard they call Cole's Lot. Yet I feel John's arms around my shoulders still, his soft eyes upon my face, the timbre of his voice in my ear. He is not gone from me.

The weakness in my shaking bones tells me that very soon I will make my way across the starry cluster in the sky to him. Mother will be there. Father. My brothers and sisters. Those I love.

I will be truly home.

Acknowledgements

T HIS BOOK HAS BEEN FORMING FOR A LONG TIME.
Around 2013, I knew I wanted to explore the life of the
famous dissident Anne Hutchinson. So much has been told of
Anne's life, mainly in nonfiction form, not with the imagination
and depth the novel form can offer. I did the research and began
a few drafts from the point of view of differing characters. One
Saturday I sat in a room in the BYU law building, serving as a
monitor for an LSAT test. In the hours of tense silence, I brain-
stormed in a notebook. What if I wrote from the point of view
of the Hutchinson daughter who survived the Indian massacre
in New York territory in 1643?

Five chapters came with great struggle. In July of 2014,
I workshopped them during a week-long writing retreat with
Dean Hughes in Heber, Utah. A major aspect of Susanna's story
stumped me: John Winthrop wrote in his journal that when
Susanna was returned as a teen to her family in Boston she had
lost the ability to speak in the English language. If that was so,
then how could I write in first person from her point of view? It
became such an obstacle that I put the chapters away, thinking I
would never be able to make the story work. I concentrated on
the edits for two novels published in 2015 and 2016, and writing
the sequel to my first. It was published in 2017.

In January 2018 I quit my part time job with the intent to
put more of my energy and time into writing. The Susanna

story kept bothering me. I had twenty-two thousand words in third person, but it felt like the novel needed to be written in first person. There had to be a way. A breakthrough came after I read that children who lost their original language returned to it very quickly. Susanna was nine years old when she was taken to live with the Indians. Before then she would have been fluent in speaking, reading and writing in the English language. I rewrote the first chapters, adding more pages daily. My husband Bryan patiently listened to my thoughts as I reasoned out the problems and then read the chapters as they unfolded. We traveled to Boston and Rhode Island and retraced the Hutchinson family's steps.

At last I completed a first draft. A friend of mine, Sue Bowen, a former history teacher, reviewed the manuscript, offering encouragement and suggestions. After the manuscript was accepted for publication, my editor at WiDo, Karen Gowen, offered razor sharp insights. "Tell more of Susanna's story before she returned to Boston, when she lived with the Indians," she told me, and I realized that what I had written lacked needed balance. The ten thousand more words that Karen suggested I include were a joy to write. The book is much better because of her wisdom. I am grateful to her and her husband Bruce for giving me the opportunity to share my stories.

In *Daughter of Anne-Hoeck*, I kept close to actual historical events. Most of the characters in the book are taken from history. Susanna. Her brother Edward Hutchinson and his two wives. Susanna's sisters Faith and Bridget. John Winthrop and his fourth wife Martha. The preachers John Cotton and John Wilson. Midwife Alice Tilley. Samuel Cole and his son John. John Eliot and his translation of the Bible into the Algonquian language and his establishment of settlements called praying towns. All of them were people of tremendous courage who shaped history for generations to come. I hope that I have treated them fairly. As I tried to explore in the book: no one is all evil or all good. Human beings are all the grays in between.

Susanna was a survivor of experiences over which she had no control, a woman of great courage and strength who moved forward in spite of great loss. She built a legacy for her children and descendants. Imagining her life gave me insights to better live my own. One thing I learned while writing this book: men and women live inside a social and political world which affects their circumstances. But our lives are much more than world events, social mores, or the interpretations of current government and religious authorities. We choose our own beliefs and opinions and actions, deciding for ourselves the truths we will follow. In doing so, we build a world of our own creation inside of our larger world. Isn't that what the designer of earth and mankind desires for each of us? Like Susanna, we choose and shape our own "space between."

About the Author

CAROL PRATT BRADLEY is an historical novelist with a Master of Fine Arts degree in Creative Writing from Brigham Young University. Her first published novel, *Light of the Candle*, was published by WiDo in January 2015, and its sequel, *Waiting for the Light*, in 2017. Her second novel, *Fire of the Word*, was originally written as her master's thesis. Carol lives in Mapleton, Utah, with her husband, Bryan, near their four grown children. You can find more about the author at www.carolpbradley.com.